PIER RATS

PIER RATS

BY

BRUCE GREIF

1.Summer--Surfing—Fiction. 2. Boys Adventure—Fiction. 3.
Humor—Fiction. 4. Ventura, California—Fiction.

ISBN 13-9781495343674
ISBN 10-1495343677

Cover art by Carla Bartow
Carlabartow.com

Back cover photo by Marty McClain
Ventura Pier, 1974

For Dick & Jacque

"Now and then we had a hope that if we lived and were good, God would permit us to be pirates"

~Mark Twain

CONTENTS

Prologue
Ventura California, Easter Sunday, 1973

The garbage cans spilled over at the Ventura State Beach after a warm and busy Easter weekend. Now, with the sun below the western horizon and no moon out yet, it was getting too dark to see. Cricket's gunnysack was heavy with treasure and his stomach full. He'd eaten a charred hamburger patty and a half tub of potato salad. In a soggy egg carton he'd found a hard-boiled egg dyed blue which he placed in his pocket for later.

Among his treasures was a torn volleyball net, two left-footed sandals, a broken transistor radio and half a bag of charcoal. He flung the gunnysack over his shoulder, felt his pocket for the egg and walked over the dune to the hard-packed sand by the water. He headed north toward the lights of the Pier a half-mile away.

A mist hung over the darkened shoreline and the waves crashed louder than usual. Ahead Cricket saw something white washed ashore. He walked closer and saw the white was the deck of a surfboard. He scanned the ocean, but could only see faint rows of white water rolling in. This wasn't a surfer's beach; he knew where the surfers went. He picked up the surfboard and continued north, over the jetties, under the Pier, around the point to the dry river bottom at the edge of town known as Hobo Jungle.

PART 1

TO SURF

Ventura, 1968

"I know what I want to be when I grow up," nine-year-old Lance Stratton announced at the dinner table. He'd spent the whole day turning it over in his mind and could come up with no reason why it wasn't the perfect job. The only puzzling thing was--why didn't everybody do it?

His dad smiled. "Well, what could it be this time?"

"I know," his older sister Ann said. "A hobo."

"Ha," his oldest sister Jean cried. "Then what would he be for Halloween every year?"

Lance sat up straight and cleared his throat. "Joke around all you want, I'm gonna be a playboy."

His dad choked and his sisters erupted in laughter.

"A playboy?" his mom gasped.

Jean pointed at him laughing. "Do you even know what that is?"

He'd imagined a playboy was someone who drove a fancy car and played sports. "I don't know, I heard mom say Joe Namath was one."

The laughter grew.

Lance sunk in his chair.

"That's enough teasing," his mom said. "Who wants dessert?"

After dinner Lance went to his room to reevaluate. His mom had recently decorated his room red, white and blue and it still smelled of fresh paint. He fell back on his bed and looked at the newly framed pictures on the wall. One was a portrait of his dad in his marine uniform from World War II. He looked young and serious. Another was a group photo of his dad with three hundred other marines aboard the U.S.S. Grimes, the ship that would deliver them to Iwo Jima.

Above the dresser was his dad's Purple Heart. It was pinned to lavender felt and hung in a gold frame. His dad had cool war scars. There were two on his right side where a bullet had gone in and come out, and a big one on his upper left arm where his triceps used to be.

Lance had thought about being a soldier, but Vietnam wasn't a good war like World War II.

Outside a train whistle blew and Lance could feel the house begin to tremble. Ann was right, he did think about being a hobo. He liked to imagine himself sitting on a log in a creek bed, under a railroad trestle, heating a can of beans over a small fire and eating them with a stick. But that wasn't something he could talk about with his mom and dad. Whenever they drove across the Main Street Bridge over the Ventura River his dad would say, "That's a Hobo Jungle down there, they'll kill you for your shoes."

The river bottom didn't look like a jungle. It was just a dry riverbed with a bunch of bushes growing in it. The train whistle sounded again and Lance put his hand on the wall to feel the vibration. Above his hand were pictures he and his mom had framed from *Life* magazine. One was of Gemini Astronaut Ed White in his silver space suit floating outside the space capsule, only a thin cord preventing him from drifting off into space.

Another picture was of a surfer riding a big wave in Hawaii. The guy stood tall on a red surfboard, white foam exploding behind him as he slid across the blue wave.

Lance tried to imagine what it would be like to be an astronaut in space, or a surfer riding a big wave. The two images filled his imagination with adventure and intrigue. He decided to do some research.

2

* * * *

The next morning Lance approached his mom in the kitchen.

"Mom, what do you have to do to be an astronaut?"

She smiled as she stirred pancake batter. "Well, I think you'd need to join the Air Force and work real hard to become a pilot. Then, if you're a really good pilot they'll give you some physical and psychological tests, and if you're at the top on those they might select you to be an astronaut."

"Hmm...that sounds hard. I think I'm gonna be a surfer."

She smiled, then her face grew stern. "For that you'll need to be a strong swimmer, that means swimming lessons. And you'll have to earn money to buy a surfboard." She put a square of butter on the griddle. "I was already planning on signing you and Ann up for swimming lessons this summer."

His mom liked to say she had salt water in her veins. She'd grown up near the beach between the Venice and Santa Monica Piers in the 1930s and 1940s. That was during the Great Depression era. She said because they lived on the beach she never felt poor. As a teenager she belonged to a paddleboard club and would watch the early surfers riding waves on redwood planks. She spoke of them as if they were gladiators. When she reminisced of those days Lance thought he could feel the warmth of sun and sand emanate from her.

* * * *

When they went to the beach that summer Lance would watch the surfers and chase after their loose boards when they washed in. If there was time he'd lie down and try to paddle.

3

After summer vacation Lance went back to school and played football and baseball with his friends. He added posters of Joe Namath and Wilt Chamberlain to the walls in his room. He asked his friends, Nicky and Martin, if they ever thought about being surfers.

"Sure, I guess so," they said.

Lance was certain they'd get more excited about surfing when he got a surfboard.

2
The Surf Shop, 1972

At age thirteen, after completing his Junior Lifeguard training, Lance's mom bought him a copy of *Surfer* magazine. He studied every wave on every page and imagined himself as those surfers. He read the interview with Jeff Hakman, who told the story of how he'd learned to surf. It was as if the magazine was speaking directly to him. There was an article on how to surf new spots and it explained the difference between beach breaks, point breaks and reef breaks. Even the advertisements taught him the latest in surfboard design and wetsuit style.

Soon the posters of Joe Namath and Wilt Chamberlain were replaced by posters of Owl Chapman and Rory Russell. For Christmas Lance got a plastic Makaha skateboard and rode it in endless figure eights on the cement patio in the backyard. He pretended every turn was on a wave.

Finally, on a Sunday afternoon in spring, Lance rode his bike to the end of Channel Drive, crossed over the railroad tracks and stood at the edge of the bluff in front of the lemon factory. There he looked out over Pierpont Bay. He could see north to the Ventura River and south to the Marina--three miles of coastline. He slipped his hand into his pocket and felt the wad of money-- thirty-seven dollars, twenty-eight of which he'd earned mowing lawns and the other nine he'd skimmed from his school lunch money.

Lance had only been by the Surf Shop once, about a year ago, when on a Sunday drive his parents drove him past. His mom said, "Look Lance, there's the Surf Shop."

Out the car window he saw an old wooden building at the end of an industrial street that ended at the railroad tracks, the paint

5

was peeling and the whole place seemed to lean to the right. There were no windows, only five wooden steps leading to a glass door. Above the door was a plywood sign cut in the shape of a surfboard, it read: Surf Shop. It was the coolest place he had ever seen.

"Now that looks like a fine establishment," his dad chuckled, then turned right on Ash Street.

Lance turned around in his seat to look out the back window. Behind the shop he could see a fishing boat sitting on blocks, and across the railroad tracks was a pedestrian bridge arcing over the 101 freeway to the Ventura Pier.

Now, standing on the bluff at the lemon factory, Lance could see the Pier a couple miles north extending into the Pacific Ocean. He took a deep breath of salt air tinged with lemon and pedaled along the bluff called Vista Del Mar. The street was lined on one side with ocean view homes and the other with eucalyptus trees that partitioned the homes from the railroad tracks. It was a mile down Vista Del Mar to Harbor Boulevard; there he continued to the Pier, across the pedestrian bridge to the Surf Shop.

He saw the fishing boat still there on blocks and the building had a fresh coat of brown paint. Several cars with surf racks were parked out front. He hoped it would be busy inside so he could slip in unnoticed and casually browse the used surfboards. He locked his bike to the railing on the wooden steps. The clang of his chain woke a large German shepherd sleeping on the landing. The dog opened its yellow eyes and closed them again. Lance climbed the stairs and stepped around the big dog. He pushed the door open and heard a round of laughter.

Lance stepped inside and the laughter quickly died. His eyes adjusted to the dim interior and he saw a large circle of guys sitting on the floor, all staring at him.

6

A guy sitting in a hanging basket chair smiled. "Can I help you find something?" The guy had shoulder length blonde hair and a fu manchu mustache.

Lance swallowed. "Do you have any used surfboards?"

There was snickering.

"Yeah, back in the corner." Fu Manchu pointed his thumb over his shoulder.

Lance looked for a place to step, two guys parted. He carefully passed through the circle.

"Don't trip, man," someone said, followed by more snickering.

Lance headed for the safety of the used board area, which was partitioned off by a wall of new surfboards standing in a wooden rack. The floor in that section was covered in bark dust and his canvas deck shoes sank into the mulch as the conversation out front started up again. Lance inspected the three rows of used surfboards.

There were longboards, short boards, skinny boards and wide boards of all colors, even psychedelic. One board looked like a needle, long and narrow and pointed at both ends. Lance walked the aisles touching each surfboard. They were all marked on the outside rail with a white sticker and a hand written price. A nice looking white board was sixty dollars, an okay yellow one was forty-five and a beat-up green board was marked at twenty-two.

The place smelled of laminating resin and Lance liked the aroma. He inhaled deep and dug his fingernails into the wax on the green board's deck. He rolled the wax into his palm and formed it into a ball. Suddenly the voices out front got much louder and the guys were talking over each other.

"Did you see how long he was in that tube?"

"I think they sped up the film on B.K."

"That wipeout sequence was far out."

7

"It was that splinter he was riding, the dude just surfs fast."

"Did you see how many chicks were there?"

Lance knew they were talking about the surf movie that had played at the Women's Center the night before. He'd almost gotten to go. His sister Jean promised to take him, but at the last minute some guy named Alan asked her to go.

Lance squished the ball of wax flat and peeked through the partition of surfboards and listened.

"Did anybody see Harmony last night in that halter top?" asked a frizzy blonde guy.

Cat calls and laughter rose up.

"Didn't McGillis take her out?"

"Yeah, he took her to the *Trade Winds* and spent thirty bucks on dinner and didn't even kiss her."

"Man, don't let him hear you say that. Anybody see him kick that guy's ass at the Pipe last week?"

"I did," said a freckled guy. "Some Souther from L.A. cuts him off and McGillis pulls the dude's board out from under him and surfs in with it. He takes the guys board and throws it on the rocks, then he picks it up and throws it again."

"That Souther came in wantin' to kill him," said the frizzy guy. "But McGillis picks up a rock and throws it at the guy's foot then punches him in the face. It was classic."

Cheers and laughter broke out.

"Yeah man, we need more stuff like that happenin' around here, seems like there's more Southers in the water everyday. I say we start slashing tires and breaking windows, make 'em think twice about coming up here."

"That's the kind of crap that needs to stop," Fu Manchu said quieting the room. "Fight on the beach all you want, but vandalizing and stealing is where I draw the line."

"Ha, Dennis, you just want more Southers surfing up here so

8

you'll get more business," said Frizzy Hair.

Dennis ran his fingers over his mustache. "Look man, I don't want crowded waves any more than you do, but you can't just randomly attack guys' cars."

Frizzy Hair shook his head. "I say whatever it takes to get 'em to surf somewhere else."

The room erupted in debate. Lance never imagined there was hostility and violence amongst surfers.

"It's the younger kids that need to step up," somebody said. "They're the ones that should be doing this stuff. The Rats need to pay their dues."

"That's great," Dennis said, "turn the kids into criminals--"

"More like pirates, you know, protecting their treasure. Plus they're minors, they can't get in trouble."

Dennis called out, "How you doing back there?"

Lance saw heads turn his direction and ducked back. He yelped, "I'm fine." Near the end of the aisle he noticed a red board that looked cool. The deck was solid red and the bottom was orange and yellow like flames. He pulled it out of the rack and another board came with it. He caught the other board before it fell, but the two surfboards clunked together.

"You break it, you buy it," someone said. Everyone laughed.

"Everything okay?" Dennis asked.

"Yeah, it's fine." He put the board back and looked at the red one. He liked it. He imagined the flames on the bottom flashing as he cranked a bottom turn. He looked at the sticker; forty bucks, crap. He put the board back and continued pacing the three aisles wishing the damn pow wow would end.

Finally someone said, "Well, I gotta get going."

"Yeah man, me too."

Lance peeked out. They were getting up.

"Later man, peace."

9

"See you in the water."

A raspy voice spoke up. "Hey, has anybody heard anything more about the body that washed up at the Pipe?"

"They think it was a bum that washed out of Hobo Jungle with the rain last week."

"I heard his skull was cracked," Dennis said.

Lance thought about what his dad always said about Hobo Jungle.

"Did they find who did it?"

"I doubt they investigated a dead hobo."

Lance saw Dennis coming his way and put his hand on the nose of the nearest board as if sizing it up.

"See anything you like?"

Lance squished the ball of wax in his hand and pointed to the red board. "Uh, I kind of like that one."

"Oh yeah?" Dennis pulled it from the rack. "This is a good board, you just starting?"

"Yeah, I'm not sure what I'm looking for, I just like the looks of that one."

Dennis smiled. "Well, you wanna like looking at it, you'll probably spend more time with it than your girlfriend."

Lance flushed. "I don't have a girlfriend."

"Yeah, you're probably a little young for that. How old are you?"

"Thirteen."

"Great age to start." Dennis placed the nose of the board on the ground and held the tail close to his face. He closed one eye and lifted and lowered the tail like a golfer eyeing a green.

"Was that a club meeting you guys were having?"

Dennis laughed. "No, just a rap session, it happens a lot." He turned the board on its side and eyeballed the rail. "Rails are soft, it'll be easy to turn. I think this would be a good first board. A

10

little hard to catch waves on at first, but you'll get used to it."

"Cool...but, I can't get it today, I've only got thirty-seven dollars."

Dennis looked at the sticker and raised an eyebrow. "Hmmm, forty bucks?" He looked at Lance. "And you have thirty-seven..." He opened his mouth and smoothed his mustache. "I think I can do that."

Lance wasn't sure he heard right. "Wow, really?"

Dennis tapped him on the shoulder. "We gotta get you in the water. I'll throw in a couple bars of wax too. Do you have a wetsuit?"

Lance shook his head.

"Well, you don't need to worry about that now, you're young, a little cold water won't hurt you."

Lance sucked in the resin soaked air. He was getting his first surfboard.

Dennis smiled. "It's a special day, you only get your first surfboard once."

Lance handed him the thirty-seven dollars and with a bar of wax in each back pocket he carried his red surfboard down the steps for the bike ride home.

It was awkward riding at first, but once he got going it wasn't bad. After a few blocks he had to stop and switch arms, then again a few blocks later. It was a lot harder than he thought it would be, but he felt like the luckiest kid in the world.

3
SANDCRAB

Nicky slid his lunch tray onto a table in the cafeteria. "I can't believe you spent thirty-seven bucks on a surfboard. When you ever gonna a use it?"

Lance put his tray down across from his friend. "I'm gonna use it today, I'm gonna use it every day."

Marty sat down next to Nicky. "I'm saving my money for a mini-bike."

"I thought you guys wanted to learn to surf too."

"No way, I'm not shiverin' my balls off just to get water on the brain," Nicky said. "I'm stickin' to throwin' touchdowns."

Lance cut into his macaroni casserole. "You can surf and still play football. I'm gonna."

* * * *

After school Lance didn't wait around for his friends at the bike racks like usual. He raced home, grabbed some food and his surfboard and pedaled down to Schoolhouse jetty. Schoolhouse was one of the seven rock jetties spaced twelve hundred feet apart between the Pier and the Marina. It was second closest to the Marina and was located in front of Pierpont Elementary School. It was also the beach his parents always took them to and he figured it was as good a place as any to learn to surf.

It was early May and the afternoon wind was cool. Lance had his swim trunks on under his corduroy pants. He decided it would be warmer just to leave the cords on. There were a handful of surfers on the south side of the jetty, so Lance kept to the north side to give himself room to practice.

As he waded into the cold water his cords became clingy and heavy. He laid on the wobbly board and tried to paddle. A wave slapped him in the face and took the board out from under him. He scrambled after it and waded back out to waist deep water. When a two-foot wave broke in front of him he turned and dove onto his belly. The board was fast, much faster than the cheap Styrofoam Waveriders he used as a kid.

He waded back out, this time he'd stand up. He caught another whitewater and struggled to get to his knees. Shivering and weighed down by his pants he groaned. He knew he wouldn't stand up today. He forced himself out to catch one more wave then went in.

Teeth chattering and wet cords clinging to his legs he climbed onto his bike and headed home. Lesson one; never wear pants in the water.

* * * *

"Man, what's the matter with you?" Marty asked. "It's been two weeks since you played football."

The plan had always been for Lance, Nicky and Martin, to play football together at Ventura High School. But Lance hadn't shown up at the football field since he got his surfboard.

"I wanna learn to surf right now. I'll play football again, just give me some time."

"I was right, he's gettin' salt water on the brain," Nicky said.

Lance endured the last few weeks of eighth grade and accepted the growing distance between him and his friends. He stopped eating lunch with them, preferring to sneak up to Cemetery Park and eat where he could see the waves breaking at the Point.

13

On the last day of school they got out early to sign yearbooks. Lance made his way around the huddles of students to get to the bike racks. He saw Nicky and Martin standing amongst a group. Nicky shouted, "Hey Lance, surf's up." He mocked standing on a surfboard and the others laughed. Lance smiled and waved. He was free.

* * * *

From the first day of summer Lance slept in his surf trunks. He'd wake up early, eat breakfast, pack a lunch, stuff it into his backpack with a towel and canteen, tuck his board under his arm and bike to Schoolhouse. He'd surf all day, come home, eat dinner, play records in his room, read *Surfer* magazine and fall asleep in his trunks again. Showers and underwear were no longer necessary.

"You can't sleep in your trunks every night," his mom said. "And when was the last time you showered?"

"I wash every day in the ocean."

"You need to rinse the salt off."

"Why? I'm just gonna get salty again."

Lance practiced standing up on his red surfboard in the whitewater until he could do it almost every time. The next step was paddling into a swell. He spent hours sitting on his board, waiting, teeth chattering. It was all about reading the waves, timing and position, but most important was staying out of the way of the other surfers. Every day they called him "kook," short for pain-in-the-ass beginner.

"What are you doing out here, kook?"

"Out of the way, kook."

"Why don't you move down the beach, kook."

14

Just catching a wave was hard, let alone trying to stand up and not pearl (nose-dive). How was he supposed to concentrate on that and keep tabs on what everybody else was doing?

He kept to himself and avoided eye contact. After a few weeks the other guys seemed to tolerate him as long as he stayed out of the way.

On July fourth Lance turned fourteen. His mom made him a cake with a surfer on it. He got a clock radio, a subscription to Surfer magazine and twenty bucks to buy a wetsuit.

That night he and his sister Ann sat on a towel on the roof of the house and watched fireworks. Ann was two years older, they had been close as kids, but now they seemed worlds apart. She was a cheerleader at the high school and had tons of friends. He was a loner trying to learn how to surf while getting heckled at the beach every day. The evening was warm and after a cluster of fireworks Ann asked, "What happened to your friends?"

"What do you mean?"

"I never see you with Martin or Nicky anymore."

Lance leaned back on his elbows. "I started surfing."

"So, you're not friends because they don't surf?"

"Yeah, pretty much."

The sky lit up with another flurry of fireworks.

Ann turned to him again. "What about at the beach?"

"What about it?"

"Do you have any friends there?"

"What do you care?" He sat up and wrapped his arms around his knees. "I go there to surf, not to make friends."

"I was just wondering." A single firework sparkled across the sky followed by a delayed *boom*. "I thought if you didn't have anybody to hang out with at the beach, maybe I could go with you sometimes."

He studied her face to make sure she was serious. "You want to come to the beach with me?"

"Sure, I get bored laying out in the backyard. It'd be fun to go the beach and watch you surf."

He smiled. "I'm in the water almost all day you know."

"Lance, I'll be in the sun with a book. You don't have to worry about me."

From the moment Ann started coming to the beach things were different. Guys who'd never given him the time of day suddenly nodded like they knew him. They asked him how it was going and started giving him pointers.

"Don't go to your knees first, jump straight to your feet."

"Work on your paddling, the stronger you paddle the more waves you'll catch."

He knew they were trying to position themselves closer to Ann, but she seemed to like the attention and he was finally accepted.

One morning at home Lance ran into his older sister Jean in the hallway waiting for the bathroom. "Hey Lance," she said. "I was at the Pier yesterday and there's a whole bunch of surfers about your age there. Christine's boyfriend calls them Pier Rats. I bet you could make some friends there." Jean was eighteen and worked at a hip clothing store called Calamity Jane. She was ultra cool and sort of a fashion maven. She convinced their mom to buy him a pair of bell-bottom pants in third grade. He got teased at first, but by fourth grade everybody was wearing them.

"I can't just go to the Pier," Lance said.

"Why not, it's just a beach." She pounded on the bathroom door. "Ann, what are you doing in there!"

"It's not just a beach it's a surf spot, there's rules."

The Pier was the closest thing Ventura had to a tourist attraction. It was the oldest and longest fishing pier on the West

Coast and had a snack bar and bait shop. As a kid Lance loved to walk out on the Pier to see what the fishermen were catching. He and Ann would get nervous walking over the wide gaps in the planks where you could see the water below.

He knew if he tried surfing the Pier he'd be back at the bottom of the barrel getting heckled.

A week later when the waves were small and Ann hadn't come with him to the beach, Lance decided to bike to the Pier and check it out. The distance was almost twice as far from home as Schoolhouse and he remembered how hard it was carrying his board home from the Surf Shop. But now he made it all the way there without having to switch arms.

He rode onto the Pier and looked out over the beach. The white sand was covered with colorful towels and umbrellas. He smelled hamburgers and french fries cooking in the snack bar. He stopped and put his foot on the railing. Kids were drinking soda pops and licking ice cream cones. Seagulls squawked and children laughed. There were girls in bikinis and kids building sandcastles. It was like an amusement park compared to Schoolhouse.

In the water there were five or six guys getting perfectly rideable waist high waves, even in the windy conditions. On the beach five surfboards stood like totems in the sand directly in line with the surf peak. Lance crossed to the north side of the Pier where the wind blew in his face. About fifteen guys were surfing the Point. He thought how cool it would be to surf the Pier, eat a hamburger, then walk up the beach and surf the Point. He rode back to Schoolhouse knowing someday the Pier and the Point would be his territory too.

* * * *

By the end of summer Lance was an accepted local at the jetties, an official *Jetty Jerk*. But still, none of the Jerks were a real friend. When school started he put on socks and shoes and long pants for the first time in almost three months. He roamed the halls of Cabrillo Junior High only thinking of the waves he was missing. He felt like an alien with nothing in common with the other kids.

In class he drew waves on his Pee Chee folder waiting for the next bell to ring. What did math and English have to do with dropping in and bottom turns? He had so much to learn about surfing. Surfing was his future, not school. He daydreamed of tropical beaches where the waves were always good and he could snorkel for food and live in a grass shack on the beach. He created that scene over and over on the backs of the zillions of handouts the teachers gave him.

When he saw Nicky and Martin talking with some classmates he nodded and smiled. They nodded and turned away. That first week was tough.

At the end of school on Friday Lance hurried to the bike racks. He saw a kid he recognized from the year before--Pee Wee--but he'd changed. Lance noticed Pee Wee's hair was longer and sun-bleached, just like his. His face sunburned and blistered, just like his. They approached each other and Pee Wee said, "You surf now?"

"Yeah. You?"

"Yeah, started this summer."

"Me too. You're Pee Wee, right?"

"Used to be, now they call me Sandcrab. You're Lance, right?"

"Yeah, still Lance. Where do you surf?"

"The Pier. How 'bout you?"

Lance's heart raced. "Schoolhouse."

18

"Cool, I've never surfed the jetties before."

"You want to?"

"Sure."

"I'm gettin' my board and going down there now, you want to meet me?"

"Is it cool?"

"Yeah, I know everybody there. You know where Surf Liquor is on Pierpont?"

"Sure," Sandcrab said. "I can be there in half an hour."

Lance smiled. "That's fast, I'll see you there."

4
SCHOOLHOUSE JETTY

Lance rode his bike on a little cement wave outside of Surf Liquor. "I beat you," he said as Sandcrab coasted up.

"I ate a banana and jammed down as fast as I could."

They pedaled down Pierpont Boulevard and cut down the lane to Schoolhouse Jetty. Sandcrab asked, "Are you goofy foot or regular?"

Lance wasn't sure, he knew he faced the wave when he went right, but wasn't sure which was which. "I don't know."

Sandcrab laughed. "Do you surf with your left foot forward or your right?"

"Left."

Then you're regular foot, like me. It's got nothing to do with whether you're left handed or right. There's twins that surf the Pier and they're both right handed, but one's a goofy foot and the other one's regular."

They locked their bikes to the railing where the street met the sand.

"Nobody's out yet, we have it all to ourselves," Lance said.

Sandcrab shielded his eyes and looked at the water. "Tide's going out, will it get better?"

Lance thought for a moment, he'd never been asked about the moods of the waves before. "Uh, it's mushier at high tide...and more peaky. It gets faster and hollower as the tide goes out, but it walls up more. Looks like high tide was about an hour ago, so yeah, it should be getting better."

They walked across the sand to the jetty and climbed over the rocks to the south side and got out their wetsuits.

20

Lance had a beavertail jacket he'd bought from a Schoolhouse local with the twenty bucks his parents gave him for his birthday. The guy had told him it was more important to keep his upper body covered, not only to protect against the cold water, but also the wind chill. The jacket zipped up the front and had a wide flat tail like a beaver's that hung in the back. The tail was meant to come up around the crotch and snap in the front, but the guy warned him, "Only dorks do that."

Sandcrab had a simple pullover wetsuit top called sleeves. It had no zipper and required the skill of Houdini to get on and off. He got his head and arms in, but Lance had to help him pull down the bundle of rubber around his chest.

Lance thought it would be fun to add a little adventure to Sandcrab's first experience surfing Schoolhouse. "You wanna try jumpin' in off the jetty? We can paddle straight into the lineup without even getting our hair wet."

"Sure, I guess, whatever you think."

Lance led the way up the rocks. He skipped out boulder to boulder over the water sending sunning purple crabs scuttling for crevices. He stopped a little beyond the breaking waves. "This is good."

Sandcrab looked down at the barnacle-covered rocks at water level. "You sure this is safe?"

"Yeah, it's easy."

Lance climbed down and stood on a rock just above the water line. He waited for a swell to pass, then jumped down to the barnacle-covered rocks where hundreds of little waterfalls spilled out around him. The next swell surged around his knees. He looked up at Sandcrab still on the dry rocks.

"Come on down, get on this rock next to me."

The water drained away exposing the jagged boulders around him. Sandcrab looked nervous but started down. After the next surge he jumped onto the rock next to Lance.

"Now we'll wait for a big swell to go in on," Lance instructed. "You don't want to hit your fin on a rock."

A small swell washed over their ankles.

"I don't know," Sandcrab said, "paddling out seems easier."

"Nah, this is cool, get ready, I'll tell you when to jump."

"You've done this before, right?"

"Yeah, a bunch of times...well, a couple...okay, here comes one, this looks good, okay...get ready...jump!"

The ocean rose above their knees and they jumped on their boards and paddled. Lance felt a jolt as his fin snagged a rock. The water receded and the bottom of his board scraped on barnacles. He rolled off the board into the water and with his foot found a rock then launched himself into deeper water. He stroked to catch up with Sandcrab who sat dry in the lineup.

"You were right, that was cool. Hey, how'd you get your hair wet?"

Lance paddled in front of him and lifted his foot. "Am I bleeding?"

"Looks like a cut on your big toe and ankle. I'll keep my eyes peeled for sharks," he joked. "Here comes a wave."

Sandcrab paddled away and to Lance's surprise caught the first wave he tried for. He rode it all the way in. Lance had expected him to struggle, at least a little. Now he felt pressure to prove he could surf too. Lance went for the first wave that came and scrambled to catch it. He dropped in late and almost pearled. He barely made the turn and had to jump to the nose of his board for speed. He surfed past Sandcrab who hooted as he paddled over the shoulder.

Lance felt embarrassed, he'd almost ate it on the takeoff, then barely made it through the section. He paddled to Sandcrab who grinned wide.

"Man, that was a killer drop you made and you powered through that section, that was hot."

Lance swelled with pride. "That looked like a good wave you got."

"Not as good as the next one I'm gonna get."

For the first time Lance knew what it was like to have a friend in the water. He knew they would make each other better.

Back on the beach Lance unzipped his wetsuit and Sandcrab pulled his sleeves up around his chest. Lance helped him yank the wetsuit over his head. "How do you get this thing on and off when nobody's around?"

"It's not easy." Sandcrab worked an arm free. "You wanna meet again tomorrow?"

"Sure, you wanna surf here again?"

"How about we try my side of town? We can meet at the Surf Shop and go to the Pier."

Lance suppressed his excitement. "Sure, what time you wanna meet?"

5
THE PIER

Lance ate a large bowl of cereal as his mom poured water into the coffee percolator.

"Slow down and chew Lance, what's the rush?"

"I'm kind of in a hurry."

"What, are the waves going somewhere?"

"I'm meeting somebody. I'm gonna surf the Pier today."

She put the top on the percolator and placed it on the stove. "I thought you said you couldn't surf there."

"Not alone, that's why I'm meeting somebody."

"Who's somebody? Did you make a friend?"

"I don't know, maybe."

His dad came in the kitchen. "Boy, what a beautiful day. We should go out for breakfast, get some huevos rancheros."

"Lance is meeting a friend to go surfing at the Pier."

"He is?" He turned to Lance. "I thought you didn't care about friends."

"I don't." Lance slurped the last of the milk in his bowl. "It's no big deal, just a guy I met at school. His name's Sandcrab."

His dad laughed. "Sandwho?"

"It's probably just a nickname Jim," his mom said.

Lance stood up. "He used to be called Pee Wee, but the guys at the Pier call him Sandcrab now."

His mom opened the refrigerator. "Do you want me to make you a sandwich to take?"

"Sure, thanks Mom. Do you think I could have a little money too? There's a snack bar there."

"Jim, get my purse on the dining room table, I have some change." She got out the baloney and mayonnaise. "You're not going to try and shoot the Pier are you Lance?"

Lance looked at her. "How do you know what that is?"

"I grew up between the Santa Monica and Venice Piers, I know what surfing through the pilings is called." She put the sandwich into a bag with a cookie and some carrots. "Be careful riding your bike on Harbor Boulevard."

His dad added, "Be sure and tell your friend Sandpebbles I said hello."

* * * *

Lance arrived at the Surf Shop first. He cruised up to the wooden stairs and put his foot on the bottom step. The shop was dark, he heard a rumbling inside and watched as a snarling mass of teeth and fur slammed into the glass. Lance leapt from his bike as the German shepherd inside went berserk trying to get him.

"Ha, ha," Sandcrab said riding up. "Diablo's pretty scary, huh?"

"That dog's insane."

"It's weird, as soon as Dennis locks the door he turns into a psycho."

Lance picked up his bike and he and Sandcrab rode over the pedestrian bridge to the Pier. The beach was mostly empty. There were two guys in the water and three boards standing in the sand by the trashcan. They pedaled onto the Pier and locked their bikes to the railing.

The bait shop was open, but the snack bar was closed. Lance put his free hand on the snack bar window to see the menu. "Do you ever get a hamburger after surfing?"

"I have, but they're kind of expensive. The best place to eat is The Galley, you can get ten corn burritos for a buck, normally they're fifteen cents each."

"Cool, where's The Galley?"

"A block up from the shop. You have any money?"

"Fifty cents."

"Me too, we can go there later."

They went down the stairs to the sand and walked toward the three surfers on the beach. "You know these guys?"

"Yeah, looks like Stoody, Q and one of the twins. Dugo and the goofy footed twin are in the water. It's mostly a left break, so the goofy-footers have an advantage."

"Are these guys cool?"

"They think so. Just ignore 'em and act like you belong. We'll get our wetsuits on and go straight out."

Sandcrab stabbed the tail of his board into the sand. "Watch where you plant your board, there's a lotta rocks around."

Lance planted his board and faced the bottom the same direction as everybody else's. He whispered, "How come everybody faces their board this way?"

"So the sun doesn't melt the wax."

Lance nodded. He liked the idea that throughout the day the surfboards would turn with the sun.

He took off his backpack and dropped it onto the sand. He shook out his wetsuit. There was a thud and Lance saw his surfboard lying on the sand. The three guys looked over. Lance picked up his board and replanted it.

A guy sitting on the sand drinking a Coke said, "Hey Crab, you bringing kooks down here, or what?" He looked about fifteen.

"He's no more of a kook than you are Stoody."

26

"Watch it little man if you want to get any waves when I'm in the water."

"Yeah, right." Sandcrab stepped closer to Lance. "He's actually a pretty cool guy."

They paddled out and stuck to the south side of the peak letting the other two guys take the lefts and they took the rights. They alternated waves and Lance got a good feel for the break.

After a while the twin and Dugo were gone and the three guys from the beach and another guy came out. As the tide came in the peak got tighter forcing everyone to sit closer together. The guys kidded and joked around. Sandcrab sat with them and joked too, they seemed to like him. Lance stayed to the inside, out of the way. Every now and then someone would give him a once over. Lance would nod and they would look away.

The atmosphere in the water was aggressive, yet more relaxed than at Schoolhouse. Here the guys teased each other and hung out. At Schoolhouse everyone was serious, caught their waves and went home.

More guys came out and Lance wasn't getting any waves. He decided to go in and warm up on the beach.

There were five guys by the trashcan now and they watched him approach. Lance avoided eye contact. He wished his towel and backpack weren't so close. He'd just do like Sandcrab said and act like he belonged. He stabbed his board into the sand, picked up his towel and looked out at the water. He could feel them staring.

"Hey man, you know somebody here?"

Lance looked over not sure who spoke. "I came with Sandcrab."

"Really?" said a guy with dark brown hair streaked blonde. He had fuzz on his upper lip. "Well, just because Sandcrab brings you down here doesn't make you cool with us, you need to move."

Lance wished he'd waited for Sandcrab by the water. *It's okay*, he thought, *I expected this. I'll respect the guy.* He took a breath. "Okay."

"Pick up your stuff and start walking, I'll tell you when you can stop."

Lance picked up his backpack and grabbed his board.

A guy with blonde ringlets said, "Oooh, do those flames make your board go faster?" They all laughed.

Lance started walking.

When he'd taken about fifteen steps the Fuzzy Lip guy said, "That's good, I can't smell you from there."

Lance dropped his backpack and towel and planted his board in the sand. He stood and watched the waves. He could hear the guys bickering and laughing, then one of them called out, "Hey!"

Lance looked over. It was Ringlets with his chest out and his hands on his hips, "You're still too close, move one more step." Lance tensed up and looked back at the water. *He's got to be kidding.*

"What are you waiting for, are you deaf? I said one more step."

If he took another step he'd look like a fool.

"Hey, dumb shit, I said move...do I need to come over there and kick your ass another step?"

Lance burned inside.

Somebody said, "Just leave him alone, Scott."

"I'm only asking the butthead to move one more step. Screw you guys, I'll make him move myself." Ringlets started towards him.

Lance's mind raced. He picked up a lemon-sized rock.

28

Ringlets stopped and grinned. "Ooh, tough guy. You gonna throw the rock tough guy?" He took another step and Lance pump faked causing him to flinch and his curls to bounce. The guys laughed. He pointed at Lance, "You little shit, you're gonna die."

Lance cocked his arm back.

"Throw the rock kid, c'mon, I dare ya, throw it. C'mon pussy, do it."

Lance looked at his jeering face and wanted to smash it. He swallowed. Ringlets took a step and Lance threw the rock just over his head. Ringlets yelped and fell back on the sand. The rock sailed passed and struck a surfboard by the trashcan. Everyone watched as the surfboard slowly fell over.

Lance's throat swelled.

Ringlets sat up. "Ha! That's Roach's board, you're dead now."

Lance watched the brown haired guy with the fuzzy lip walk over and look at the damage, then glare his way.

"You stupid asshole." Angry and red Roach came toward him.

Lance prepared for a beating, but Roach stopped at Ringlets sitting on the sand and slapped him on the head. "You're an idiot, you're always taking shit too far."

"Hey, why you hitting me?"

"You couldn't leave the kid alone. You had to be the tough guy. You're fixin' my board and I'm riding yours 'til you do." Roach looked at Lance. "Watch where you're throwing rocks kid."

Lance sat down in the sand and hugged his knees and stared out at the ocean.

A while later Sandcrab came running up from the water. "Why are you sittin' over here?"

Lance squinted in the sun's glare. "That guy Roach told me to move."

"What for?"

"I hit his board with a rock."

"You what?"

"How about we go get those corn burritos?"

"Why were you throwing rocks?"

"It's a long story, I'll tell you on the way."

"Geez, I can't wait to hear this."

INITIATION

The corn burritos at The Galley were buried in melted cheese and red sauce.

"Those were the best things I've ever tasted," Lance said licking his fingers. "I wish we had another dollar."

Sandcrab ran his finger along the bottom of the cardboard boat scraping up what was left of the cheese and sauce.

"Hey, save me some of that."

Sandcrab handed Lance the empty boat. "So, what are you gonna do when we get back to the beach?"

"Nothing," Lance said licking the container. "I'll just keep my distance."

"Yeah, I don't think anybody's gonna bother you again today." Crab stood up and gathered their trash from the table. "You want to stop by the Surf Shop and see what's going on? I've got a dime and there's a candy machine there."

"Sure." It was hard to believe he could surf the Pier, eat corn burritos at The Galley and go to the Surf Shop all before the day was half over.

As they came around the corner from Ash to Front Street Sandcrab pointed to the fishing boat on blocks behind the Shop. "That's where Dennis lives."

"Whoa, what a righteous pad. Is that his Karmann Ghia too?"

"Yeah. See the ladder on the ground, that means he's not there. He's probably working, he's always working."

"Whose van is that?" Lance pointed to a beat up brown Volkswagen van parked in front of the Shop.

"That's Scarecrow's, we call it the Turd."

Lance laughed. "It looks like a turd. Why do they call him Scarecrow?"

"'Cause he looks like one."

Diablo slept at the top of the steps and barely opened his eyes as they came up. They walked in and Sandcrab yelled, "Anybody home?"

No one was around and Sandcrab turned to the candy machine. "Dennis is probably in back." He slipped his dime into the slot and pulled the handle for a candy bar. A guy appeared from behind a rack of surfboards with a red bandana around his face like a bandit. He was lanky and his hair was yellow and stiff like straw. He held a trowel. "Hey Crow," Sandcrab said. "Where's Dennis?"

Crow pulled down the bandana. "He's buffing out a board in back, I'm watching the front."

Sandcrab looked at the trowel. "What are you doing?"

"I'm laying some carpet back there. Dennis got a bunch of scraps for free and I'm piecing 'em together. You been down at the Pier?"

"Yeah. This is my friend Lance. Lance, Crow."

"Hi," Lance said.

Crow nodded and looked at Sandcrab's candy bar. "Man, I'm starved, can I have a bite of that?"

Sandcrab peeled back the wrapper and held out the candy bar. Crow grabbed it and stuck the whole thing in his mouth and handed the wrapper back to Sandcrab. "Um-flanx," he said, and disappeared behind the surfboards.

Sandcrab squished the empty wrapper. "You're a jerk Crow!"

Dennis came out of the back with a big smile, "Hey Sandcrab, what's up man? How's the waves today?"

Sandcrab scowled. "I just bought a candy bar and Crow ate the whole thing."

32

From behind the racks Crow said, "Consider it payment for the ride home I gave you the other day."

"Screw you, Crow."

Dennis shook his head and smoothed his mustache. He walked behind the counter and opened the register. "Here's a dime, I'll take it out of his pay." He looked at Lance. "Hey, how's that red board working for you?"

"Uh, it works good, thanks." *Wow, he remembers me.*

"Listen to this," Sandcrab said slipping the dime into the candy machine. "Today's his first time surfing the Pier and he throws a rock at Scott and hits Roach's board."

Lance's face grew hot and he wanted to strangle Sandcrab.

Dennis grinned. "How'd you manage that?"

Crow came back out with the bandana covering his mouth. "If that's true how come your face isn't rearranged?"

"It was an accident, the guy with the ringlets was hassling me, I threw a rock to scare him and it hit Roach's board. I guess Roach blamed him more than me."

"Did you call Scott, Ringlets?" Crow laughed. "That's funny...yeah, he can be an ass."

Dennis came out from behind the counter. "Well, sounds like you made an impression. Hey, I left a couple of games on the pinball machine if you guys want 'em."

Sandcrab's eyes widened. "Thanks man. Come on, I got first game."

This is too cool, Lance thought following Sandcrab to the pinball machine.

* * * *

Lance started going to the Pier every day. After a couple weeks he knew who all the Pier Rats were and had a grasp on the

33

undefined hierarchy. Age, size and ability had the most to do with it. Dugo and the twins were the oldest at seventeen and though they had authority they were on the way out. Sixteen was the prime age, which Crow, Roach and Q were. Nobody messed with them. Stoody, Bill and Ringlets were all fifteen and jostling for position while Sandcrab was fourteen and at the bottom of the barrel. Lance was fourteen too, but he wasn't even in the barrel. There were others, mostly older guys, but they didn't hang out much. There was McGillis who was nineteen or twenty, and Dennis, who was like, twenty-six, and other older guys.

Lance continued to keep his distance on the beach and he followed the rules in the water giving no one reason to hassle him.

By mid-October the surfers were the only ones on the beach except for the occasional strollers and fishermen. With the sun setting earlier and the air getting colder Lance knew he would need more wetsuit soon if he was going surf through the winter.

On the day before Halloween, with the sun fading, Lance came out of the water shivering. Roach, Stoody and some other guys had made a fire in the trashcan and were warming themselves. Lance picked up his towel and held it to his mouth to feel the warmth of his breath. He wished he could go by the fire. He watched as Sandcrab and Dennis came in and went to the trashcan.

Sandcrab looked over. "Hey Lance, come and get warm."

"Yeah, come by the fire," Dennis said.

Lance waited for the reactions of the others. Stoody and Roach looked up in the firelight. Nobody else seemed to pay any attention. Dugo and one of the twins were gathering their stuff to leave. Lance figured he could go over since Dennis invited him, no one would argue with Dennis. He walked over and put his hands to the flames. "Man, that feels good."

34

With the light disappearing guys were coming out of the water one after the other. McGillis stopped at the fire for a second then ran to catch up with Dugo. Then Bill came in, and Scarecrow. When Dennis picked up his board to leave, Lance was alone with the Rats. He listened to them talk about their waves and joke around, he laughed and tried to be cool. Then Ringlets came out of the water.

"Hey man, make some room it's freezing out here." The circle opened and Ringlets stepped up and put his hands to the fire. He noticed Lance. "What the hell is he doing here?"

"Same thing as you," Sandcrab said, "getting warm."

"So what? He just gets to waltz in here?"

"What are you talking about?" Sandcrab sneered.

"This is bullshit. We need to make some rules around here. If somebody wants to surf the Pier they should have to go through an initiation or something."

Lance tensed up as everybody waited to hear what Ringlets had in mind.

"What are you ranting about?" Sandcrab said. "We don't need any initiation."

"I say we start now." Ringlets looked directly at Sandcrab. "With you and your friend."

"Me!" Sandcrab protested. "It's a little late for that, you're an idiot."

"And you're a pussy. I say you and your friend cigarette wrestle so we can see who the bigger pussy is."

Sandcrab swatted the air. "You're crazy."

There was a sudden buzz around the fire.

"I've got a cigarette," Bill said.

"I'm not doing it." Sandcrab looked around for support. "This is stupid."

The guys gathered round.

35

"Okay, put your arms together," Roach said.

Bill lit a cigarette.

Roach put a hand on each of their shoulders. "Okay, first one to pull away loses."

Sandcrab looked around in desperation. "You guys, come on, this is stupid."

Sandcrab's fear somehow calmed Lance. "Let's just get it over with," he said and raised his forearm.

Sandcrab frowned and lifted his arm. Lance pressed his against it. Bill took a drag on the cigarette and dropped it between their arms. The cherry glowed on their skin and before Lance could feel anything Sandcrab pulled away. "Screw you guys, I'm not doing this."

As the cigarette hit the sand Lance felt the sting on his arm.

"Oh geez, what a pussy," Ringlets said.

Sandcrab clenched his fists and swung at Ringlets who was a head taller.

Ringlets stepped back and laughed. "Oh, looks like I pissed off the Sandflea." He looked down at Sandcrab. "Don't make me squish you."

Lance stepped up to Ringlets. "How about you do it then?"

Ringlets scoffed, "I'm not doing anything, I don't even want you in, why would I bother?"

"Come on, it was your idea," Roach said, "let's see you do it."

"Look, if Sandpussy, or anybody else won't do it then I say he's out."

"I'll do it," Scarecrow said.

Ringlets laughed. "Don't mess around Crow."

Scarecrow put his arm out. "I'm not."

"Don't be silly, man. You don't have to."

Lance put his arm up to Crow's.

Ringlets backed away. "What are you doing man?"

36

Crow looked at Ringlets. "Don't start something you're not prepared to finish. You want an initiation? Then we'll all get initiated. Me and Lance'll go first, and the loser'll go against you, and we'll go right down the line, Roach, Bill, everybody."

"You're blowing this way out of proportion," Ringlets said. "Now it's getting stupid."

"Let's do it," Roach said. "You guys ready? Light the smoke Bill."

Lance and Crow pushed their arms together, Bill took a drag on the cigarette and dropped it between their arms.

Again there was a moment before Lance felt anything, then it came. He clenched his teeth and sucked in air through his nostrils. Breathing was his only defense. He huffed and puffed as the pain increased extending his lips like a cartoon kisser. He sucked in smoke with every breath. He heard Crow hissing through clenched teeth. Their breathing synched. Lance glared at Crow. Crow gritted his teeth. "You ready to give up?"

Lance clenched back, "Nope...feels good."

Crow smiled and gritted, "Yeah...tickles."

When the cigarette stopped smoking Roach inspected it. "I think it's out."

Lance looked at Crow, "Go ahead, pull away."

"I'm not pulling away, you pull away."

Bill plucked the cigarette from between their arms and puffed on it. "Yep, it's out."

Lance looked at the burn on his arm, it was oval and white with black around the edges. Not as ugly as he thought it would be. He wanted to hoot and holler, but he took his cue from Crow and just acted cool. Crow looked at his wound too. Lance said, "You're pretty tough."

Crow laughed and slapped him on the back. "Yeah, you too." He turned to Ringlets who stared into the dwindling fire. "You're off the hook Ringlets, no loser. We're all done."

Everyone cheered.

"Hey Ringlets," Roach said. "You wanna go a round just for fun?"

Ringlets turned to gather his stuff. "Screw you."

Crow turned to Lance. "We're gonna have some hellashish blisters tomorrow. Probably be a good idea to put Vaseline or something on it before surfing."

Sandcrab looked at their burns. "You guys are nuts."

7
SURF SACRIFICE

On an early morning in November Lance opened the front door prepared for the autumn chill. Instead he was hit by a gust of hot desert air--the Santa Ana winds. Though the winds swept over the southland every fall from California's eastern deserts, they always came unexpected.

Lance watched as the wind lashed at the fig tree across the street and static electricity collected on his wool sweater. He yanked off the sweater and felt the charged wool pull at his hair.

For the next several days Southern Californians would have to endure the hot dry winds and rampant wild fires they often fueled. Many considered the winds a curse, but for the surfers the Santa Ana's were a blessing. The strong offshore winds blew from the east hitting the waves straight on, holding the faces up for steeper, faster rides.

After school Lance raced to the beach on his bike with his board. He could see the waves were flat, but with the hot air and offshore winds he could feel something brewing. Speeding down Harbor Boulevard his front wheel veered off the pavement onto the sandy shoulder, his tire slid out and he went down. Lying there he groaned and lifted himself up. He saw no major damage to his board, picked up his bike and pedaled on.

At the Pier he laid his surfboard on the trashcan for inspection. He'd had worse wrecks, like when he hit the sprinkler coming down the dirt path around the lemon factory. He'd flown over the handlebars and smashed the nose of his board. That was his first big ding repair too. It wasn't pretty, but it was still holding up.

Relieved to find only minor scratches he stuck the tail of his board in the sand and turned to study the water. "Damn...flat as a pancake." He pulled the canteen from his backpack and took a long cool drink of water. He'd heard there was a brushfire in Fillmore twenty miles east and now the wind was spreading a smoky haze over the crisp autumn view of Santa Cruz Island twenty miles off the coast.

A gust of wind blew his surfboard over. He replanted the tail and laid out his towel. He sat down and shaded his eyes with both hands. The hot wind dried the sweat in his armpits as he scanned the water for any sign of a wave.

The ocean was dark blue and textured with wind ripples. "Come on waves!" he yelled. A seagull glided overhead toying with the wind. Lance heard a surfboard grind into the sand behind him and turned.

"Man, where's the waves?" Sandcrab said. "These winds are insane."

"They'll be coming any minute, I can feel it."

"Okay Nosferatu, but I'll wait to see one before I put my wetsuit on."

"It can't stay flat forever." Lance saw Scarecrow's brown van roll up the hill at the base of the Pier. "There's the Turd."

Roach and Crow came down with towels around their necks. Roach squinted at the water. "How come you guys aren't out there, too big for ya?"

"That's so funny I forgot to laugh," Sandcrab said.

Lance stood up and unstuck his trunks from his butt. "You guys didn't even bring your boards down? You've got no faith."

"When I see you get a wave I'll run up and get mine," Crow said. "How's your arm?"

Lance held up his cigarette burn. "It's healing."

Crow grimaced. "What happened to your elbow?"

40

Lance turned his arm over and saw a bloody scrape. "Oh geez, I ate it on my bike coming down here."

"Did you hurt your board?" Roach asked.

"It's okay, I landed mostly in the sand."

They turned to the ocean and the warm wind blew at their backs.

Crow picked up a rock and threw it in a high arc to the water. "Man, Santa Ana's revenge is going to waste."

Lance picked up a rock. "What revenge?"

Crow waited for his rock to splash. "They say when we took California from Mexico General Santa Ana cursed us with these winds."

Roach heaved a rock. "Right now we're being cursed by this flat spell. We gotta do something."

"Like what, pray for surf?" Sandcrab laughed.

"Exactly." Roach said. "Stand back, we need to appease the surf gods." Roach found a stick and tied his towel to it. He held the stick toward the water. "Oh mighty surf gods, why do you withhold your precious waves. We beg you, oh powerful ones, please release the waves we crave. Feed us from your infinite bounty and we'll be eternally stoked to you." He began hopping in a circle, one foot to the other, chanting, "Surf, surf, surf..."

"That's good," Lance said giggling.

Roach stopped. "It's not gonna work if it's just me, come on."

Crow held his towel up and joined in. "Surf, surf, surf..."

Lance looked at Sandcrab and shrugged. They picked up their towels and fell in line, "Surf, surf, surf..." They widened the circle around the trashcan and the surfboards. They swung their towels over their heads and amid the chanting let out an occasional howl. A small group of people watched from the Pier and a hobo down the beach looked up from a trashcan.

They chanted and danced until their throats were dry. Lance got out his canteen and took another long drink. He handed it to Crow and as their sweat turned to salt they watched the ocean for a wave. Nothing.

Another gust of wind blew Lance's board over. This time he jabbed it into the sand hard and twisted the tail. Something cracked. He lifted the board, the fin was no longer at a ninety-degree angle and jagged fiberglass jutted from one side. This couldn't be. He laid the surfboard on the trashcan.

"Damn. You must've fractured the fin when you wrecked," Crow said.

"But it didn't hit that hard."

"You didn't think you scraped your elbow either."

"You think I can fix it?"

Roach bent the fin back to look. He shook his head. "The whole thing's gotta come out. You're gonna have to strip all this glass off and redo the whole tail."

Lance felt a lump in his throat.

"You buy the materials and I'll help you do it," Roach said. "I've got some dings to fix too."

Crab held his towel by the corners and let it flap in the wind. He fell to his knees and laid the towel out in a ritualistic manner. He pulled down the top two corners of the towel and started to roll it.

"He's making a rat tail!" Crow shouted.

They scrambled for their towels and frantically folded and rolled.

Sandcrab went after Crow who squirmed away while still trying to roll his. Sandcrab zapped him on the leg.

"Ouch, you son-of-a-bitch!"

Lance saw Roach coming and scrambled to his feet and ran. He felt a sting on his ass. "Eeee-yow!"

42

They chased each other laughing and hollering.

It ended when Sandcrab broke the above-the-chest-rule and snapped Crow on the chest.

"That's it," Crow cried. "He got me on the tit." They stopped to look and sure enough there was a red welt the size of a cigar butt above Crow's left nipple.

"Okay, truce," said Roach. "But Crow gets a free shot at Crab."

"No way!" Sandcrab said. "It was an accident."

"Doesn't matter, he gets a free shot."

Crow re-rolled his rattail as Sandcrab watched nervously. Crow circled him like a shark snapping the towel randomly to feel for the sweet spot. Sandcrab closed his eyes and put his hands over his genitals. Crow pulled back and struck him on the back of the knee. Sandcrab hollered and hobbled clutching his leg.

"Let me see it," Crow said. "Did I draw blood?"

"Get away from me," Sandcrab howled and limped toward the water.

Roach turned and sat in the sand staring at the ocean. Lance sat down next to him and again he felt the dry wind turn his perspiration to salt. Crow plopped down next to them. "Man, I got him good, there was blood coming up."

"That was harsh," Lance said watching Sandcrab rub water on the back of his leg.

"He deserved it," Crow complained. "Look at this welt. What if that was my eye?"

"Look!" Sandcrab hollered. "A wave!"

A hundred yards out a swell was rising from the water. They watched in amazement as the shoulder high wave pushed in against the wind. The wind battled to hold it back and it seemed the wave would never break. The lip finally began to feather and the wave pitched sending a plume of spray high in the air as if exalting victory. A beautiful left peeled toward shore and Lance thought it was the greatest thing he'd ever seen.

They hollered and danced and laughed. It was a miracle. "Our plea to the gods worked," shouted Roach.

Sandcrab ran up from the water, "I'm gettin' my wetsuit on."

"Let's wait for another one," Roach suggested.

They stared out certain another wave would come. They waited, but no second wave came. They plopped down in the sand.

"Must've been a rogue," Crow said.

Roach frowned focusing on the water. "It was a message."

Lance looked at him.

Roach narrowed his eyes. "They want a sacrifice."

Crow nodded thoughtfully.

Lance frowned. "What kind of sacrifice?"

Crow and Roach turned to Lance's board on the trashcan. "A surfboard."

"No way! Not my board!"

"It's etiquette to sacrifice the most thrashed board."

"You've gotta do it Lance," Sandcrab said. "It's for the greater good."

Lance stood and looked at his board. A cold chill ran down his spine as the hot wind blew in his face. He looked to Roach. "You said you could fix it."

Roach dug his fingers into the sand. "Yeah, but it would never be the same."

"Think about that wave," Crow said. "Imagine sets like that coming in." Crow stood up and brushed his hands on his trunks. "We have to do this. Get a rock Lance, you should have the first throw."

44

The hot wind swirled around Lance's head. *That wave came out of nowhere; it had to have been sent by the gods.* He thought of the patch job he'd done on the nose. Roach was right; his board would never be the same.

Lance picked up his surfboard and leaned it against the trashcan. He frowned. *This is how a cowboy must feel when he has to shoot his horse.* He looked for a big rock and thought of all the time he'd spent learning to paddle, to stand up and turn. The countless hours shivering together waiting for another wave. He picked up a rock the size of a football and looked down at the jagged fiberglass around the fin, he could see the white foam and wooden stringer exposed underneath; it was a mortal wound. He lifted the rock over his head as tears welled in his eyes. *Thanks for helping me learn to surf!* He heaved the rock down and the board snapped in two.

Immediately his friends began pummeling the board with rocks and Lance hurried to get in some throws before the board disintegrated.

After the flurry Sandcrab karate-kicked the last piece of foam that looked big enough to break and Crow and Roach gathered pieces to burn.

"Who's got matches?" Roach asked.

"I've got some in the Turd," Crow said carrying a stack of foam pieces to the trashcan.

Watching him Lance got an idea. "How about we stack the bigger pieces on the water and light 'em, then let the Santa Ana's carry 'em out to sea?"

Crow, Roach and Sandcrab all looked at the flat ocean.

Roach nodded. "Hell, yes!"

Crow dug through the trash for the biggest pieces. "A floating pyre to the surf gods. We'll get waves for sure."

In knee-deep water they stacked the five largest pieces of foam and put newspaper between each layer. They lit the paper and waited for the foam to burn orange and billow black, then let the Santa Ana's push it to sea.

They swam in the cold water briefly then stood on the sand and watched the flame grow and black smoke thicken as the pyre shrank in the distance. Before the Santa Ana's could dry their bodies the orange flame passed beyond the end of the Pier into open-ocean toward Santa Cruz Island. "This is going down in sacrifice history," Roach said. "Let's go home and let the surf gods work their magic."

Lance wrapped the jagged fin in his towel and stuffed it into his backpack.

The next morning he awoke and looked to the empty corner where his surfboard would've been. Had it been for nothing? He stuffed his wetsuit into his backpack just in case and on his way to school rode to the bluff at the lemon factory. There he saw three and four foot waves pushing into the Santa Ana's. His heart pounded and an overwhelming feeling of gratitude swept through him. He squeezed his handle grips. "Thank you surf gods!"

8
LONGBOARDING

Lance was ditching school today for sure. He pedaled down Harbor Boulevard stoked by the plumes of spray blowing off the waves as they broke into the Santa Ana's.

He thought maybe Dennis would lend him a surfboard, but it was only eight-thirty and the shop didn't open until ten. He rode over the pedestrian bridge past Dennis's boat hoping to catch him on deck. The Karmann Ghia was there, but the ladder was on the ground, he was probably surfing. Lance rode his bike around the boat to the garbage barrels behind the shop. He decided to rummage through the trash while he thought about what to do. They were mostly full of foam scraps and empty cans of resin.

He heard a train whistle blow and saw a locomotive coming north on the tracks. He got back on his bike as the train passed and looked for hobos. It was a short train and he didn't see any. He watched the caboose disappear into the steel trestle over the 101 freeway.

"Can I help you?" asked a female voice.

He looked up and saw a girl looking down from a hatch on Dennis's boat. Her arms were folded on the deck and her shoulders were bare. He wondered if she was naked. The Santa Ana's blew her long brown hair around her face. "Is a...Dennis around?"

"Hold on," she said and ducked below. She came back up wearing a t-shirt. "He's surfing," she said wrapping her hair with a rubber band. "Who should I say came by?"

"Uh, I guess you could tell him Lance, but I'll see him when he opens the shop."

"Shouldn't you to be in school?"

"Uh, yeah, but the waves..."

"Sure, I know the story. So where's your surfboard and why are you looking for Dennis?"

He was flattered she had so many questions. "I was gonna ask him about borrowing a board. Mine got sacrificed yesterday."

"Sacrificed?"

"Yeah, we did a surf sacrifice...you know, to the surf gods, for waves."

"Ooh, and there's waves today." She smiled. "You must have good vibes."

Lance blushed. "It was lucky."

She ran some chap stick over her lips and tilted her head. "Oh my god, isn't this cosmic."

"What?"

"Don't you hear it?"

"What?"

"*Good Vibrations*, on the radio." She ducked below again and the Beach Boys' song rose up from inside the boat. She popped her head back out. "See, isn't it crazy? I love this song."

Lance liked the song too and he thought he might be falling in love with her. "Yeah, that's weird."

"Well, good luck finding a board. I'll tell Dennis you stopped by...Lance, right?"

"Yeah, thanks."

"I'm Noelle, see ya Lance." She disappeared down the hatch.

Lance pedaled up the pedestrian bridge and the song faded behind him. *Man, she's hot.* He tried to imagine what it must be like to be Dennis. Living on a boat, being a good surfer, owning a surf shop and getting to see Noelle naked. It was too much to comprehend. Dennis had it made.

Lance sang as he coasted down the other side of the pedestrian bridge to the Pier. "*I'm picking up good vi-bra-tions, she's giving me ex-ci-tations...*" A bunch of guys were out at the point so he rode up there to check it out. He cruised up the promenade and locked his bike at Inside Point. He made himself comfortable on an ocean front bench. Guys were getting long rides, taking off way out at the Point and riding all the way to Inside Point. The Santa Ana's seemed to be helping line up the waves.

The wind blew his hair around his face and Lance took off his shirt. The hot air felt good on his back. He watched a guy knee paddling on a longboard and giggled to himself; *what kind of kook still rides a longboard?* Then the guy caught a wave and did a nice fade back turn. He cross-stepped to the nose then walked back and did a stall, then ran back to the nose through a section. The guy was good. As he surfed to the beach Lance realized it was Dennis. He met him as he came up the stairs. "That was a good wave."

"Thanks man, those are great longboarding waves. You going out?"

Lance folded his arms. "I don't have a board, mine got sacrificed yesterday."

"Oh yeah, I heard. Crow and Roach came by the shop, they said it was a flaming sacrifice at sea. So, what are you going to do for a board?"

"I don't know. I was gonna come talk to you. I just rode by your boat. I met your girlfriend."

He grinned wide. "Noelle? She's a hottie, huh? She was dressed I hope."

Lance blushed.

"Well hey, cool, I'm going in...do you wanna ride this?" He held out the longboard.

"I've never ridden a longboard before."

"It's easy, just make your turns slow 'til you get used to it. This thing'll be a tank for you. Just try not to lose it into the rocks. Bring it by the shop when you're done."

Lance took it by the rails; it was heavy as hell. "Wow, thanks. How big is it?"

"Nine-six, it's a Yater. Don't be afraid to go to the nose. Have fun, I'll see you later." Dennis took a few steps then turned around. "And hey, looks like the sacrifice paid off."

Lance grinned and put the longboard down on the planter. He put on his wetsuit and carried the hulking surfboard down to the water. His arm could barely get around the thing and in the wind it was like carrying an airplane wing. Sweating in his wetsuit he plopped the board on the water. He pushed it into a small wave, the wave didn't budge the heavy plank. Lance jumped onto his belly and stroked. It was like paddling a log, but once it got going the board really moved. He cruised past everybody on their short boards. He didn't even need a wave to stand on it; he could stand with his hands on his hips and look for sets.

Once he reached the line-up at the Point he stopped paddling and glided past the other guys. He sat up on the board and noticed the warm wind had dried his hair and wetsuit. He didn't see any waves and worried the swell had died. He glanced back and saw he was sitting about thirty yards too far out, the offshore winds were blowing him out to sea.

He paddled back toward shore stroking hard against the wind, enjoying the board's momentum. A swell rose beneath him and he accelerated with it--he'd caught the wave. He was still so far out the other guys hadn't even turned to paddle yet. He cruised along on his belly relishing the speed of the heavy board as the wave built up under him. He stood up as he entered the pack of surfers and when the wave started to break he leaned into his turn, but the board didn't follow. It was more like he fell

50

overboard than wiped out. Luckily he got an arm around it so the board didn't wash in.

He felt like he could catch anything on this board. He started taking off at an angle to avoid having to bottom turn. It didn't take long to get a feel for it. Soon he was turning on the tail and taking a step or two forward to trim, then back to the tail, not so much maneuvering as just keeping the board in position, all the while getting the longest rides of his life.

He went in to eat his lunch and drink some water and soon after that heard Sandcrab calling him from the inside. He was knee paddling now to keep his shivering body out of the water. He waited for Sandcrab to catch up.

"Holy crap man, have you been out here all day? Dennis is worried you took off with his board."

"The waves just keep getting better and the rides are so long. Is school out already?"

"Yeah, damn, I wish I'd ditched today."

* * * *

Lance couldn't carry the longboard on his bike in the wind, so he walked it back to the shop on his head. By the time he got to the steps he thought he might collapse.

"Man-o-man, you get any waves out there?" Dennis helped him haul the longboard inside.

"Yeah, plenty. I only lost it a couple of times, I don't think I got any dings."

Dennis did a quick survey of the rails. "So, did you get to the nose?"

Lance wanted to blurt out how well he thought he'd done, but he knew how irritating it was when guys blabbered about how great they surfed. "I got up there a few times, I wasn't hanging ten or anything, but I got some nose rides."

"That's great. I love short boards, but I could never stop riding my Yater." He carried the board to the back corner opposite the used surfboards and put it in a rack with what must've been his other boards. "So, what kind of board you thinking about getting?"

"I don't know, whatever I can find, depends on how much money I can scrape up."

"Well, I've been thinking, I'd like to see all you Rats riding my boards and you're about to be the first to hear my offer." He smoothed his mustache. "I'll make you a custom board with one color and a pinstripe for ninety bucks."

The thought of a new board made Lance dizzy. He'd never considered a new board; they were normally a hundred and twenty-five or more. Even ninety was a lot, but this was too good a deal to pass up. "Wow, a new board."

"I can help you design it, here's a form you can fill out: Height, weight, what length and width you want, what kind of tail, the waves you like to ride. You can draw the basic design here. Then we can talk about it...once you place the order it'll take a couple weeks."

It was happening so fast. Could he do it? He had to do it. He was gonna have a brand new surfboard. He'd already been skimming from his school lunch money for a wetsuit. "I've got seven dollars saved."

Dennis grinned. "Maybe your folks can help you. And I could let you clean the shaping room once or twice a week at two-fifty a shot, that would help."

Lance flew home on his bike. Maybe he could negotiate some early Christmas money from his mom.

Man, yesterday the waves were flat and my surfboard wrecked, he thought, *and today I got killer waves and I'm ordering a custom surfboard. Man, the surf gods are lookin' out for me.*

9

SOUTHERS

The next day was Saturday and Bill, Stoody, Q and Ringlets stood around the planter on the promenade at Inside Point. Lance locked his bike to the railing by the stairs and looked out at the water. It was crowded. It seemed the hot dry winds and clean swell had lured everyone with access to a surfboard to the beach.

"Hey Lance, heard you got your board sacrificed." Ringlets laughed. The warm wind blew his blonde locks around his face.

"Somebody had to do something so you slobs could get some waves. You should be out there, you're wasting my magic."

"I'm waiting for the tide to go out," Q said, "it's only gonna get better."

"Look at all the Souther kooks out there," Bill said. "The Santa Ana's brought 'em out of the woodwork."

Stoody glanced over his shoulder at the parking lot behind them. "You see how many Souther cars are in our lot?"

Inside Point had a small semiprivate parking lot nestled between two condominium complexes, one of which was still under construction.

"How do you know they're Souther cars?" Lance asked. He'd heard the complaints about Southers, but there were never Southers at Schoolhouse or the Pier.

"The license plate frames," Stoody said. "Go look, you'll see Encino, Topanga, Sherman Oaks, all in our lot, right now."

"I got an idea," Ringlets said. "Since you don't have a board Lance, why don't you make yourself useful and write Southers Go Home on the windshields with wax?"

"Hey, that's a good idea," Q said. "You think of that?"

"Sure, I think of a lot of stuff."

"Why don't you do it?" Lance sneered.

Ringlets pulled his hair into a ponytail then let it fall back onto his shoulders. "Hey, I'm just trying to think of stuff for you to do while we're surfing."

Bill pointed to the ocean. "Look at that wave McGillis is getting."

Lance jumped up on the planter and saw McGillis streaking down the line on a beautiful wind blown wave, then some dufus dropped-in on him.

"That guy's dead," Q said.

McGillis shot his board at the guy, but missed and the guy surfed on unaware.

"That's McGillis' new board, somebody should save it before it hits the rocks."

"I'll do it," Lance said jumping down from the planter. "Hey, I didn't tell you guys, I'm getting a new board. Dennis is making me a custom board for ninety bucks."

"Bullcrap," said Ringlets. "That barely covers materials."

"He'll do it for you guys too, he wants us all riding his boards." Lance turned and ran down the stairs splashing into the water to save McGillis' board.

McGillis high stepped toward him.

"That was a nice wave you had 'til that Souther cut you off," Lance shouted.

"That bastard's lucky I have to split." He reached for his board. "Did it hit the rocks?"

"Nope, I saved it."

"Thanks man. Do me a favor, if you see that guy out there, cut him off for me, okay?"

Lance smiled. "I'll try, which one is he?"

"He's the goon on a blue board, you can't miss him."

Lance nodded and followed McGillis up the stairs.

Ringlets ran up. "You're not gonna let that Souther get away with that are you?"

McGillis glared at him. "I'm late for work man. Did you wax any windshields like I told you to?"

Ringlets slouched. "Not yet, I was just talking to these guys about it."

"I'm telling ya man, if you guys don't start doing something it's gonna be like this every weekend."

"I don't want to mess up anybody's car," Lance said.

"You *need* to mess up some cars!" McGillis snapped. "Slash some tires, break some windows! Get in a fight on the beach. Send these Southers home with a story to tell their friends." He looked out at the water. "Look man, I'm getting too old for this, you guys are the young bloods, you need to protect this place for your own future." McGillis shook his head, turned and walked toward the Point.

Ringlets faced the group. "You guys heard him, come on, we gotta do something."

"I'm not gonna vandalize Southers just because McGillis says to." Lance looked at the three boards lying on the flowers at the end of the planter. "If none of you guys are going out, can I use somebody's board?"

"I'm going out," Ringlets said.

"I thought you were gonna slash some tires."

"Not right now."

"You can use my board," Bill said, "I'm going to *Johnny's* to get a burrito. But, you better come in when you see me waving."

Lance was already getting his wetsuit on.

Bill's board was a 6'2" diamond tail. Paddling on it felt squirrely after riding Dennis' longboard the day before.

In the water Lance was more aware of the faces he didn't recognize. He saw Dugo and the Twins sitting out where the

56

Point unofficially turned to Inside Point. He paddled toward them as a set was rising outside. Everyone began to paddle. The regular-footed Twin got the first wave. Lance watched him come down the line and gave him a hoot as he paddled over the shoulder. Dugo got the second wave and the goofy-footed twin was in position for the third, and best wave of the set. But a guy on a yellow board was paddling for it too. The yellow board took off in front of the twin and faded back on his drop forcing the backhanded Twin to get swallowed up in the whitewater. It was outright theft. The Twin popped up yelling at the back of the wave.

Tension was growing.

Lance couldn't catch a wave. With so many guys out and the wind in his face he hadn't caught one yet and Bill was already on the beach waving him in. Out of desperation he paddled into a wave late. He jumped up and ahead of him some bozo was taking off too. "Hey, hey, coming down," Lance called. The guy surfed on without looking back. Lance stayed behind him eating his spray as the guy gyrated and flailed. The guy kicked out and was surprised when Lance kicked out too.

"Sorry kid, I didn't think you were gonna make it."

Lance saw it was the goon on the Blue Board, the same guy that had cut off McGillis.

"I called you off."

"Yeah, but like I said, I didn't think you were gonna make it." The guy paddled away.

"You didn't even look!" Lance yelled.

The guy sat up on his board and turned around, he inflated his chest. "Look kid, consider that wave a free lesson, next time it'll cost you."

Lance spotted Sandcrab and paddled to him. "Did you see that guy cut me off?"

Sandcrab shook his head. "He's been snakin' everybody." He looked at the board Lance was on. "Is that why Bill's jumping up and down on the beach?"

"Oh crap. I gotta go in."

Lance paddled and caught a small wave. The inside was a slalom course of kooks. They splashed and kicked to get out of his way. Ahead a guy held his board in waist deep water, Lance trimmed high to charge past him, but the guy panicked and ditched his board into Lance's path, Lance dove as he ran over the board.

Bill came running down the beach screaming. "You idiot! What are you doing?"

Lance wasn't sure if he was referring to him or the other guy. He flipped over Bill's board and checked the bottom. "Just some wax."

Bill took his board. "You're damn lucky nothing happened. I've been waving you in for twenty minutes."

"Sorry man, I couldn't get a wave." Up the beach Lance saw Blue Board getting out of the water. "Hey, I'll be right back, I gotta check something."

Lance followed Blue Board up the cobblestones to the dirt parking lot at the Point where cars lined the five-foot ledge facing the ocean. Blue Board opened the side door of a blue Chevy van. Airbrushed on the side was a tropical sunset with palm trees and islands. Painted in cursive on the back door was, *If this van is rockin', don't bother knockin'*. The license plate frame said Simi Valley Chevrolet. Lance watched as the guy leaned his board on the floorboards and pulled out a towel. Another guy was in the passenger seat with wet hair and there was an orange surfboard on the racks. Lance walked to the ledge two cars down and pretended to watch the waves. He tilted his head away from the wind to better hear.

58

"...that's why I like coming here, these guys don't know how to compete for waves." Blue Board put a cigarette in his mouth and lit it. "We can dominate this place, and it's way better than county line."

Lance was beginning to understand the fuss about Southers. The crowd itself was a problem, but add a few jerks and things could really get out of hand. He casually jumped down from the ledge and hurried down the beach back to Inside Point.

A new crew was gathered around the planter. The Turd was parked in the roundabout in the Inside Point parking lot and Crow and Roach were watching the waves with Dugo and one of the Twins.

"Where'd you guy's surf?" Lance asked.

Crow scratched his armpit. "Overhead, it's good there at high tide."

Lance could only imagine how cool it must be to able to drive to other surf spots. "Was it crowded?"

"Not like this." Roach pointed to the water. "Look, Q's getting snaked."

It was a guy on a yellow board dropping in on him. Q was forced to go straight. He shook his fist at the guy and dropped to his belly to come in.

"That was the same guy that cut me off," Twin said.

Q came running up the stairs and tossed his board onto the planter. "Anybody got any wax?"

Crow dug a bar from his pocket.

"That guy cut me off twice," Q said. "I know which car he came in."

They followed Q to a yellow Datsun station wagon. He jumped on the hood and wrote, "GO HOME SOUTHER" across the windshield.

"Let me write something," Twin said. He scrawled, "SNAKE" on the back window.

Twin broke the bar in half and handed a piece to Dugo. "Let's block out the side windows." They began waxing the windows solid.

"I'll be a lookout in case somebody comes," Crow said. Roach followed him.

Q picked up a rock and smashed the driver side window.

Lance started to back away.

Q reached in and opened the door. He pushed the passenger door open and called out, "Lance, come over here."

Lance looked around then walked to the door. He saw Q going through the glove box.

"Get in the back and take anything you can find, he's gonna pay for surfing here."

Lance climbed in the back. There was a wad of clothes on the floor behind each seat. He unravelled some pants and coins fell on the floor. He gathered the quarters and dimes. He felt a wallet and fished it out. He opened it. The guy's driver's license picture stared at him. He took the money from the wallet and dropped it.

"Anything back there?" Q asked.

"Just money." Lance picked up the other pants; no wallet.

Dugo stuck his head in the car. "Come on, let's get outta here."

They closed the doors and walked back to the promenade, Lance clutched the money in his fist. Q carried a Buck knife and some 8-track tapes and was now wearing sunglasses.

"I'm gonna stash this stuff in the island," Q said. He stepped into the large island planter in the center of the turnabout and squeezed between the bird of paradise plants to where three palm trees grew from the center. He stashed the loot between the palm trees. Lance came around the Turd and Dugo opened the side

60

door. "Get in, let's count the money." Lance, Q and Twin climbed in and Dugo slammed the door.

Lance opened his fist. "Whoa, seven dollars and seventy cents."

"A small price to pay to surf Ventura," Q said.

Scarecrow cupped his hands on the window to look in. "What are you guys doing?"

"Getting ready to get some corn burritos for lunch," Q said. "Come on, you drive, Southers buy."

10

PILLAGE

At The Galley, Dugo, Q, Twin, Scarecrow, Roach and Lance each carried a paper boat of ten corn burritos and a fountain soda to a booth at the back of the diner. Lance devoured eight sauce and cheese soaked corn burritos before telling them what he'd heard Blue Board say. "He thinks every wave is his and if you're behind him when he takes off, that's your problem."

"I'd like to see him try and cut me off," Crow said.

"He's pretty big," Lance warned.

Dugo tilted his cup back and shook the ice. "We need to find his van and do to it what we did to that Datsun."

"They're gone by now," Lance said. "Hey, I need to go to the shop and talk to Dennis about my new board, anybody want to go?"

"Nah, the waves'll be getting better," Crow said.

"Yeah, I'm goin' back out," said Roach.

"Me too," Q and the others agreed.

That was fine with Lance, he'd prefer to talk to Dennis alone anyway. He walked down Ash Street to Front and stopped when he saw the blue Chevy van parked outside the shop. He looked back for the Turd; it was gone. He thought about heading for the beach. *No way, I'm going in there to hear what that jackass is saying.*

Diablo sat at the top of the steps sniffing the air. Lance patted his head and walked in. Dennis was leaning on the customer side of the counter and Blue Board was standing in front of the mirror modeling a long john wetsuit. He puffed his chest out and rubbed the smooth rubber. The zippers on the legs weren't zipped and they flared out. Blue Board's friend sat in the hanging basket chair with one foot on the floor rocking himself.

"Hey Lance," Dennis said, "you been in the water?"

Blue Board and his buddy looked over.

"Yeah, I borrowed Bill's diamond tail; I didn't really get any waves though, it's pretty crowded out there."

Crowded?" Blue Board smirked. "You don't know what crowded is. We come up here to get away from the crowds."

"Well, it's crowded for here, it's hard to get waves."

"You just gotta be more aggressive," Blue Board said. "You might as well get used to it, more people are gonna be surfing up here."

Lance's stomach turned. "I don't want to get used to it."

"It's only a matter of time kid, it's happening." Blue Board looked at himself in the mirror, inflated his chest again and rubbed his pecs. "I'll be able to stay out all day in this."

Dennis turned to Lance and rolled his eyes. "So, you give any thought to your new board?"

"Yeah. I've just gotta work on getting the money, I'll come back later, when you're not so busy."

"Cool, I've got some ideas."

* * * *

Lance walked back to Inside Point thinking about more Southers like Blue Board invading Ventura. Maybe McGillis was right, maybe targeted Souther attacks were a good idea.

Back at Inside Point everyone was in the water. Lance walked up the grass hill that elevated the new condominium complex above the promenade. He stood and looked out at the ocean. How great would it be to live here, just look out the window to check the surf. But man, to afford living here you'd never have time to surf. Forget that. I'd rather live in a hut on the beach for free and surf every day, that's what it's all about.

Lance turned and looked over the parking lot. The yellow Datsun was gone, there was broken glass on the concrete where it'd been parked. He counted ten cars in the parking lot with surf racks, but only recognized three. He sat down and laid back on the grass feeling the warm wind blow over him. He closed his eyes.

He awoke to Sandcrab yelling, "Crow's getting in a fight! Crow's getting in a fight!"

He sat up and saw Sandcrab running up the stairs, he scanned the beach. "I don't see anything."

"They're coming in right now, Crow nailed a guy in the back with a flyaway, the same guy that cut you off."

Lance jumped to his feet and ran to the rail. Sure enough Blue Board was high stepping from the water toward Crow who was holding a rock over the blue surfboard on the shoreline.

"You drop that rock you die," Blue Board hollered.

Crow raised the rock. "You need to leave, Souther."

Blue Board stopped and pointed at Crow. "As it stands kid, I'm just going to kick your ass, you drop that rock, I'll kill you."

"We gotta help him." Lance started down the stairs.

Crab followed behind. "What are we gonna do?"

"Get a rock."

Blue Board had a good thirty pounds on Crow and when he took a step Crow faked dropping the rock. "I'll do it asshole."

Lance and Sandcrab took positions on either side of Crow holding fist sized rocks.

Blue Board's face turned purple with fury. "You little shits have no idea what you're getting yourselves into." His eyes shifted to the side and he called out. "Hey Josh, we've got some pests here that need to be exterminated."

64

Lance saw the guy with the orange board coming in from the water.

"You disturb the natives, Cal?" Orange Board joked.

"I don't think one guy is enough to help you, asshole," Crow said.

Lance was surprised at Crow's bravado. They were bigger and all they had to do was pick up rocks too. Then he saw Roach, Q and both twins hurrying in from the water. Behind them were Bill, Dugo, Stoody and Ringlets. They closed in around Cal.

"What's this, your pussy posse?" Cal looked side to side. He moved slowly toward Crow. "Okay man, you win. I admit, maybe I get a little aggressive sometimes."

"You're a wave hog and you surf like a goon." Crow dropped the rock inches from the surfboard.

Cal flinched then took a deep breath. "We're cool then, right?"

Crow picked up the blue surfboard. "Go home, Souther, and don't come back." He heaved the board over his shoulder onto the cobblestones.

The clunking of the surfboard caused a crowd to form along the ledge of the parking lot and the surfers in the water craned their necks to see.

Crow picked up another rock. "Split, now!"

Cal snorted and walked over the rocks to get his surfboard. The group followed him and his friend to the Chevy van. Cal slammed his board on the racks and started to take off his wetsuit. A rock bashed the side of the van.

Cal yelled, "What do you think you're doing man?"

"Leave now!" Crow said.

Cal clenched his fists. "Okay! We're leaving you little shit, but you haven't seen the last of me." He got in the van and backed out, then hit the gas spewing dust and pebbles over the boys.

Rocks pelted the van as it sped away and the boys hooted and cheered. A smattering of applause came from the older surfers parked along the Point.

This was exactly what McGillis had called for. They ran down the promenade back to Inside Point jumping on the benches and planters retelling their versions of how it all went down.

Most of the guys returned to the beach to retrieve their boards and head back into the water. Lance and Sandcrab stood on the promenade as Ringlets came up from the beach with his board and a bar of wax. "Come on Lance, let's do this."

"Do what?" asked Sandcrab.

"Wax some windows," Lance said. "We might as well keep it going while we're on a roll."

Ringlets looked at Sandcrab. "You stand lookout in case anybody comes." He broke the wax and handed half to Lance. "You do this side I'll do that one."

In typical fashion Ringlets chose the side with fewer cars.

The wax went on easy in the hot air. Lance used the wide side of the bar to get thicker letters. He wrote *Southers Go Home* and *Locals Only*. When he finished he took the last of the wax and put an X on all the side windows until it was gone. He smooshed the last bit onto the passenger window of a green Volkswagen squareback. Inside he noticed a bill rolled up in the ashtray, he cupped his hands to the glass, it was a twenty.

Sandcrab howled a warning. Lance hurried back to the promenade where Sandcrab and Ringlets were leaning on the rail. Lance looked around. "I don't see anybody."

"You were taking too long. Ringlets was done a long time ago."

Lance scowled. "I did all the windows on my side, plus I had more cars."

"You didn't have more cars, you're full of crap," Ringlets argued.

"Who cares," Sandcrab said. He looked at Lance, "You want to go get something to eat?"

"Naw, I already had corn burritos with Q and those guys earlier."

"Well, I gotta eat." Sandcrab unlocked his bike. "You can use my board 'til I get back."

"Thanks man." Sandcrab's board wasn't one Lance could ride very well. He thought about the money in the car. Even if his mom agreed to give him the fifty bucks for Christmas it would still take him weeks to get the rest of the money. That twenty bucks would really help. No way, just go surfing. He picked up Sandcrab's board.

Ringlets came out of the bushes from taking a leak.

"Hey Ringlets, you do me a favor?"

"I don't know, what?"

"Be a lookout for me. I want to finish the windows on that last car."

"I guess so, just make it quick."

Lance went to the island planter where Q had stashed the loot from the yellow Datsun.

"Hey, what're you doing?" Ringlets called.

"I'm looking for something, just keep a lookout." Lance found the Buck knife and went to the squareback. He stuck the blade between the glass and the weather stripping of the wind wing and popped the latch. He reached in and lifted the lock. He took a quick scan around; Ringlets was watching him. He opened the door, the car smelt of stale smoke. He leaned over the passenger seat, grabbed the bill and slipped it into his wax pocket. He closed the wind wing, locked the door and shut it. He dumped the knife back into the palm trees and met Ringlets on the promenade.

"What the hell did you just do?" Ringlets sneered.

"Nothing."

"Don't give me that, I saw you get into that car. What'd you take?"

"Nothing man, I--look, I need money for my new board, there was a twenty in the ashtray. I took it, it's just a Souther--"

"Lemme see it."

"See what, you know what a twenty looks like."

"Prove it, lemme see it."

Lance reached into his pocket and pulled out the bill. "Holy crap, two twenties!"

"I knew you were lying, give me one."

"Get outta here."

"You couldn't have done it without me, one of those is mine."

"No way! I need this money for my new board, get away from me."

"You want me to tell whoever owns that car who took it?"

Lance got in Ringlets face. "You know Scott, I really want to like you, but it's because of crap like this you're an asshole. I need this money for my surfboard. That's the only reason I did it. I did all the work and I'm not giving you crap!"

"Okay, geez, relax. Keep your damn money you selfish bastard, see if I ever help you again."

Lance shook his head and stuffed the money back into his pocket. He picked up Sandcrab's board and headed for the stairs.

"Hey Lance," Ringlets called out, "For your information, nobody calls me Scott anymore, it's Ringlets...and you owe me one."

11
HOME

Lance dug the two twenties from his pocket and sat on his bed. He smoothed the damp bills on his knees and reached for a mahogany box between the magazines on his bookshelf. Inside the box were seven one-dollar bills. He counted them, placed the twenties underneath the ones and replaced the lid. He slid the box back between the magazines and went to the kitchen for dinner.

At the table Lance picked at his ravioli. Until now, thirty-seven dollars was the most money he'd ever had--how would he feel if someone had stolen that much money from him?

"Lance, you're not eating," his mother said. "Usually you'd be on your second helping by now. Do you feel all right?"

"I'm fine, just thinking."

"About what?"

"Oh, there was a Souther at the beach today that Crow got into a hassle with."

Ann put down her milk. "I don't think Souther is a word."

"What kind of hassle?" his mom asked.

Lance jabbed a ravioli with his fork. "Everybody from the valley came to the beach today because of the Santa Ana's and one guy was cutting everybody off. Crow almost got in a fight with him."

Lance's dad wiped his mouth. "These Santa Ana's drive me bananas. It's miserable getting in and out of the car all day in a suit, perspiring, hair's a mess, static electricity--"

"They're good for the waves though," Lance said.

Ann looked at her mom. "Susan's cousin lives in Thousand Oaks and he won't surf in Ventura because he says the surfers threw rocks at him."

Lance sat up in his chair. "That guy doesn't surf, he's a hodad. He dyes his hair and drives around in his race car with a surfboard on top."

"Is it true Lance, did people throw rocks at him?" his mom asked.

Lance frowned. "One guy threw a rock because he was cruising the Point gunning his engine. Can you pass the parmesan, Mom."

She handed him the grated cheese. "You would never do that, would you Lance?"

"Of course not." He glared at Ann.

"I think they just don't like cute guys coming down there," Ann said.

Lance rolled his eyes. "That's so retarded. Do you have a crush on that guy or what?"

"Jim, are you listening to this?"

"Mom, if Southers follow the rules they don't get hassled. There's a thing called surf etiquette."

"Surf etiquette?" Ann laughed. "Why don't you try using some of that around here."

"Honey," his dad said, "this is typical, boys need rivalries. You've seen *Westside Story*--"

"Oh that's a great example."

"I'm just saying this kind of thing is normal, young men need adversaries. That's why they join the military."

His mom put down her knife. "I don't want Lance going to Vietnam."

Lance's dad looked at him. "You *will* have to register for the draft you know."

70

"Dad, I'm only fourteen, there might not even be a draft then."

"Yes, we have a long time before we have to worry about that." His mom stood up and picked up her dish and Lance's. "Ann can you bring your father's plate?"

"Can I finish eating?" His dad sighed.

His mom walked to the sink. "I don't want you getting into any hassles with Southers, Lance."

"Believe me, I avoid hassles. Hey, did you guys talk about the fifty bucks for my board?"

Ann stood up. "You're giving him fifty dollars?"

"Bring your plate over here Ann. Lance asked for fifty dollars for Christmas to put down on a new surfboard. You got a bike last year, remember?"

His dad crumpled his napkin. "How much is this surfboard?"

Lance straightened up. "Ninety dollars."

"So, where are you going to get the rest of the money?"

"Dennis said I could do some work at the shop."

"Well, I like that idea." His dad scooted his chair out. "But I don't see what the big hurry is. Why can't you just wait until Christmas?"

"Dad, that's more than a month away, I can't go that long without a surfboard."

His dad chuckled. "God knows how I've gotten by all these years without one."

Lance faked a smile. "Anything for dessert mom?"

* * * *

The next morning Lance's mom wrote him a check for fifty dollars.

Out of gratitude and guilt he hung around for breakfast.

"No waves today?" his mom asked. "I can't believe you're still here at nine thirty."

"The Surf Shop doesn't open until eleven on Sundays and I don't want to leave the check in my backpack on the beach."

She stacked four pancakes on a plate. "Don't tell me people are stealing down there too?"

"No, it's just a lot of money, I don't want to take any chances." He eyed the pancakes and she handed him the plate.

"You can have these, Ann's not up yet."

The back door opened and his dad came in. "Hey Lance, I thought you'd be up to your ears in salt water by now."

His mother put a square of butter on the griddle. "He's joining us for breakfast."

"Two meals in a row, how 'bout that, we should call the Star Free Press."

"Oh brother, Dad."

"Maybe after breakfast we could run you up to the barber shop."

"Jim, don't bother him about his hair, it's the style these days."

"Who cares about the style. Doesn't that hair bother you when you're surfing?"

"I'm starting to lose my appetite."

"You know there's a man cutting hair at my salon now," his mom said. "His name is Max, maybe you could have him cut your hair Lance. He could keep it long but layer it so it stays neater."

Lance sat silent.

"You want Lance to go to a beauty salon?"

She put another plate of pancakes on the table. "Sit down, Jim. A lot of men are going go to salons now."

72

His dad shook his head and sat down. "So, what kind of work will this Dennis have you doing?"

"Just some clean up once a week for a couple hours."

"Well, that's great. How much is he going to pay you?"

"I think ten bucks."

"For a couple hours of work? What are you going to be cleaning, a septic tank?"

"The shaping room and stuff. Maybe he didn't say ten, maybe it's only five."

"That's still a lot of money," his dad said. "Minimum wage is only a dollar twenty-five."

"A dollar *thirty*-five," Ann yawned as she entered the kitchen in her robe.

"Hey sleepyhead, why are you so tired?" Lance asked changing the subject.

"Because I got woken up at two in the morning last night when Jean came sneaking in."

His mom sighed. "She wasn't sneaking in, she's eighteen and it was only one thirty."

"Whatever," Ann said, "just don't complain when I start coming home that late."

"You're only sixteen." She put a plate of bacon on the table. "You're going to miss your sister when she moves to San Diego."

"Oh yeah, it'll be horrible having my own room."

Lance ate his last bite of pancake and grabbed a piece of bacon. "Well, you don't have to worry about me, I'm always home early."

Ann rolled her eyes. "Oh yeah, mister angel."

"What? You don't think your brother's a good boy?"

Lance stuck out his tongue at Ann and took his plate to the sink. "You guys talk about me all you want, I'm going to the shop to put money down on my new surfboard. Thanks Mom, thanks Dad."

12
NEW SURFBOARD

It was the fourth day of the Santa Ana's and a brown haze lay over the horizon from the wildfires in Fillmore and Agora. Flakes of ash drifted in the wind like snow. Dennis propped open the door to the Surf Shop as Lance rode up. "Hey Lance, you ready to talk about your new board?"

"I'm ready."

"All right, come on in. I've got a surprise for you."

Lance hopped up the steps and was surprised to see Noelle leaning against the counter. She had on short cutoffs and a beige crocheted bikini top. She stopped applying chapstick and said, "I know you."

Lance's throat seemed to swell.

"Yeah, didn't you guys meet the other day?" Dennis asked.

"That's right," Lance squeaked. He felt hot.

A strand of hair fell in her face. "Nice to see you again." She held out the chapstick. "You need some? It's so dry out."

He took the chapstick and ran it over his lips. "Thanks." She smelled like coconuts. He stared at her abalone necklace that pointed like an arrow to her cleavage.

"So Lance," Dennis said. "I shaped your board last night."

Lance turned from her breasts and took a deep breath. "You did?"

"You don't have to take it, I was playing around and did something you might like."

"Can I see it?"

"Sure. Noelle can you watch the front?"

She stepped behind the counter and Dennis pulled open the door to the back room. Lance followed him into the sacred shaping area. Against the wall was a row of foam blanks, the raw material for making surfboards. On the other side was a stack of newly shaped boards ready to be glassed. Dennis opened another door and flicked on the lights. Two florescent bulbs mounted horizontally on opposite walls illuminated the room. In the middle, floating on a wooden stand, was a newly shaped surfboard.

It was a sculpture as much as a surfboard--smooth, symmetrical and white as marble. The side lighting showed off the curves of the rails and the lines running from the nose to the tail. Lance swallowed. "Wow, this is radical."

"I call it an arc tail," Dennis said, "something between a round pin and a diamond tail. It'll be good for a little bigger surf this winter, but should work in smaller waves, too."

All Lance knew about surfboard design was that the bigger the waves, the longer and narrower you wanted your surfboard. "This is cool Dennis. I'll take it."

"You know what color you want?"

"I wanna stick with flames. Maybe a fireball on the bottom with flames coming off it."

Dennis chuckled. "I was thinking something a little cleaner, like a light gray bottom and rails with a white deck and dark blue pinstripe."

Lance thought it sounded boring. "Hmmm..."

Dennis smiled. "Whatever you want it's your board, but flames would have to be airbrushed and that would cost extra."

"How much?"

"Depends. The whole bottom like that, probably fifteen bucks, so you'd be up to a hundred and five total."

76

Lance took off his backpack and unzipped the outer pocket. He handed Dennis the fifty-dollar check. "Do you still think I could clean the shaping room?"

"Sure, you could start now if you want."

"Cool, I'll get the flames."

"You got it, big spender. I'll call Julio and see when he can do it. It might take an extra week or two depending on his schedule, but you'll need time to round up the rest of the cash anyway."

A week or two? Lance thought. *I wish I could tell Dennis I've got the money now.*

Dennis unlocked a latch on the back wall then slid the wall open. Sunlight poured in and the warm Santa Ana's whipped up the foam dust. They were standing on an old loading dock.

Lance stepped to the edge and looked out at the railroad tracks and Dennis's boat. Below him were the trash barrels he'd pilfered through a few days before.

Dennis pointed to them. "Break the foam chunks as small as you can and toss them in these barrels. Dump the dust and shavings into that one with the lid, the broom and dust-pan are over there. There's goggles and a mask on that nail, wipe everything down with this rag after you sweep it all out. You'll never get it all, but do the best you can. Pull the door shut and lock it when you're done. I'll be out front if you need anything." He picked up Lance's new surfboard. "I'll put this in the other room." He stopped in the doorway. "What kind of wetsuit do you have?"

"A beavertail jacket."

"You know, a fireball isn't going to keep you very warm this winter. Just something to think about."

Dennis left and Lance stood on the edge of the loading dock. Beyond the railroad tracks bougainvillea's grew through the chain-link fence. The sound of freeway traffic beyond the bushes mimicked the sound of the ocean two hundred yards beyond that.

Lance put on the mask and goggles and gathered the biggest foam pieces. He broke them up and dropped them into the barrels. *It's stupid to pay extra and wait longer for the airbrushing.* He saw Noelle walking to the boat. Dennis was right about the wetsuit too. He lifted the goggles and watched her climb the ladder. "I gotta go talk to Dennis."

Lance approached Dennis at the front counter. "I think I'll cancel the fireball and go with the gray bottom and blue pinstripe."

Dennis smiled. "You sure? That's not very exciting."

"I think I'd rather go clean and put that fifteen dollars toward a wetsuit like you said."

"Good call, you can't surf if you're frozen stiff."

After an hour Lance finished cleaning the room. He pulled the door shut and locked the latch. Sweaty and itchy with foam dust he walked to the front room and saw Dugo, Q, Stoody, Roach and Scarecrow all sitting on the floor talking with Dennis. Dennis swung around in the hanging basket chair. "Hey Lance, how'd it go?"

"Good, I think I'm done. I closed the door and locked it."

"Thanks, come have a seat. Crow's telling me about the run-in you guys had with Cal yesterday."

Lance eased onto the floor next to Roach, the foam dust felt like sandpaper on his skin.

Crow stretched his legs out on the floor. "So then we followed him to the van and he starts to take off his wetsuit--"

"That's when Crow threw the rock at his van," Roach interrupted.

"I thought his head was gonna explode," Q added.

They hooted and laughed.

78

"So anyway," Crow continued, "he peels out in the dirt and dusts us, and we pounded his van with rocks."

They smiled and congratulated each other, but Dennis just shook his head. "I admit the cat's a piece of work." He looked at each of them. "Did it stop there?"

"We waxed some windows in the parking lot at Inside Point," Lance said, glad Ringlets wasn't there to elaborate.

"Most of us just went back in the water," Crow said. "I tell you, the vibe was a lot different after that." He crossed his legs and leaned back on his elbows. "Hey, Dennis, tell us about the time you guys pushed that van over the ledge at the Point, that was classic."

Dennis shook his head and frowned. "Now that's a good example of things getting out of hand. I wish I could forget that story."

"No way, that was huge for Ventura's reputation."

Dennis got up from the basket chair and walked behind the counter as if he were a judge taking the bench. He looked down at them.

"My buddy Ray got into it with a guy on the beach, they were rolling on the sand pulling each other's hair, it was ugly. Bob and I paddled in to help and it turns out the other guy had a couple of friends there too. We were throwing threats back and forth, then little McGillis and one of his buddies smash a window on their car. They ran up to get 'em, and by that time more guys were coming in from the water to help us. The Southers decide to split and we threw rocks at 'em driving away, just like you guys. But now we're amped up and we see a van parked there with Torrence plates. So, we break the window and Bob gets in and puts it in neutral and we pushed the front end over the ledge."

"That's so cool," said Crow. "And then you spray painted Souther Go Home on the side and it sat there all day."

Dennis scowled. "It wasn't cool at all. Turns out, the guy was from Ojai and was just out for a morning surf. It was his daughter's fifth birthday and it screwed up all their plans."

"You know him?" Roach asked.

"Now I do, he comes in sometimes, still drives the same van. We've talked about it. He's a history teacher at Nordoff High. He did nothing to deserve it, he was just a nice guy with an out-of-town license plate out for a surf."

"Ouch," Roach said.

"Surfing is a territorial sport," Dennis said, "nothing's going to change that. Cal's an ass and he asked for it, but random vandalism and stealing is just wrong. We're fortunate to live here, but that doesn't give us the right to violate others just because they want to surf here too." He came out from behind the counter.

Lance stared at the ground.

"Hey Lance, you want to show these guys your new board?"

"Uh, yeah...sure."

"I'll put it back on the rack."

Lance followed everyone into the shaping room. Stoody turned to him. "I hear you got a nice down payment for it yesterday at Inside Point."

Lance grabbed his arm. "Don't say anything. Who else did Ringlets tell?"

"I don't know, we rode home together and he told me." Stoody put his hand on Lance's shoulder. "Relax, nobody's gonna say anything. Come on, let's go look at your new board, maybe you can learn to surf on this one."

13
NORTH SWELL

It was now late November, the warm Santa Ana winds had passed and Southern California had returned to its normal seasonal chill. Dennis laid the six-foot six-inch arc tail on the carpet at the front of the shop. The dark blue pinstripe was the perfect accent between the gray rails and white deck. It was as clean and pretty as Dennis said it would be.

"You got the money together fast," Dennis said. "You didn't do anything illegal did you?"

Lance forced a laugh. "My mom found some extra work for me."

"Good for you." Dennis smiled. "So, let's see, you swept the shaping room four times, and with the fifty dollar check and this forty, I owe you ten bucks." Dennis hit a button on the register and took a ten from the drawer.

Lance pulled eight ones from his pocket. "There's a used short john on the rack for twenty bucks. I was hoping I could clean the shaping room one more time and get it."

Dennis grinned. "Bring it over here."

When Lance came back with the wetsuit there were three bars of wax on the counter.

"Take this wax and that wetsuit and go surfing," Dennis said. "You owe me one. Come back and tell me how it rides."

Lance felt like the luckiest guy in the world, not only did he have a new board and wetsuit, but he had Dennis' friendship.

* * * *

The first solid north swell hit on Saturday the following week. Five and six foot lines were wrapping into the Point and Lance was surfing better than he ever had. His new surfboard was everything he'd hoped for--smooth, fast and responsive. The quality of the waves had everyone surfing better and everyone was saying the swell was only getting bigger. Lance felt ready, he was handling everything the ocean was dishing out and wanted more. He couldn't wait for bigger waves.

* * * *

The next morning he packed an extra big lunch and rode down Channel Drive to the lemon factory. The air was misty and cold as he carried his bike and board over the railroad tracks to the bluff. There he saw huge waves breaking across Pierpont Bay. His heart pounded. A wave exploded off the breakwater at the marina engulfing it in white foam. Looking north he saw rows of whitewater rolling into the Point from far beyond the Pier. Swell humps were visible moving across the horizon toward Oxnard and further south. This was a big north swell.

Inside Point was buzzing. The stoked vibe of the day before was gone, no one was joking around. It was as if the game had been moved from the sandlot to a stadium and these waves were hundred mile per hour fastballs. Guys dripping and shivering were giving reports to those getting their wetsuits on. Stoody stood trembling as he told Dugo, "It was the biggest wave I've ever seen..."

Lance leaned on the rail and looked out. A foamy mist hung over the water and the waves were breaking so far out it was hard to see anybody out there.

Sandcrab came up and leaned on the rail next to him. "What do you think?"

82

"I think we need to get our wetsuits on," Lance said trying to sound confident.

"You think we can make it out?"

"I don't know, but we've gotta try."

McGillis came bouncing up the stairs from the water. "This is what it's all about boys, I just got a wave from Stables to the Pier." Stables--named for the horse stables at the fairgrounds visible from the water--was one of the four surf spots that made up the whole of the Point. The northernmost break was the Pipe, where the Ventura River fed into the Pacific, then Stables, the Point and Inside Point. McGillis jogged away toward the Point.

"Hey, where you going?" Lance yelled.

McGillis turned running backward. "Back to the Pipe to paddle out."

Lance pulled his new short john wetsuit up under the towel wrapped around his waist. He walked over to Ringlets and Bill sitting on the planter while snapping his shoulder strap. "Why's McGillis going all the way to the Pipe to paddle out?"

Ringlets was using his hand to replicate his surfboard on a wave, he froze it in mid air and looked at Lance like he had two heads. "Because dip-wad, you see the current? You paddle out from here and you'll get sucked into the Pier in about two seconds."

Bill added, "You gotta start at the Pipe to give yourself room. I got drilled by a set paddling out and lost my board. By the time I got in my board was a hundred yards up the beach."

Sandcrab came up with his wetsuit bundled around his chest.

Ringlets picked up his surfboard. "My advice to you guys is-- be prepared to get your asses kicked and you won't be disappointed." He trotted off toward the Point.

"Thanks a lot," Lance said. He helped Crab pull his wetsuit down. "You ready?"

"I guess so."

They walked up to the dirt parking lot at the Point where they hopped and skipped around the mud puddles from the recent rain. Between the cars lined along the ledge they could see guys paddling and being swept south in the current. For as many waves that were breaking hardly anybody was riding them.

"Do you think we're ready for this?" Sandcrab asked.

"We'll never know unless we try. Let's just see if we can make it out."

"Hey look, there's the Turd, lets go talk to 'em." Sandcrab headed to the van.

Crow's legs were sticking out the side door as he sat naked pushing his feet into his wetsuit. He rolled onto his back lifting his legs to pull the wetsuit on.

"Hey, nice butthole," Sandcrab said.

Crow rocked forward, stood up and pulled the long john up over his chest. "You guys are feelin' brave, huh?"

"I don't know about that," Lance said, "but we're going out."

Roach turned around in the driver's seat already in his wetsuit. "You guys ever been out in waves like this?"

"No."

Crow pointed to the water. "Look at this set."

Way outside a monster wave was beginning to crumble. A small figure on a yellow surfboard rose up on the shoulder.

"Somebody's going."

"I bet that's Dennis on his yellow gun." Roach put his hands around his eyes like binoculars. "That's gotta be him."

They watched as Dennis dropped in and disappeared in the trough then cruised back up the wave's face and kicked out in front of a massive section.

"That wave was huge," Lance said.

84

"Come on, let's get going." Roach picked up his board. "I hope you guys are prepared to do a lot of paddling."

Scarecrow gave them his observations as they walked to the Pipe. "The bigger sets are coming in about every thirty minutes and smaller ones about every ten, there's four to five waves per set. My plan is to start paddling when the first wave of the set breaks, then I'll be deep into the impact zone by the time the last wave breaks."

Roach pointed to a guy being swept south in the current. "That's gonna be us in a minute. You want to get away from shore as fast as you can, that's where the current's worst. If you get dragged past the stairs at Inside Point go in. You don't want to get sucked into the Pier."

They stopped near the mouth of the Ventura River and waited for a set. Crow shaded his eyes looking out. "Once you get out there you can relax a little, but because the waves are bigger, everything is bigger. When you're paddling for position what would normally take two or three strokes, might now take ten or twelve. When you see a set coming paddle your ass off, you do not want to get caught inside."

"Here comes a set," Roach said. "Let's get out there, the wind's starting to pick up."

Lance turned to Sandcrab. "Try to stay together."

Stepping into the water was like stepping into a rushing river. Lance struggled to keep his footing as the current swept around his legs. In thigh deep water Roach and Crow jumped on their boards and started to paddle. Lance and Crab did the same. They crashed through whitewater after whitewater trying to make headway.

Soon Lance lost track of Crow and Roach, but Sandcrab was still behind him to the right. Lance flung his hair from his face and caught sight of another big set breaking outside. He looked to shore. They were only about two hundred feet out and the current was now sweeping them around the Point to Inside Point. They'd been swept three-quarters of the way down from the Pipe.

His arms were tired and soon they'd have to give up and start over. He bore down stroking hard through each whitewater before the next one knocked him back. He stared at the deck of his board and concentrated on breathing--inhale, exhale. He listened for the next wave before bracing for its impact. Only a couple more and he'd turn to go in. He stroked deep, hugged his board, got bashed back, gathered himself and paddled again. One more and that'd be it; he'd given it everything he had. He crashed through the whitewater and would now let the next wave carry him in, but there wasn't a next one. There were no waves breaking in front of him. He paddled over a swell and beyond that was open ocean. As long as a set didn't come he'd make it out. His arms felt like noodles, but he had to stroke. "Paddle, paddle, paddle. I'm gonna make it." He looked around for the Pier to get his bearing; it was behind him to the left. The Pier was a thousand feet long, more than three football fields. How the hell did he get clear out here?

After battling the endless whitewaters, he was now paddling in a wild undulating calm. He allowed himself a moment to rest and feel the swells pass beneath him. *Those are the small ones,* he thought. Looking toward shore he saw the tiny stairs at Inside Point and realized--*the only way in is to catch a wave, oh Jesus.* He wished he was one of those dots on the promenade staring out. He looked around for somebody. *Crow, Roach, Ringlets somebody else has to be out here...keep paddling.*

He spotted a guy on a red board a hundred yards away. Lance put his head down and stroked ignoring the soreness in his shoulders. He inhaled and exhaled pulling hard. He looked up to

86

get a fix on the red board. The wind was picking up and the chop splashed in his eyes. He put his head back down. *I'll catch up to him...maybe I know him...keep paddling, stroke, stroke...I wonder how deep the water is out here? Damn it's cold.*

Okay...where'd Red Board go? Don't get nervous, he's here somewhere. Lance rose on a swell and darted his eyes over the water. He spotted Red Board paddling out. Lance saw huge swells rising on the horizon. His heart pounded. The waves were like mountains rising from the water, he cursed himself for being out here. Why hadn't he just turned and gone in like Sandcrab. The waves kept rising, big and slow. The guy on the red board paddled up the face of the first wave and Lance breathed easier knowing he'd make it too. Stroking up the face he tingled in awe of the wave's sheer size and energy.

His relief was short lived; the next wave was a dark horrendous mass. This was not good. His heart sank as all the fear of all the boogeymen he'd ever imagined were now combining into one very real and threatening monster. The wave was going to break and he was in immediate danger. Paddling toward it would only put him closer to the impact. He turned and paddled for shore trying to distance himself from the crushing whitewater. But the wave didn't break, it kept rolling; he'd made a critical mistake. The towering wave was now sucking him and the whole ocean into its maw. He turned to face it; the wave was going to break right on him. "Oh shit, oh shit, oh shit." He ditched his board and swam for the bottom.

He stroked down but was lifted up with unbelievable force and heaved over backward as if being flung over a waterfall. It slammed him down and in a violent rush picked him back up only to heave him over again. When he felt the wave releasing its grip he struggled through the turbulence upward. The harder he fought the more he needed air. After four desperate strokes he broke the surface and got two quick breaths before the next wave tumbled over him.

His breath was short. It seemed an eternity before he was able to get back to the surface. He was grateful for every swimming lesson his mother had forced him to take. Shaking the hair from his eyes he was surprised to see the guy on the red board sliding down the face of the next wave, his hair blowing back on possibly the ride of his life. Lance dove back down struggling for his.

Each wave dragged him further in and now with the big set past he used the momentum of the inside waves to help get him to shore. Exhausted and frozen he struggled in the shoreline current to stay on his feet.

He stumbled onto the sand dangerously close to the Pier pilings. A group of spectators looked down from the fenced off Pier and applauded his arrival. He waved and thought if they weren't there he might kiss the sand. He looked around for his board and saw it up the beach. He laughed out loud, but fear still clung to his bones. He'd gotten a taste of big waves and right now all he wanted to do was sit on the solid promenade and relish the fact that he'd made it out and he'd made it in, still breathing.

Sandcrab met him at the top of the stairs. "Man, what happened to you? When that set came and your board washed in I thought you were a goner."

Lance walked past him and put his board on the planter. "I gotta to sit down." He was trembling from cold and fear. "Where is everybody?"

"They're all splittin' cause of the wind." Sandcrab sat next to him. "Ringlets broke his board."

"He did?"

"Yeah, he took it to the shop, we should go over there, I bet that's where everybody is."

14
RATTED OUT

The Turd and several other cars were parked at the shop and Q and the twins were standing on the steps.

"What's going on?" Lance rubbed Diablo behind the ears.

"Everybody's in there looking at Ringlets' broken board," Q said.

Lance and Crab walked in and a circle of guys stood around the two broken pieces of surfboard. It reminded Lance of the first time he'd entered the Surf Shop except now he knew everybody. Crow turned to them. "Hey, what happened to you guys? Did you make it out?"

Crab pointed his thumb at Lance. "He did, and just about got killed."

Everybody looked at Lance. Roach punched him in the shoulder. "You made it out, a punk kid like you?"

"Good for you Lance," Dennis said. "Did you get a wave?"

Lance smiled. "No, I got drilled by a set. It was pretty damn scary."

"I didn't make it out, you did better than me," Bill said.

Ringlets swung in the hanging basket chair. "Big deal, anybody can get lucky and make it out."

"Luck is part of it," Dennis said. "The key to surfing big waves is--"

"Having balls," Sandcrab quipped.

Dennis grinned. "That definitely helps, but it's the right board. If you want to surf big waves you've got to have a board that can get you out there and get you into a wave."

"Sure, but who can afford to have a big wave board," Ringlets groaned.

90

"I know, I'm just hearing a lot of frustration and you guys are blaming yourselves when a lot of it is just having the right equipment."

"So, you gonna give me the same deal you gave Lance on his board?" Ringlets asked.

"Sure, the deal stands for all you guys."

"Ninety bucks is still a lot of dough," Stoody said.

"Yeah, but you guys are surfers, what's more important than having a good board. Lance is younger than all you guys and he scraped up the money. Fast, too."

"Well, it's not like he earned it," Ringlets said.

Lance felt his face flush and he stared at Ringlets begging him with his eyes not to say anything.

"I'm sure your mom will give you fifty bucks for Christmas," Crow said.

"That's not what I'm talking about. Tell 'em Lance. Tell 'em where you got the rest of the money."

Everyone looked at Lance. He wanted to smash Ringlet's face. There was no way out, they were all staring; it was like being held under by a wave, except now he didn't want to come up. He looked at Dennis. "I stole it. I stole forty dollars from a Souther."

There was a moment of silence then Roach said, "That's it, you stole forty bucks from a Souther, so what?"

"I don't care either," Ringlets said, "I'm just saying, he didn't earn it."

"That's earning it if you ask me," said Q.

"No, it's not," said Dennis glaring at Q. "Stealing is not cool and I won't take stolen money from any of you. Damn you Lance, this bums me out."

A lump rose in Lance's throat. "I knew it was wrong, but the money was there and I needed it to get my board, things were crazy that day." He looked at Dennis. "What do you want me to do?"

"I want you to earn forty dollars and make this right."

"You can't make him pay twice," Sandcrab said.

Dennis ran his fingers over his mustache. "Dammit! Let me think about this." He squinted, concentrating. "Okay, you give me forty dollars you've *earned* and I'll give you forty dollars in store credit. I don't see any other way to fix it."

Lance swallowed and nodded. "All right, I'll get you the money."

"I don't want to see you around here until you have it. Now go." Dennis looked around the room. "I hope you're all getting the message here."

Lance hung his head and walked out of the shop.

PART 2

THE CURSE

15
EASTER BREAK

It was the end of February when Lance walked back into the Surf Shop and handed Dennis half of what he owed him. It had taken him that long to skim twenty dollars from his school lunch money. He hadn't surfed much during that time either. Without full wetsuits he and Crab found themselves riding cement waves on their skateboards rather than freezing their asses off in the cold winter water.

It wasn't until March that they started surfing regularly again. The big winter swells were over, but there were still plenty of good waves and Lance was happy to find he hadn't lost any of his skill.

Easter break came with a heat wave and it felt like summer. The snack bar on the Pier reopened and girls in bikinis reappeared on the beach.

Lance paddled out in the water and surprised Crab.

"What are you doin' here?" Crab asked. "I thought you had to go to San Diego to visit your sister."

"I got out of it, Ann just got a job at Whataburger and couldn't go, so my parents wanted me stay home with her. I've got a whole week to do whatever I want."

"Lucky dog. You gonna let me spend the night?"

"Every night if you want. The fridge is stocked with T.V. dinners. We can gorge."

Crab sat up on his board. "Hey, you wanna hit the Holiday Inn for breakfast later?"

"Yeah, we haven't done that in a long time."

94

They surfed until eleven when they figured the breakfast rush would be over. Lance jabbed the tail of his board into the sand and picked up his towel. "I want eggs benedict."

Crab rubbed his towel over his hair. "I want pancakes...you remember the routine, right?"

"We take turns with the trays?"

"Yep, no food fights."

Lance put his shirt on and called over to Stoody and Bill who were sitting on the sand. "You guys watch our stuff while we go get something to eat?"

"You gonna let me try your board?" Bill asked.

Lance hesitated.

"Come on, it's not new anymore, you owe me."

"Oh all right, but don't go shooting the Pier or anything."

They walked across the sand to the first set of stairs to the promenade where the high rise Holiday Inn overlooked the beach. Crab peeked over the fence to the pool. "Whoa, check out the chick in the green bikini."

Lance looked over. "Oooh, she's hot."

They continued to the hotel entrance where the automatic doors opened. The carpeting in the lobby felt plush under their bare feet. Lance picked up his pace. "Come on, hurry, the front desk is busy."

They turned down the elevator corridor where a Mexican maid waited with an empty cart. Lance smiled and pointed up.

She smiled. "No, down."

Crab hit the 'up' button and they waited.

A red arrow pointing down lit over the center elevator. The doors opened and the maid pulled the cart in. Lance watched the arrows. "Come on elevator, hurry." *Ding*, a green arrow lit over the right elevator as someone called out, "Excuse me, are you staying at the hotel?"

Down the hall a guy in a monkey suit and cap speed walked toward them.

The doors opened and they rushed in. Crab pounded the number two button.

The voice approached. "Excuse me, are you guests of the hotel? Excuse me?"

As the doors closed Crab frowned. "Well, they know we're here."

"Hit five, we'll start there and work our way up."

"All right. If we have to split up just meet back at the Pier."

The doors opened on the second floor and a man and woman stood waiting.

"Going up?" Crab asked.

"Uh, no down," the man said.

Lance hit the five button and the doors closed.

On the fifth floor there were two trays in the hallway waiting to be picked up by room service. "You take the first one," Crab called.

Lance lifted the plate covers and grabbed half an omelet and a piece of bacon. He took two bites from the uneaten end of the omelet and stuffed the bacon in his mouth. He hurried down the hall past Crab biting into a hunk of hash browns. Lance pushed open the stairwell door and they climbed to the sixth floor. They gobbled eggs, pancakes and ham as they continued up to the seventh, eighth and ninth floors stuffing anything into their mouths decent enough to eat.

"Man we're piggin' out," Crab said chewing on a slab of ham. "I'm stuffed."

Lance rolled up a pancake and took a bite. "Yeah, let's get some toast and stuff to huck from the top floor."

From the twelfth floor stairwell Lance looked over the ledge to the promenade below. "See that hobo diggin' in the trash, let's bombard him."

They hurled English muffins and toast one after the other. The bread spiraled down crashing around the bum. They ducked back when he looked up.

"He probably thinks it's food from heaven," Crab joked.

They corkscrewed their way down the stairs leaping from landing to landing until they got to the bottom and the familiar two doors. One read: LOBBY, and the other: WARNING, EMERGENCY EXIT ONLY, THIS DOOR WILL SOUND ALARM.

"Let's be polite and take the lobby," Lance said. "They're probably still looking for us upstairs."

Lance opened the door and not ten feet away was Monkey Suit and a security guard.

"Stop there!" Monkey Suit shouted.

Lance shoved Crab back into the stairwell and they pushed open the emergency door. The alarm sounded and they ran to the promenade past the hobo, up the stairs to the Pier and over the pedestrian bridge where Crab slowed down holding his side.

"I gotta cramp."

Lance looked back. "I don't think they even chased us."

Crab rubbed his ribs. "Wanna go to the shop?"

"I don't know. I still owe Dennis twenty bucks."

"He doesn't care, he knows you'll pay him."

They continued down the pedestrian bridge and saw Noelle come around the corner from the shop heading to Dennis' boat.

Lance hoped she'd look over so he could wave. Crab wasn't so patient. "Hey Noelle!" he called out.

She smiled and waved. "How are you guys doing?" She was wearing a white blouse and tight jeans.

"You want us to help with the ladder?" Lance asked.

"Well, aren't you chivalrous."

Lance and Crab fumbled with the ladder trying to lean it up evenly for her.

"Thank you gentlemen."

They watched her climb up then effortlessly pull the ladder aboard. She looked over the rail. "I gotta warn you guys, there's a real head case in there blabbering about his trip to Hawaii."

"Ha, this should be good," Crab said.

They turned and walked to the shop. "Did you see her butt?"

"Man, Dennis is lucky."

Parked in front of the shop was a white El Camino with surf racks and two boards on top.

"Pfff, what kind of hodad puts racks on an El Camino?" Crab sneered.

Diablo, the German shepherd, slept on the landing and as they stepped around him they heard voices inside; they paused to listen.

"I was hanging with all those guys--BK, Hakman, Lopez--and they're like, hey Cal, you should come with us..." Lance and Crab looked at each other, giggled and walked in. A guy was standing in front of the mirror trying on a wetsuit. Dennis was leaning on the counter with his arms crossed and another guy was in the hanging basket chair. To Lance the scene felt weirdly familiar.

Dennis stiffened when he saw them.

The guy in the wetsuit turned, his face-hardened. It was Blue Board.

Lance froze as Blue Board came toward them and grabbed them each by the throat. "I should break both your necks right now."

Dennis raised his voice. "Let go of them Cal, not in here!"

98

Suddenly there was a thunderous roar as Diablo charged in barking.

Cal fell backward into a wetsuit rack with the dog snarling over him.

"Get him off! Get him off!"

"Diablo, no!" Dennis called and grabbed him by the collar. The dog stopped barking and Dennis rubbed his head. "It's okay, good boy, easy now, go lay down."

Diablo retreated to the doorway and lay down inside facing the group with a low growl.

Dennis turned to Cal. "Deal with your issues on the beach, not in here."

Cal stood up. He looked at Lance and Crab then Dennis. "Look man, those little shits aren't gonna get away with throwing rocks at my van and tellin' me where I can surf. I just spent three months in the islands surfing with brahs who wouldn't let these punks wipe their ass."

Dennis rolled his eyes. "That's great Cal, but that doesn't mean anything to anybody here."

"I'm sure they let you wipe their asses plenty," Lance said.

Cal clenched his jaw and started at Lance. Diablo jumped up and growled.

"That's enough!" Dennis said. He looked at Lance and Crab. "You guys, split, now."

They went out and from the landing looked down at the El Camino. There was an orange surfboard over the driver's side and on the passenger side was a brand new *Lightning Bolt* from Hawaii. "No way, he got a *Lightning Bolt*," Lance said. "I've never seen one in real life before."

"Me neither, those things cost like two hundred bucks."

"I've got an idea." Lance jumped down the steps and ran around the car. He began unstrapping the *Lightning Bolt*.

"You can't take it!" Crab protested.

"I'm not, just unstrapping it."

"Oh, shit...should I undo the other one?"

"Naw, that guy's never done anything, let's get outta here."

"Wait." Crab bent into car window.

"Forget it, let's go."

They ran over the pedestrian bridge and saw the Turd parked on the hill at the base of the Pier. Crow and Roach were inside checking the waves. Lance whipped opened the sliding door. "You guys won't believe who we just saw!"

"Geez dude, slow down, you scared the crap out of me," Roach said.

"The Souther with the blue van," said Crab, "he's at the shop right now."

"That guy's back?" Crow punched his fist into his palm.

"They're in his buddy's car," Lance said, "a white El Camino."

"He's got some balls. We gotta do something."

"We already did." Lance grinned. "He's got a brand new *Lightning Bolt* on the car and we just unstrapped it."

"Oh damn!" Crow and Roach looked at each other and laughed. Crow asked, "Should we take 'em with us?"

"Sure, sounds like they need to get out of town."

Crow put his elbow over the back of his seat and looked at them. "You guys want to go on an overnight surf trip to Jalama?"

Lance and Crab turned to each other. "A surf safari, hell yeah! Where's Jalama?"

Crow grinned. "It's north of Point Conception in the middle of nowhere. The beach break's almost always fun, but if there's waves there's a left down the beach called Tarantulas."

Crab looked at Lance. "I can tell my mom I'm spending the night at your house."

"Okay," Crow said, "we'll pick you guys up in an hour at your house Lance. You guys have any money?"

Crab held up some one-dollar bills. "I've got four bucks," he said grinning at Lance.

"We've got a couple bucks too," Crow said. "We'll need gas and the camping fee is three bucks. Grab some food and sleeping bags."

Lance and Crab ran down the hill to get their stuff.

"Where'd the money come from?" Lance asked.

"The El Camino, just now."

"That was good timing. You can call your mom from my house and borrow my sister's sleeping bag--oh crap, Bill's got my board." Lance ran to the shoreline to wave Bill in.

16
YOGI BEAR

Roach turned around in the passenger seat as Crow veered the Turd onto the 101 freeway. "So what'd you guys bring for food?"

With no back seat in the van Lance and Crab sat in the rear on a plywood bed cushioned by a foam pad and a sleeping bag. Lance opened a paper sack. "We've got two baloney sandwiches, some Cheez-its, Captain Crunch and a couple root beers. What'd you guys bring?"

"Nothing," Roach said. "We're pretty low on food 'til Crow's mom gets back from Palm Springs. We're gonna stop at EL Cap and get supplies." He reached back. "Let me see that bag."

Lance handed him the sack.

"This'll be a good snack for the road." Roach took out a sandwich and ripped it in two. He handed half to Crow and stuffed the other half in his mouth.

"Hey that's all we brought," Lance complained.
Roach tossed him the other sandwich and swallowed. "You guys can split that one." He opened the Captain Crunch and poured it into the Cheez-its box and shook it.

"Hey, you're ruining the Captain Crunch," Crab said.

Roach handed him the box and opened a can of root beer. "Don't knock 'til you try it."

"We're coming up on Rincon," Crow said.

Lance knew Rincon Point was one of the premiere surf spots on the Pacific coast. He and Crab pulled back the side curtains to look out at the small waves peeling into the cove.

"You know in the old days Rincon was one of the most dangerous places on the El Camino Real," Crow said. "You know what that is, right?"

Lance saw Crow eyeing them in the rear view mirror and answered, "Sure, I watched Zorro. Isn't it the road that connected all the Missions?"

"Yep, the first California Highway." Crow pointed out the windshield. "You see how the mountainside comes down to the base of the point? Back then a stagecoach could only get around there at low tide, and even then it was slow going over rocks and sand. That made it a good place for bandits to hideout and wait for an easy ambush."

"How do you know?" Crab asked.

"I read it."

Roach turned in his seat. "He's always reading about stuff like that."

Crow continued, "Sometimes, if a stage was comin' through with a lot of gold or valuables, they'd hire a gun ship to sit in the cove to protect it."

Crab shook his head. "Man, think of all the great waves that went unridden back then."

They all looked out at Rincon Point and nodded.

Going through Santa Barbara the freeway became boulevard and they had to stop at a couple of traffic lights. Hitchhikers lined the grass along the roadside holding signs for San Francisco, Portland and even Vancouver B.C.

The Turd caused a stir. Hippies waved and held their fingers to their lips indicating they had marijuana. Crow held up two fingers indicating they were only going a short distance.

"Man, why you showing 'em how small your wiener is?" Roach chuckled.

"I'm not, parakeet penis, I'm showing 'em how big your brain is."

Leaving Santa Barbara the street became Highway 101 again and as Crow accelerated Lance had a strange thought. "It's weird to think that right now my parents are driving to San Diego and we're driving north. That means every second I'm further away from them than I've ever been."

"So?" Crab said. "You gonna cry cause you miss your mommy and daddy?"

"No dip-wad. I'm just saying it's weird."

After passing through Goleta they drove mostly in silence until Crow pointed across the highway to the ocean. "You see that tip of land there? That's El Cap Point. When it breaks it's a flawless tube that wraps all the way down the point with a lip so thin it's like glass."

Lance looked out the window at the unimpressive tip of land. There wasn't a ripple on it. "Have you surfed it?"

"No, it hardly ever breaks."

"Well, it ain't breaking again today," Roach said.

Crow veered off the highway onto the El Capitan State Beach exit.

"Why we pulling off here?" Crab asked.

Roach put a sandaled foot on the dash. "You guys ever watch Yogi Bear?"

"The cartoon?"

"Yeah, what's Yogi do?"

"He steals picnic baskets," Lance said.

"Exactly, but in our case it's gonna be an ice chest."

"You can't steal an ice chest," Crab said. "If you get caught we'll all get in trouble."

Roach turned to face him. "We're not doing it, you guys are. So don't get caught and we won't get in trouble."

104

"I'm not doing anything," Crab said.

"So, what are we supposed eat?"

"We've got the Captain Crunch and Cheez-its."

Roach tossed the empty box on the floor.

Crab looked at Lance and frowned.

Roach smiled. "Come on, it's part of the surf trip adventure. Everybody should know how to Yogi Bear."

They pulled up to the ranger booth at the entrance of the state park. A skinny guy in a green uniform pushed back his hat. "Man, that is some brown van you got there."

Crow leaned out the window. "Yeah, we call it the Turd."

"I wasn't gonna say it. You guys camping or day use?"

"We just wanna just check the surf."

"Sure, I'll give you ten minutes."

"Thanks." Crow drove in and parked near the camp store. They got out and looked over a hedge to the beach. There were people sunbathing and wading in the water. The waves were small well-formed peaks. The coast here was a barren strip of white sand that ran along the foot of an eroding bluff.

"Okay, that's enough sightseeing," Roach said.

"What's the hurry?" complained Crab. "We've got ten minutes."

"We've got business, remember?"

"He's right," Crow said. "We gotta get going."

They got in the van and drove into the campground. Roach looked left, then right as they cruised past the campsites. "This should be easy--looks like everybody's at the beach. There's one, park in the next empty site."

Crow parked a few campsites down and shut off the engine. He turned to Lance and Crab. "Okay, walk through the bushes like you're looking for the bathrooms then wander through that campsite. If nobody's around peek in the ice chest and make sure it's got stuff in it, grab anything else that looks good and get back here."

"I can't believe we're doing this," Crab said.

Lance slid the van door open and jumped out. "Come on, let's get it over with."

They walked through the bushes to the campsite and strolled past the tent. No one was around. Lance opened the ice chest; it was full of stuff. They each took a handle and Lance grabbed a loaf of bread off the picnic table, Crab grabbed a package of napkins. They carried the ice chest through the bushes to the van.

"See, nothing to it," Roach said.

Driving past the booth on the way out they waved to the skinny ranger. On the highway Roach climbed in back and opened the ice chest. "Whoa, a six pack of beer, you guys did good. Okay, so we've got six beers, four hot dogs, a package of ham, some cheese, mayonnaise, mustard, half a quart of milk and a loaf of bread. Good eye getting the bread Lance...oh yeah, we've got napkins too."

"What, you don't wipe your mouth?" Crab asked.

"That's what my towel's for. Why couldn't you grab a bag of chips or something?"

"I didn't see any chips--and I use my towel to dry off."

"Pfff, I use mine for everything."

"You even wipe your ass with it?"

"No, I use your towel for that."

17
JALAMA

Highway 101 turned inland through the rolling hills of central California and after a few miles they took Highway 1 north toward Lompoc. The Turd sped down the long strip of highway as golden sunlight poured in through the driver side windows and the wind whipped their hair around their faces while they sipped cold beer.

"Look at all this ranch land," Crow said. "Almost all of California used to be giant cattle ranches like this."

"Here we go again," Crab said.

Lance sat up. "Go ahead, I wanna hear."

"During the rancho days a single ranch could be hundreds of thousands of acres, like on *Bonanza*." He took a drink of beer. "Anybody ever read *Two Years Before the Mast*?"

They all shook their heads.

"The guy who wrote it sailed on a ship up and down the California coast in the 1830s, back when California was still Mexico."

"Were they looking for gold?" Lance asked.

"Nope, they were collecting cow hides to take back to the east coast, thousands of 'em. The guy's name was something Dana-- I'm pretty sure they named Dana Point after him. They'd anchor wherever there was a Mission, row ashore and buy up all the cowhides they could. They did it from San Diego to San Francisco and back again until the ship was full."

"What'd they want 'em for?" Crab asked.

"Leather goods, boots, saddles, they made everything out of leather back then."

"Boy, that sounds like a real page turner," Roach said.

107

"He even mentioned Ventura, said our Mission was the prettiest on the coast."

Lance sipped his beer. "Did he say anything else about Ventura?"

"He said it was a lousy place to land because the boats would get swamped going ashore. That's why they eventually built the Pier."

Crab leaned forward. "So what happened to all the cattle ranches?"

"I don't know. I guess they discovered how good citrus grew and everybody planted orchards."

"And everyone wonders why the condors are going extinct," Roach said. "They can't eat lemon carcasses."

The sun disappeared behind the western hills and a sign appeared on the highway: Jalama 15 miles. Below that an arrow pointed to the hills. Crow down shifted and turned left. "Here we go, Jalama Road."

The Turd gasped and sputtered as it wound through the ups and downs and around blind corners on what could hardly be called a two-lane road. The ice sloshed back and forth in the ice chest as Crow constantly worked the clutch and gas. In the shadow of the hills it got dark and Lance continually shifted his weight in the swerving van. Suddenly Crow hit the brakes and turned sharply, two tires went off the pavement. Lance and Crab fell to the floor.

"What the hell was that?"

"That pickup almost hit us," Crow said.

Roach wiped his hair from his face. "Maybe you should slow down and turn on the headlights."

Crow restarted the engine and flicked on the lights.

"Whoa, wait!" Roach flung his door open and jumped out. He ran in front of the van and bent down in the headlights.

108

"What the hell is he doing?" Crab asked.

Roach came back to the van cradling something in his hands. "Open up, I'm getting in back."

Crab slid the side door open. "What is it?"

Roach leaned in and held his hands open. "A tarantula."

"Oh shit, get that thing away from me!" Crab yelled.

Crow reached over and petted the spider with one finger. "Don't be a baby, Roach used to have one of these for a pet."

"That's sick, who keeps a tarantula for a pet?"

Roach cupped the spider in his hands. "Relax Crab, you're getting her excited."

"Come on Lance, tell 'em you don't want that thing in here either," Crab protested.

"I don't care as long as I don't have to touch it."

Roach stepped into the back of the van. "Scoot over, I'm sittin' back here."

Crab stood up. "Then I'm sittin' in front." He jumped out, closed the side door and took the front seat.

Roach laid back on the bed petting the spider and Crow put the Turd in gear and pulled back on to the pavement.

Crab turned around in his seat. "How do you know that thing won't bite you?"

"She won't, as long as you don't scare her."

"How can you tell it's a girl?" Lance asked.

"'Cause man, she showed me her boobs. Look she's crawling up my stomach."

Roach sat still as the spider crawled up his bare chest to his neck. He leaned his head back and let the tarantula crawl over his chin and onto his face. It stepped slowly over Roach's mouth, nose and eyes and came to rest on top of his head.

"That was freaky," Lance said.

"Man, you're sick," said Crab, "What if that thing had peed on your face?"

Crow shifted gears as they came over a rise and the van filled with orange light from the setting sun. "There's the ocean, we're almost there."

The road switch-backed down the hillside and by the time they entered the campground the sun had vanished below the horizon leaving an orange and pink sky. The campground was mostly empty and Crow pulled into a beachfront campsite. "Let's check the waves real quick, then you guys can round up some firewood while there's still some light. Me and Roach'll get camp set up."

"How come we have to get firewood?" Crab complained.

"Because you want a ride home," Roach said. "It's called paying your dues."

"Let's hurry and check the waves," said Lance.

The waves looked rideable but sloppy and Lance and Crab wandered into the darkness to find wood. Roach called out. "See if you can find a mate for my spider while you're out there."

Crab frowned. "There's probably tarantulas all over the place, especially in the wood."

"Let's check the empty campsites first."

The waves pounded in the distance as they rummaged through old campfires for half-burnt logs. Lance wished he'd worn tennis shoes instead of thongs. On his third trip back with a load of wood Crow had the fire burning and Lance settled near the heat. The concrete fire pit had a grate on one side for a kettle or frying pan. Lance and Crab put hotdogs on sticks and roasted them over the fire. Roach sat on the floor of the van with his legs out and the tarantula on his lap.

Crow held a stick out to Roach. "You ready for a hot dog."

110

"In a minute. I'm trying to get her to relax, I think the smoke is freaking her out."

Crab blew out the flame on his hotdog. "Aren't those things nocturnal?

"Sure are," Roach said.

Crab took a seat at the picnic table. "Great. I'm sure it's poisonous too"

"Not to humans, they use their venom to liquefy their prey then suck it up with their stomach."

"That's appetizing." Crab laid a napkin out on the table and wrapped his hotdog in a slice of bread. "That thing just better not end up in my sleeping bag."

Roach stood up cradling the tarantula; he walked to the picnic table.

Crab stopped chewing. "Don't bring that thing over here."

"I'm gonna help you get over your fear. Just look at her, she's an amazing creature." Roach held the spider out for Crab to see.

"Get that thing away from me."

"Just look."

Crab held his hot dog off to the side and peered into Roach's hands. "That thing's ugly and it's probably got parasites." Crab turned away in disgust and Roach dropped the tarantula on his lap.

"AHHHH!" Crab tossed his hotdog and rolled over backward into the dirt. He scrambled to his feet swatting his body. "You asshole! I knew you'd do that!"

"Sorry man." Roach laughed. "I couldn't resist. Do you see her?"

Lance spotted the spider cowering against the cement wall of the fire pit. "There it is."

Crab grabbed a pile of napkins, snatched up the tarantula and flung the heap onto the grill. The napkins ignited and the spider's legs erupted in a frenzy from the flames as it shrieked like grating metal then fell silent on the grill.

"What the hell was that?" Crow said.

Roach shoved Crab. "What the hell have you done?"

"I got rid of it, that's what."

Lance stared at the charred spider remains on the grill. "Did you hear it scream?"

Roach shook his head and sat down at the table. "That's a curse man, that's an omen." He looked at Crab. "You've done it now, you better watch it, we all better watch it."

"Relax," Crow said, "that thing could've easily died on the road."

"But it didn't 'cause I saved it. You heard that scream." Roach looked across the sky. "Evil's been cast over us, you can forget about getting waves tomorrow. We better just worry about getting home safe."

"You shouldn't have thrown it on me," Crab said.

"I was trying to teach you something."

"By throwing a spider on me? Right. Only thing that taught me was you're an asshole."

Roach got up and opened the ice chest. He took out a hotdog, stabbed a stick through it and walked to the fire. "It's cool, I'm just glad I'm not sleeping on the ground tonight with a tarantula curse on my head."

Lance and Crab looked at each other.

* * * *

Through the fabric of his sleeping bag Lance could feel every pebble. He rolled up his beach towel for a pillow and pulled the sleeping bag over his head. It was almost impossible to sleep.

112

When dawn finally came Lance stretched out pressing his feet against the bottom of the bag. He lay there listening to the waves and tried to determine if they were louder than the night before. He poked his head out; the air was cool and moist. He saw Crab wrapped tight in his sleeping bag on the picnic table. "You bastard." Lance climbed out and walked across the cold sand to the water. It was glassy and the waves were dark hollow peaks. With no one out it was hard to tell how big they were, but it looked good.

He ran back to camp, unzipped Crab's sleeping bag and flung it open. "Wake up the waves are good."

"What the hell are you doing?" Crab pulled the sleeping bag back over himself.

"Get up, the waves are good, you're wasting time."

"Okay, give me a second will'ya."

"Let's hurry and get our wetsuits on before those guys wake up."

Before leaving for the water Lance opened the Turd's sliding door. "Waves are good, see you guys out there." He ran to catch up with Crab.

"Omen shmomen," Crab said walking to the water. "Look at those waves."

Peaks were pounding up and down the beach. The sky was grey and so was the water. The waves were breaking close to shore, an easy paddle out. They ran splashing into the water, jumped onto their boards and paddled. The waves were powerful and Lance battled to get out. When he finally made it past the whitewater he heard yelling on the beach. He turned and saw Crow and Roach waving their arms and yelling like lunatics. He wondered what the hell they were doing. They didn't even have their wetsuits on yet. Lance stroked over a swell and looked for Crab. He saw him bellyboarding in on a whitewater. "What the

113

hell is he doing?" Lance sat up on his board and turned to the outside. There he saw a large fin rise from the water not fifty feet away. The tail fin thrashed the surface and the dorsal turned his way.

"Shark!" he screamed. He sank the board's tail and swirled around plunging his arms into the water knowing his splashing would only attract the shark--stroke, stroke. He lifted his feet. The shark would be on him any second. He felt a jolt from behind and was thrust forward. It was a whitewater. A wave had picked him up and was carrying him in. He continued to paddle until his hands hit sand.

The other boys ran up shouting, "Did you see it? That thing was huge."

Lance stood up trembling and looked back out. They watched for the fin, but it didn't reappear.

"I'd say that's an omen," Roach said. "Can't be too bad though, you guys both made it in."

"Come on," Crow said, "we better tell the ranger."

18
GIRLS

It was almost ten when they finally got on the road and drove the many turns from Jalama back to Highway 1. The overcast skies mirrored their gloom. Lance busied himself making sandwiches. With no utensils he rummaged around the van for something to spread mayonnaise with. He pried a popsicle stick from a crevice on the floor.

"You can't use that," Crab said. "That's gross."

"It's all I've got." Lance wiped it with his towel and dipped it into the mayonnaise where it left a dirty smear. He spread mayonnaise on the bread, threw on some ham and held the sandwich out to Crow.

Crow downshifted while turning then straightened out, shifted up and took the sandwich. "Maybe we should stop at El Cap and surf the beach break just to shake the sharkies."

"I vote for that," Lance said.

Crab reclined in the back of the van. "You know the average person has a better chance of being killed by lightning or a bee sting than a shark."

Roach turned in his seat. "Yeah, but the average person doesn't go surfing every day either." He looked down at Lance. "Put the works on mine."

When they reached Highway 1 the sun broke through. They weaved through the rolling hills back to Highway 101 then rounded the bend at Gaviota and were back on the coast. Soon they passed the palm trees at Refugio State Beach then turned off again at El Cap.

A Chevy Blazer loaded with beach gear waited at the booth. The same young ranger was working and did a double take when he saw the Turd.

"Ha, he remembers us," Crow said nudging the van forward as the Blazer pulled away.

The ranger lifted his hat and scratched his head. "I didn't expect to see you guys here again."

Crow handed him a dollar. "Yep, we're back. We'll take a day pass."

"Whatever you say." The ranger handed him a quarter and a receipt. "Put that on your dash."

Roach looked back as they pulled away. "Was he acting funny?"

"He's probably stoned," Crow said. "Wouldn't you be if you had that job?"

They parked a few cars away from the camp store, got out and stood at the hedge surveying the scene. It was close to eleven and the beach was filling with people. Roach tore off a piece of bread and tossed it to a hovering seagull. Another seagull appeared. Lance grabbed a piece too and tossed some in the air. Seagulls came from all directions and swarmed over them. Lance held up a whole slice of bread and two seagulls ripped it from his hand. "Did you see that?"

"I see girls," Crab said.

Four girls were standing in front of the camp store watching them.

The boys stopped and stared.

The girls instantly looked away and huddled together. They each wore shorts with bikini tops.

Crow whistled lightly. "Look at the rack on the blonde."

"Okay, I know which one you want," Roach said.

116

The girls started down the path toward the beach. One with curly strawberry-blonde hair picked up a surfboard lying on the bushes and followed the others.

"Ha, a surfer girl," Roach said.

Before they disappeared Crow called out, "Hey, where you guys going?"

"What are you doing?" Lance gasped.

The girls stopped and looked back.

"Don't worry," Crow said. "Just let us do the talking."

"Yeah, all you guys have to do is--nothing stupid," Roach added.

As they walked toward the girls a white glob splatted on Crab's bare shoulder.

"Haha," Lance laughed. "A seagull just crapped on you."

"Perfect timing, go wipe it off," Roach ordered.

Lance waited as Crab flung open the side door of the van and wiped his shoulder with Roach's towel, then they ran to catch up.

"Great, now I smell like seagull crap."

"You can rinse off when we get to the beach," Crow said.

Roach walked with a new swagger. "They all look pretty hot."

The girls whispered to each other as they approached. The redhead was the only one not smiling.

"Can we help you with something?" asked the busty blonde.

"We were wondering if you guys would want to hang out on the beach." Crow said.

Her brow narrowed. "Uh...you mean with you?"

"Well, yeah...us."

She folded her arms. "Why would we want to do that?"

"Well...because, there's four of us and four of you."

She smiled and looked at Crab. "Did a seagull just poop on you?"

The girls giggled. Crab blushed.

Roach looked at the redhead with the surfboard. "You surf?"

She shifted her weight. "Yesterday was my first time."

The blonde rolled her eyes. "For some reason she feels the need to act like a boy."

"It's better than looking at myself in the mirror all day."

Crow smiled. "You guys must be sisters."

"Unfortunately," said the blonde.

Crow nodded to the surfer girl. "If you need some pointers my friends here, Lance and Sandcrab can help you, they're just learning to surf too."

"Hey, we've been surfing almost a year," Crab protested.

The blonde reached up and pulled her hair back and the motion of her breasts brought the attention back to her. "Did you just call him Sandcrab?"

"Yeah," Crow said. "We usually just call him Crab, but his full name is Sandcrab."

She laughed. "I'm Ashley and that's my thorny little sister Briar, and these are our friends Kim and Kari."

"I'm Steve," said Crow, "but everybody calls me Crow and this is Roach, which is short for Richard, and Sandcrab...well, that's just his name--"

"It's Mike," Crab said, "but I like Crab better."

Ashley and the other girls looked at Lance.

He shrugged. "I'm just Lance."

Briar switched the surfboard to her other arm. "Can we go now?"

"Yeah," Crab said. "I need to rinse off."

They headed down the path to the beach and a couple of kids came barreling down behind them. They moved aside to let them run through. Two adults followed carrying plastic beach toys and gear. Lance and Crab stood on either side of Briar. She wrinkled her nose at Crab. "You smell like rotten fish."

118

Lance laughed. "I think it's an improvement."

She grinned and they headed to the water.

Her surfboard had a funny shape--a wide twin fin with a square tail and fat pointy nose. It looked homemade. "Is that your board?" Lance asked catching a whiff of her Coppertone.

"It's my cousin's, he left it at our house last summer."

"Where do you guys live?"

"Santa Barbara."

"Oh yeah? We're from Ventura. You ever been there?" Lance joked.

"Sure," she replied. "We drive through it every time we go to L.A."

On the beach Crab dove in the water and took a couple of strokes out.

"Shark!" Roach cried.

Crab scrambled for shore and they all laughed. Roach turned to Kim to explain why that was so funny.

Crab ran up from the water and picked up a piece of dead jellyfish lying on the wet sand. He flung it at Roach; the tentacles wrapped around his shoulder and chest.

"Ow, you bastard!" Roach peeled off the jellyfish and ran after Crab. The tentacles wrapped around his arm as he ran. "Aaaahhh!"

Crab laughed so hard he couldn't run anymore and Roach slapped the jellyfish onto his back. Crab wriggled and shimmied. "Somebody get it off."

Lance stood between Kari and Briar laughing.

"I'll help him," Kari said. She walked over and examined his back. "It won't sting me will it?"

"Just don't touch the tentacles," Crab said.

She placed one hand on his back while peeling the jellyfish off with the other.

119

"Hey Crab," Roach called, "let me know if you want me to pee on it."

Briar grinned in disgust.

Lance shrugged. "They say urine is good for a jellyfish sting, but I've never tested it. Hey, we're going up to get our boards and stuff. When we get back I could help you learn to surf."

She frowned. "Did anybody help you?"

"No."

"Exactly. So why do you think I need help?"

"I don't, I just thought--"

"If I need your help I'll ask."

Ashley looked to Lance. "She doesn't like being treated like a girl."

"You don't get it Ash."

Lance admired Briar's spunk, and her curvy body.

"Well," Crow said, "where you girls gonna put your towels?"

Ashley pointed up the beach. "Somewhere over there, away from the crowd."

"Oh, that's too bad," Crow said. "That's exactly where we were gonna go."

"Well, maybe we'll see you over there." She smiled.

The boys hurried back to the van to get their stuff.

"Damn, those chicks are unreal," Roach said. "I dig Kim."

"Did you see Kari touching my back?" Crab grinned. "I was afraid I was gonna get a woody."

"Ha! Control yourself there little man," Crow said. "What about you Lance, you like the surfer girl?"

"Uh...yeah, she's okay." He couldn't wait to get back and try to make her smile again.

They started up the path to the parking lot and Roach clenched his fists. "Damn, how lucky are we?"

120

"No kidding," Crow agreed. "Four chicks, four guys, this never happens."

"So much for that curse," Crab said. "This is our lucky day."

At the camp store two rangers stood out front.

"Hello boys," said the taller ranger.

"Hello," they said. The ranger looked like Andy Griffith.

"Is that your brown van there?"

"Sure is," Crow said proudly.

The other ranger was the skinny kid from the booth.

"I understand you fellas were here yesterday," said Ranger Andy.

"Yeah," said Crow. "We just stopped in to check the surf."

The ranger raised an eyebrow. "Is that all you did?" He tipped his hat back. "There's a red ice chest in your van, we'll need to take a look at it."

They walked to the Turd and Crow slid the side door open.

The ranger leaned in and opened the ice chest. "It matches the description, and the contents check out, minus a few things." He stood and faced them. "We'll need you fellas to come to the station." He looked at Crow. "You bring the vehicle over to the Ranger Station with your driver's license and registration. The rest of you boys come with us."

19

RANGER STATION

Lance felt queasy as he followed the rangers across the parking lot to the station. He could only hope this would be over quickly and they could get back to the beach and the girls.

The skinny ranger held the screen door open as they filed into the Ranger Station. It was a wooden cabin with a lot of windows. From inside they could see the booth, the parking lot, the camp store and the entrance of the campground. The skinny guy set up folding chairs in the small reception area and they sat quietly while Crow was outside in the van, probably looking for his registration.

Sitting there didn't feel much different from being in the principal's office, except this was real life. Lance whispered to Roach and Crab, "Let's cooperate and get this over with quick."

Crow came in and sat down. The clock on the wall read 11:16. Ranger Andy sat at a desk behind the counter filling out paperwork. He scooted his chair out and came around, he took Crow's license and registration and looked at the rest of them. "Anybody else have identification?"

They shook their heads.

Andy looked at Crow's driver's license. "All you boys from Ventura?"

They nodded.

He took a moment and looked at each of them. "My name is Buck, and the four of you are in a bit of trouble. I presume you're all under eighteen. Have any of you been to juvenile hall before?"

The words felt like a punch in the stomach. Lance groaned audibly and Buck looked directly at him.

"Is something wrong young man?"

"Uh, no sir...I just feel ashamed."

"Well good. Maybe we can make this a learning experience for you and you can move on and live happy productive lives. I've gotta make a phone call to get the ball rolling, you boys just sit tight. If you need anything, Gil here can accommodate you." He nodded at the skinny kid.

Gil sat on the windowsill and touched the brim of his hat. Buck went to his desk and picked up the phone. He read Crow's driver's license and registration information into the reciever. "Okay, no hurry, I'll wait to hear back."

No hurry? Lance groaned again and looked up at the knotty pine ceiling and the slowly spinning fan.

Buck hung up the phone, shuffled some papers on his desk and stood up. "You boys are either very bold or not very bright. We put an APB out on your vehicle yesterday after the ice chest was reported missing. We didn't have a license plate number, but that van is a pretty easy one to spot. When there was no word from the highway patrol this morning we figured you'd gotten away. Then you come prancing back in here. Would you care to explain your actions?"

There was silence, then Crab said, "Shouldn't we speak to a lawyer or something before we say anything?"

Buck tipped his hat back and smiled. "You don't need to answer my questions son, I'm just trying to make an assessment here. You were identified in the campground around the time of the crime and you've been caught with the stolen property in your vehicle. Now, I'm allowing you an opportunity to present your side before I assume the worst."

"I can explain, sir," Crow said. "We were probably just a little too excited about making this surf trip. I think we each hoped somebody else brought enough food or money. It wasn't until we

123

stopped here that we realized we barely had enough money to cover the camping fee at Jalama and we'd already eaten all the food we brought. So, then we were thinking about what to do and happened to see that ice chest just sitting there."

Buck sat down on the corner of a table, folded his arms and squinted at Crow. "Just sitting there? On a picnic table in a campsite?" He shook his head. "You didn't discuss food or money before you took this little adventure?"

"No sir. It was all pretty spontaneous and at the time food didn't seem all that important, but once we got this far we knew we had a problem."

"Basically sir," Roach interrupted, "we couldn't see aborting the trip and the opportunity for waves on account of a lack of nutrition. None of us are quitters, so we saw no choice but to kick it into survival mode and resort to Yogi Bear tactics."

Buck closed his eyes and massaged the bridge of his nose. "I'm not even going to try to decipher what you just said." He held up Crow's license and studied it. "Let's see, it says here you're almost seventeen Mr. Helman. Do you work?"

"Yes sir, I have a lawn service."

"Well, good for you. I can only hope you're getting this kind of nonsense out of your system because for you the game's going to change very soon. You don't want mindless stunts like this going on your permanent record." Buck stood up. "I'm waiting to hear back from the Sheriff. While we're waiting I'll need to get all of your personal information, I have forms you can fill out. Meanwhile, I have to write up a report, then decide what to do with you. Can you get the paperwork and some clipboards, Gil?"

Gil opened a file cabinet and fingered through it.

Lance imagined the four girls sitting on the beach. He imagined sitting next to Briar on the sand, asking her what she

124

liked to do after school, what music she liked. He looked up at the clock; it was 12:02.

Gil handed out the paperwork. It was a general information form: name, age, address, telephone number, parents or guardian's name. They filled in the information and handed the forms back to Gil who gave them to Buck.

Out the window Lance saw the girls standing by the camp store. Ashley had her hands on her hips surveying the parking lot. Lance sat up in his chair. "There they are."

The boys craned to see. Ashley looked their way and pointed to the Ranger Station.

"They see the van," Crow whispered.

The girls huddled together.

Roach waved his arms and Buck stood up. "What the hell's going on?"

"Sir, we need to talk to those girls," Roach said.

"Who are they?"

"They've been waiting for us on the beach," Crow explained, "they don't know what happened to us."

"Well, you're not going anywhere."

The girls started toward the Ranger Station.

"Looks like I'd better deal with this. You boys don't move, I'll be right back." Buck pushed open the screen door and let it slam behind him. He met the girls halfway.

Gil leaned on the counter looking out the window. "Man, you guys just met those girls? Who got the one with the rack?"

"Hey, come on," Crow said.

"Sorry man, no offense. I'm not even a boob guy."

Buck folded his arms and Briar pointed to the Ranger Station. Buck shook his head and waved them away. The girls turned back toward the beach.

"Man, that's a bummer for you guys," Gil said.

"Yeah, we blew it," said Crow.

Gil shook his head. "I can't believe you guys came back to the scene of the crime."

Crow shrugged. "We thought we got away clean." He looked out the window. "It was almost worth it."

Buck flung the screen door open and let it slam again. "I told them you boys were being detained and awaiting removal." He went to his desk, sat down and put his feet up. "As soon as I hear back from the Sheriff, presuming he has nothing to tell me, I'll release you boys to the custody of a parent."

Crow stood up. "What about my van, sir?"

"As long as a parent comes to claim you, you're free to drive it home."

Crab squirmed in his chair. "I don't want my dad to have to come get us."

Buck chuckled. "I wouldn't want to have to come and get you either, but somebody's parent has to come." He pulled out his wallet and gave Gil a couple of dollars. "Go to the store and get these boys some sandwiches and soda pop, we're going to be here a while."

At two-twenty the Sheriff finally called back. Buck hung up the phone and said, "Your record's clean Mr. Helman. Whose parents should I call first?"

"I live with my grandma and she doesn't drive," Roach said.

"My parents are in San Diego," said Lance.

"My mom won't come," Crow said.

Buck tipped his hat back. "What do you mean she *won't come?*"

"She's kind of checked out of family life since the divorce, she's got a boyfriend now and--"

"Okay, what about your dad?"

"He lives in Chicago."

126

"Well, I'll call your mom anyway just to let her know what you've been up to, maybe it'll get her a little more involved. I'm calling everybody's house until somebody comes."

"Oh no," Crab said. "It's gonna be my dad. Can't we just go to juvenile hall?"

"Same situation there, except you'd all have to be claimed individually. Believe me, this is simpler and a lot less paperwork."

It was four-thirty when Crab's dad finally pulled up outside the ranger station. Buck went out and shook his hand, they talked briefly and as they came in Mr. Shaw thanked Buck for his trouble. He glared at the boys and followed Buck to the counter.

"I've issued them all citations," Buck said. "On it is a date for an appearance in juvenile court."

Mr. Shaw turned and looked at them. "I hope you're proud of yourselves."

Crow stood up. "We're sorry Mr. Shaw, thanks for coming to get us."

"I didn't have much choice, did I?"

Crow shook his head and looked at the ground.

"Mike, get in the car," Mr. Shaw said.

"But, all my stuff is in the van."

"We can bring it by in the morning," Crow offered.

Mr. Shaw looked at Crow. "What the hell were you thinking?"

"We weren't, sir."

The boys followed Mr. Shaw out and went to the van. Lance slid the side door open and climbed in. "Man that's gonna be a long ride home for Crab."

Crow started the engine. "Hey, what's this?" He reached out and removed a piece of paper from under the wiper blade. He read it. "No way!" He handed the paper to Roach.

Roach stomped his feet. "Oh yeah!"

"What is it?" Lance asked.

Roach handed him the note.

In loopy girl writing it read, *We'll be here until Friday. Will we see you again?*

20
ANN

It was six o'clock when Crow and Roach dropped Lance off at his house. He walked in and saw Ann sitting on the couch eating a T.V. dinner and watching *I Love Lucy*. She sat back and crossed her arms.

"Well, look who's here."

"Are you mad?"

"Lance, it's kind of a big deal for mom and dad to leave us here alone and the first night I get a note saying you're going off all night with your friends. I'm supposed to be watching you."

"You're not watching me. I'm here so you won't be alone."

"Great, and the first night you leave me alone. Just remember, you'd be in San Diego right now if it wasn't for me."

"I know." He dropped his backpack on the floor and sat down. "But Crow and Roach asked me and Crab to go with 'em on a surf trip to Jalama--"

"With who, where?"

"Jalama, with Crow and Roach, it's up north. It was my first surf trip, I had to go."

She rolled her eyes. "Sounds like you went to magicland with your animal friends."

"I've told you about Crow and Roach before."

"How old are those guys?"

Lance folded his arms. "Sixteen."

"Why are they hanging out with you?"

"I don't know, I didn't ask 'em. Maybe they think we're cool."

"Seems weird."

Lance paused. "Ann."

"Yes?" Her eyes narrowed.

"We were...kinda thinking about going back up there tomorrow."

"No way Lance."

"Come on Ann, I have to--"

"Forget it, just because mom and dad are gone doesn't mean you can do whatever you want."

"Please Ann, just one more night, I swear I'll stay home the rest of the week."

"What's so important, were the waves that good?"

"We...met some girls."

Ann gasped. "You met a girl!"

"It's no big deal."

"Is she cute?"

Lance rolled his eyes.

"Okay, of course she's cute. What school does she go to?"

"I don't know. She lives in Santa Barbara."

"Uh-oh, long distance romance could be difficult on your bike."

He picked up his backpack. "I'm going to my room now."

"Oh Lance, I'm just teasing. Look, It's okay. I can spend the night at Tracy's or Susan's."

"Thanks Ann."

"The oven's still hot if you want to put in a T.V. dinner. *The Andy Griffith Show* is on next."

* * * *

The next morning Lance sat at the table eating cereal when he heard the Turd pull up. He opened the kitchen window and hollered out, "Come on in, the door's open, you guys want some cereal?"

130

"Do bears crap in the woods?" Roach replied.

Lance put two more bowls on the table and got out two more boxes of cereal. Roach and Crow came in and sat down.

"So, we've got a plan," Crow said pouring milk. "You remember what I was saying about the fire road that runs along the railroad tracks?"

"Yeah, you said there's no way we could get on it without being seen."

"Well, I thought of something."

"Listen to this," Roach said with a mouthful of cereal.

Crow continued. "Those railroad tracks run through El Cap and up through Refugio, the next state beach north. All we have to do is drive to Refugio, get on the fire road there and drive back down to El Cap. We park on the bluff just north of the campgrounds, walk in on the beach and never even see a ranger."

"It's perfect," Roach said. He slurped the milk from his bowl and got up and went to the fridge. "We should make some sandwiches, what've you got?" He pulled out baloney, jam and mayonnaise.

Lance got out the bread and peanut butter.

"What are you doing?" Ann asked standing in the doorway with her hands on her hips.

"We're making sandwiches," Lance said, "we're going back up north, remember?"

"I don't remember saying it was okay to feed the neighborhood."

"This is my sister, Ann," Lance said.

"Lance, this is all the food we've got until mom and dad get home."

Lance laid out the bread on the cutting board. "We're only making a couple of sandwiches, and remember I won't be home for dinner."

The phone rang at the back of the kitchen and Ann darted around the boys to answer it.

"It's always for her," Lance said.

"Quiet, it might be mom and dad." She picked up the phone. "Hello...oh, hi Susan...yeah, they left the day before yesterday...hey, can I call you back? My brother has a bunch of friends over and they're all here in the kitchen...okay, bye." Ann weaved her way out of the kitchen. "You'll be home tomorrow, right Lance?"

"Yep."

Roach opened the refrigerator again. "She seems cool." He took out a jar of mustard. "I want some of this on mine."

"On peanut butter and jelly?"

"Yeah, and put some jelly on my baloney and cheese too, I like to mix things up."

Lance wrapped the sandwiches in wax paper and stuffed them into a grocery bag, he tossed in a couple of cans of pork 'n beans and a can opener then they headed to Crab's house.

21
CRAB'S HOUSE

The morning sun pulsed through the palm trees lining Poli Street as they drove to Crab's house. Crow turned left on Santa Rosa and parked across the street. Mr. Shaw's car was in the driveway.

"Damn, doesn't that guy work? It's after nine," Crow said.

Roach looked back at Lance. "Good luck in there."

Lance opened the side door and walked to the house. As he stepped on the porch the front door flew open and Mr. Shaw charged out. "No trouble today, right Lance?" he said as he marched past.

"Uh, no sir." He watched Mr. Shaw toss his brief case into the car while staring across the street at the van.

"Good morning Lance," Mrs. Shaw said appearing in the doorway. "That was quite a day you boys had yesterday."

"Yes ma'am, I'd like to forget it."

"We all would. He's in his bedroom, you can go in."

The T.V. was blaring in the den and Crab's little brother and sister were sitting on the floor in their pajamas watching *Tom and Jerry* cartoons.

"You guys are robbers," said Crab's little brother Timmy.

"Are you going to jail?" his sister Cathy asked.

"That's enough you two," Mrs. Shaw said. "They are not going to jail, and turn that down."

Lance continued to Crab's room and found him peeking out the curtain. "What are you lookin' at?"

"My dad's out there talking to Crow and Roach. He was in a big hurry to leave, but now he's got time to sit around and talk to them."

Lance looked out the curtain. Mr. Shaw leaned on the van with both hands over the driver's door.

"Is he still mad?"

"He'll be mad for a week, let's go rescue 'em before he chews their ears off."

"Crow wanted you to ask your mom for a buck."

"Are you kiddin' me?"

"Come on, I made us some sandwiches."

When they came out Mr. Shaw was backing out of the driveway. Crab opened the sliding door. "So, what was my dad hassling you guys about?"

"He was guilt trippin' us, about being better role models," Crow said. "He says you guys are impressionable and that we should be aware of our influence over you."

"Yeah, he's trying to lay his parenting responsibilities on us," Roach said, "but I straightened him out. I told him you guys were the bad influences and that everything would be fine and dandy if you hadn't fried my tarantula."

"Hey, you're the one that put the curse on us," Crab said.

"No, you did when you torched my spider."

Lance slammed the sliding door. "We can forget about that now, our luck's about to change. Get this piece of crap moving."

Crow turned around. "Hey, what have I told you about taking the Turd's name in vain?"

"Sorry man, I'm just excited."

Crab looked skeptical. "What are we doing?"

Roach handed him the note. "This was on the windshield when we came out of ranger station."

Crab unfolded the paper. "This is from the girls?"

"Yeah, they want us to come back."

"We can't go back up there."

Lance rubbed Crab's back. "Think about Kari dreaming about rubbing jellyfish on you."

"Get your hands off me, homo. You guys are nuts, Buck said we're not allowed up there for the rest of the week."

"We've got a plan," Lance said. "We're sneaking in."

"Oh right, this van's about as discrete as a diarrhea fart."

Crow looked back. "Hey, enough with the blasphemies, and we're not going to El Cap, we're going to Refugio and taking the fire road back along the bluff. We'll park north of El Cap and walk in on the beach."

"It's perfect," Roach said.

Crab shook his head. "I'm telling you guys right now, no matter what happens, we are not calling my dad."

"Pfff," Lance said, "nothin's gonna happen."

22

BACK TO EL CAP

Crow turned into the Mobil gas station on Seaward Avenue and coasted to a pump.

"What about that APB Buck put out on us?" Crab asked. "You think the highway patrol is still looking for us?"

Crow leaned out his window and handed the attendant cash. "Dollar twenty-five regular please." He looked back at Crab. "I don't believe him. Why would he put an All Points Bulletin out for stealing a stupid ice chest?"

"Yeah," Roach said, "he was just trying to scare us. And even if he did, I've watched a lot of *Adam 12*, APB's are only hot for a little while."

They rolled out of the gas station and Crow turned onto the 101 freeway heading north. An hour later they passed the exit to El Cap and a few minutes later saw the palm trees at Refugio State Park. Crow veered the Turd onto the off-ramp, looped around in a sweeping turn under the freeway and hit the brakes.

"Oh no, what's the ranger booth doing there? I thought it'd be down below on the other side of the railroad tracks like at El Cap."

Roach pounded the dashboard. "Damn, we gotta turn around!"

A ranger came out of the back of the booth and climbed into a truck.

"Oh crap," Crow said. "It's too late. Play it cool."

"They're coming to get us," Crab said.

"Shut up," said Roach.

The truck started toward them.

Crow crept the van forward. "I'm just gonna drive to the booth like nothing's wrong."

136

The truck cruised past and a female ranger smiled and waved.

Roach watched as she drove by. "I didn't know they had chick rangers."

"Be cool, I'm pulling up to the booth."

"We weren't supposed to see any rangers," Crab said.

"Pipe down!" Roach snapped.

Crow eased the van up to the window and frowned. "Oh no."

Inside the booth sat Gil, his arms crossed shaking his head.

"Are you guys retarded? Didn't I hear Buck tell you not to come back for the rest of the week?"

"Yeah...but, he didn't say anything about Refugio," Crow said.

"I think he said *all* Santa Barbara State Beaches. What were you planning on doing, walking two miles to find those chicks?"

Roach reached over and handed Gil the note from the girls. "Look, they left this on our windshield."

Gil leaned back on his stool and read the note. "I should turn you guys in, man."

"Look," Crow begged, "all we want is to see the girls, get their phone numbers and split."

Gil tipped his hat back. "I can't do it, if Buck finds you guys I'll be in trouble."

"Does he come up here?"

"Yeah, he does rounds in the morning and afternoon."

"What time?"

"Usually ten and three, but forget it--"

"We'll be way gone by three."

"Hey, I'm not losing my job just so you guys can see your chicks."

Roach leaned forward. "Couldn't that chick ranger have let us in?"

Gil scratched his cheek. "Hmm...I guess so, she has been working all morning."

"Come on man be cool. We drove all the way back up here. Just give us a couple hours and I swear you won't see us again," Crow pleaded.

Gil stuck his head out the window and looked both ways. "I don't know why I'm doing this. You guys have got to be gone by one o'clock."

"We promise." Crow pulled away from the ranger booth.

"Outta sight!" Roach said.

Crab shook his head and grinned. "I can't believe we did it."

Roach turned around in his seat. "The curse is definitely over."

"Are we really gonna leave by one?" Lance asked.

"Hell no," said Crow. "We're just gonna disappear."

The Turd bounced over the railroad tracks and they looked for the fire road. "Damn, I thought it'd be right here."

"Just keep going," Roach said. "It's gotta be up here."

"I'm sure glad you guys know what you're doing," said Crab.

"Quiet dip-wad, we're trying to concentrate."

Crow continued to the south end of the campground and found the unpaved fire road. He turned and drove about a mile and a half before veering off the dirt road into the foot tall grass. He weaved around clumps of giant rye grass and parked at the edge of the bluff next to a stand of oak trees. He turned off the engine and sat back. "They'll never find us here."

Lance opened the sliding door and he and Crab jumped out. The bluff was covered in green California brome and flowers bloomed on the purple sage and coyote brush. "It's like our own paradise," Lance said.

He stepped to the edge of the cliff and looked up and down the coastline. No people, no buildings. Twenty feet below a strip

138

of white sand stretched north and south. The glassy ocean sparkled in the still air and little waves rolled in.

Crow unstrapped the surfboards from the racks, they draped their wetsuits and towels over them and headed down the beach to El Cap.

The waves lapped at their feet as they came around a bend. In the distance they saw a crowd of umbrellas and towels on the beach. They walked closer past a few stray sunbathers then Crow planted his board in the sand. "We should be able to see 'em from here."

They spread their towels and plopped onto their elbows to watch for the girls.

After a few minutes Roach said, "I don't see 'em."

Crow stood up. "Lets go check the campground." He looked down at Crab and Lance. "You guys stay here."

"What for?" Lance complained.

"Four of us going up there is too many, and somebody needs to stay here in case the girls show up."

Crow and Roach walked down the beach along the base of the bluff then cut up through some bushes.

Lance picked up his wetsuit. "Feel like riding some ankle slappers?"

"Sure."

The waves were small and breaking close to shore. They surfed their way down the beach to better view the crowd, but the girls were nowhere to be seen. Lance picked up a piece of floating tar, balled it up and threw it at Crab's head. "What time do you think it is?"

Crab sat up on his board and squeezed a seaweed bulb back at Lance. "I don't know, but those guys are taking too long."

"Yeah, let's go find 'em."

Back on the beach Crab wriggled his wetsuit up to his armpits and bent over for Lance to pull it off. "I hope they didn't get busted."

"Don't even say that," Lance said.

"Well, what could they be doing?"

"I don't know, but we'll find out." They left the four surfboards and wetsuits on the beach and walked along the bluff to the bushes where Crow and Roach had gone up. At the top they found themselves in a hollow under a willow tree behind the camp store.

"This is a cool spot," Crab said.

"Pssst, hey." Above them Crow peered down from the store roof, he motioned for them to come up. They climbed the willow tree onto the roof under the cover of it's branches.

"Why aren't you guys on the beach?" Roach hissed. He was lying on his belly looking out over the parking lot.

Crab hunkered down next to him. "We couldn't wait down there forever."

Lance plopped down next to Crab. "You guys been up here the whole time?"

"No." Crow laid down next to Lance. "We scoped out the campground then came up here."

Lance could see across the parking lot to the booth and ranger station.

"Here comes a ranger truck," Roach said.

The truck sped up to the booth for a moment then continued into the parking lot.

Crow craned his neck. "It's coming this way."

The truck drove up to the store and parked right below them. They ducked back and listened to the truck door open and slam shut. Lance peeked over and saw Buck hurry down the path to the beach.

140

Roach whispered, "This is weird."

"Maybe there's a lost kid or something," Crow said.

Crab pointed to the park entrance. "There's the girls!"

Roach put his hand over Crab's mouth and they watched silently as the girls walked into the park on the main road and split up. The older girls, Ashley and Kim, went to the campground while Briar and Kari headed for the store.

"They're coming this way," Lance said.

Below them the truck door opened and the engine turned over. Buck backed out and passed the girls on the way back to the station.

"We gotta get down and meet 'em," Crab said. He and Lance started to get up and Crow grabbed Lance's arm.

"Okay, you guy's go down first and tell the girls to meet us on the beach." He glanced at the ranger station. "We'll wait a few minutes then meet you down there."

Lance shimmied onto a branch and swung down landing on the leafy dirt. Crab dropped down beside him. They squeezed through the bushes and came out on the side of the store next to the path. Lance and Crab peeked around the corner as the girls were entering the store. "Psst, you guys."

The girls turned and Lance waved them over.

"I can't believe you guys are here," Briar said. "Are you in trouble?"

"Only if we get caught. Look, our stuff is up the beach. Can you get your sisters and meet us up there?"

Briar grinned and took Lance's hand. "Yeah, we'll get them now."

Crow looked down from the roof. "Get out of here, Buck's coming!"

Lance squeezed Briar's hand. "We'll see you up there."

He and Crab ran down the path to the sand. Lance's heart pumped less from fear of Buck than excitement over Briar. They ran up the beach and stopped when they saw Gil and the chick ranger gathering their surfboards and wetsuits.

"What the hell?"

"Quick, back to the bushes," Crab said.

"It's no use, they've got our boards, we're caught."

Gil saw them and waved them over. "Sorry guys, you're busted, the van's getting towed."

"Towed?" *How could this be happening?* They walked toward the rangers.

The girl ranger held a surfboard under each arm. "The tire tracks in the grass were pretty obvious," she said. "I found the van and reported it. Somebody else would've found it if I hadn't. Everybody uses that road to get between the parks."

Suddenly Gil's walky-talky came to life. A static voice reported, "We found two of 'em on the store roof."

Gil took his walkie-talkie from its holster and pressed a button silencing the static. "We got the other two on the beach, we're bringing 'em in."

* * * *

It was two thirty when they reached Crab's mom, but then had to wait for Mr. Shaw to get off work. He didn't arrive until six thirty. With the Turd impounded the four boys had to pile into Mr. Shaw's Toyota station wagon. They slid the four surfboards down the middle and over the passenger seat and everyone squeezed into the car for the long drive home. Lance opted for the very back of the wagon where he scrunched down under the stack of surfboards farthest away from the wrath of Mr. Shaw.

142

Mr. Shaw's rant went on uninterrupted for twenty minutes. Lance lost track of his words as they morphed into grunts and barks like a yammering dog. He covered his mouth and snickered.

"Is that you Lance? Do I hear you giggling back there? You think this is funny?"

There was a moment of silence while Mr. Shaw waited for Lance's response. Lance squelched another snicker, then someone else giggled and Lance exploded into laughter. Mr. Shaw's shouting then became more fuel for his hysteria.

Lance's gut ached and his cheeks hurt when he'd finally exhausted himself. He watched the shadows from the streetlights move across the car in a steady rhythm as the ride home continued in nervous silence. Lance hated that they had to bother Mr. Shaw again. He felt bad for Crab. The whole thing had been a bad idea. Even if he and Crab hadn't shaken the tree like a bunch of orangutans, as Buck put it, the van was already being impounded and Gil and the girl ranger were already walking down the beach looking for them. He wasn't sure if they were cursed or just stupid.

When Mr. Shaw finally stopped at Lance's house they unloaded their surfboards and wetsuits and Mr. Shaw announced, "Mike is on restriction from the beach indefinitely, he's not to see or talk to any of you. Is that clear?"

"Yes sir," the boys said.

Crab looked up and raised a hand good-bye as the car pulled away.

23
DENNIS

Lance, Crow and Roach stood on the front lawn of Lance's house with their surfboards and wetsuits scattered on the grass. Roach picked up his towel. "Wow man, restriction indefinitely. That's a bummer."

"It's because of you and that damn curse," Lance said.

Roach tossed his towel in Lance's face. "Don't blame me. You were the one that pissed off his dad, laughing like a lunatic."

Lance smelled seagull crap on the towel and threw it back at Roach. "Can't you stop the curse?"

"You guys are so gullible. I just said that 'cause I was mad."

"Then why does bad junk keep happening?"

"How am I supposed to know?"

Crow gathered his stuff. "All I know is things can't get much worse. Our luck's gotta change."

Roach gathered his stuff too. "You got anything to eat?"

"T.V. dinners. My parents are out of town and my sister's staying at her friend's house, you guys can spend the night if you want."

"Cool, I'm starved." Roach headed to the house.

"*Hawaii 5-0's* on tonight," Crow said.

Roach turned. "The only thing good about that show is the theme song and the wave."

"I like seein' Jack Lord's hair get messed up."

"I gotta warn you," Lance said, "our T.V. is black and white."

"Black and white?" Crow scowled. "You guys are livin' in the stone age."

* * * *

In the morning they sat at the kitchen table eating cereal. Roach filled his bowl. "So, what's the plan?"

Crow poured the milk then handed it to Roach. "Buck said it'd cost twenty-five bucks to get the Turd out of impoundment. So, the first thing is to get the money, then thumb up there. You got any sugar, Lance?"

Lance passed the sugar jar. "Maybe Dennis would lend it to you?"

"Hey, that's a good idea," Roach said. "Dennis'll do it."

Crow shrugged. "Can't hurt to ask."

After three bowls of cereal each they walked down Channel Drive to the railroad tracks. A freight train was moving slowly northbound in a steady rhythm of iron clangs. Roach looked south down the tracks. "This thing's long. We could be here all day."

"You guys ever hop a train?" Crow asked.

"Me and Crab have talked about it," Lance said.

"This'll be easy, come on." Crow trotted alongside a freight car, grabbed hold of a ladder and jumped on.

Lance ran behind Roach and they each caught up to a ladder. Lance grabbed the iron rung and jumped up. He felt the solid bar under his canvas deck shoes and shook the hair from his face. He saw Roach and Crow looking back at him and he yelled out, "Yee-haw!"

It was a two-mile ride to the Surf Shop and the train clunked along slowly. Lance looked down the line of railroad cars and pretended it was a big wave snaking ahead.

He got a rush of fear as the train approached the San Jon Bridge and he clung tight as they passed over traffic thirty feet below. When they got to the Wharf Crow jumped off onto a patch of grass and ran to a stop. Roach jumped and Lance followed.

"That was too easy," Lance said.

"Beats walking," said Roach.

The freight cars continued to clunk by as they walked around the back of the shop. Lance looked at the windows of Dennis's boat hoping for a glimpse of Noelle.

They walked around to the front where Diablo slept at the top of the steps. Inside Dennis sat at the front counter doing paperwork. He looked up as they came in, but didn't smile. "Hey, how was Jalama?"

"How'd you know we went up there?" Roach asked.

"Stoody told me." He focused on Lance. "I've been looking for you."

"How come?"

"I've got something to show you, follow me."

They followed Dennis into the shaping room and Lance wondered if Dennis hadn't shaped him another board.

"You recognize this surfboard?"

On the rack was the *Lightning Bolt*--the Souther's board he'd unstrapped. The nose had major repair work done and there were lots of patches on the rails.

"Whoa, a *Lightning Bolt*," Crow said.

Roach looked at Lance. "Is that the board...?"

Dennis narrowed his eyes at Lance. "Did you unstrap this board?"

"Uh..."

"This really pisses me off Lance. I spent all day yesterday fixing it, you're damn lucky the fin didn't break."

Lance took a deep breath and fought back emotion.

Dennis frowned and smoothed his mustache. "You can forget about that forty bucks credit I was gonna give you, you just spent

146

it, and you still owe me twenty." He walked around the board sliding his hand over his repair work. "You know what crap like this does for the shop's reputation?" He raised his voice an octave in mock conversation, "Hey man, look what happened to my board while I was at the surf shop in Ventura, somebody unstrapped it. Dammit Lance, what the hell's the matter with you?"

Lance's mind raced, how could he have been so stupid to bring this on Dennis? He opened his mouth and heard himself say, "Crab did it." *Oh crap, I can't believe I just pinned it on Crab.*

Dennis' eyes narrowed. "Crab did it?"

Lance could feel Crow and Roach staring at him.

"This was Crab's idea, you had nothing to do with it?"

Lance looked at the floor and half truthfully said, "I stopped him from unstrapping the other guy's board."

Dennis raised an eyebrow. "Well, you're both guilty as far as I'm concerned, you were with him." He picked up the board. "Keep your idiotic antics away from my shop. You understand?"

Lance nodded.

Dennis led them out of the shaping room and placed Cal's board in his personal rack. He went back behind the counter.

There was awkward silence, then Dennis asked, "Where's the Turd? I didn't hear you guys drive up."

Crow ran his hand down the rail of a new purple board in the display rack. "It's a...in Gaviota."

"Gaviota? Did you break down?"

"Yeah, sorta. It's at the gas station there."

"What happened?"

"It was the fan belt," Roach said shifting his weight. "They didn't have one that fit and Crab's dad had to come get us."

Dennis raised an eyebrow again. "Volkswagens are air cooled, they don't have fan belts."

"Oh, uh..." Roach stammered.

"You must mean the alternator belt," Dennis said.

Crow looked at Roach. "Yeah, that was it. We're going up there to get it now." Crow paused and turned to the purple board. "We were kinda hoping you'd lend us the money to get it."

Dennis groaned and shook his head. "Don't you guys have parents?"

They looked at each other. Lance said, "My parents are in San Diego."

Crow dug his hands into his pockets. "My mom's with her boyfriend in Palm Springs."

Roach didn't say anything. They all knew when he wasn't at Crow's house he lived with his grandmother in the trailer park by the drive-in theater.

Dennis closed his eyes, filled his cheeks with air and blew out. "How much do you need?"

"Twenty-five dollars."

"Okay, but you need to pay me back ASAP." He opened the register and wrote something on a small piece of paper and had Crow initial it. He put the paper under the change compartment and handed him two tens and a five. "How you gonna get to Gaviota?"

"Hitchhike, I guess."

"Not all three of you I hope."

"Hmmm, you're right." Crow looked at Lance. "You better stay here, it'll be easier for two of us to get a ride."

Lance scowled.

"It's not like you're going to miss anything," Crow said.

"Yeah knucklehead." Roach punched his shoulder. "You get to stay here and surf while we're standing on a freeway onramp."

148

"Come on, we'll walk back to Seaward with you, it's the best onramp." Crow waved to Dennis. "Thanks man, I'll pay you back as soon as I can."

Lance stopped at the door and turned to Dennis. "Sorry about all the hassle, we never wanted anything to come back on you."

Dennis picked up the papers he was working on and tapped them on the counter. "I know you didn't Lance, just try and think a little more."

Lance looked down and nodded. "Just so you know, Crab's already in pretty big trouble. He didn't tell his parents he was going to Jalama and then his dad had to come get us...he's grounded for a while."

"Okay, I'll go easy on him...and hey, I'd steer clear of Cal if I were you."

Crow hollered from outside, "Hey Lance, you coming or not?"

Lance waved to Dennis. "Thanks, I'll see ya around." He ran down the steps and caught up with Crow and Roach.

Crow turned to him. "I can't believe you pinned that on Crab."

"I didn't mean to, it just came out." He looked at Crow then Roach. "At least he won't be around for a while, hopefully it'll blow over by then."

Roach shook his head. "Man, I'm watchin' my back around you."

24
RETRIEVING THE TURD

A hippie couple stood on the Seaward onramp. The guy wore a headband, leather vest and sunglasses. He was smoking a cigarette and had one foot on the curb and one in the street with his thumb out. The girl held a cardboard sign that read Big Sur. At their feet was an aluminum framed backpack and a suitcase. The girl looked pregnant. The guy grinned and said, "Beautiful day, man."

"Sure is," Roach said as he and Crow continued down the ramp to give them room. Spray painted on the cinderblock wall next to a peace symbol was the message "Nixon kills." Crow had seen it a thousand times getting on the freeway, but never this close.

"We're lucky there's nobody else here," Roach said. "Those guys should get a ride quick."

On the second stream of traffic a beat up Dodge van pulled over for the couple and after a short discussion they climbed in. Crow and Roach moved up the ramp to their spot.

In the next flow of traffic a Volkswagen bug pulled over and a girl in the passenger seat rolled down her window, the guy driving leaned over. "Where you guys going?"

"Gaviota," Crow said.

"We can drop you in Carpenteria."

"Thanks, but we'll wait for a ride all the way."

The bug sputtered away and Roach put his hands on his hips. "What'd you say that for? Carpenteria's a good ride."

"No way, we'd be sittin' there all day."

The next car that stopped was going to Santa Barbara. "No thanks," Crow said.

150

"You're crazy," Roach complained. "We're gonna be here all day if we don't take a ride."

"Look we're the only ones here and there'll be a million hitchhikers in Santa Barbara, stay cool."

A while passed before a rusty pickup truck pulled over. Crow ran up to the passenger window. The driver looked tired, his eyes were red. The cab was loaded with plastic buoys and ropes. Crow waited for him to roll down the window, but the guy just pointed his thumb to the back.

"How far you going?" Crow shouted. The man stared at him as if he had to think about it. "Santa Maria."

"Great. Can you drop us off at the Gaviota gas station?"

The man nodded and pointed his thumb to the back again.

Roach was already climbing over the fishing net and crab traps in back. "It's all wet."

"You wanna wait for another ride?"

"No, get in."

Crow stepped around the mound of net and nestled into a corner behind the cab. The guy drove slowly and had a hard time staying in his lane. Car after car came up behind them, turned on a blinker and sped past. When they finally saw the palm trees at Refugio Crow looked over the mound of fishing gear and groaned, "Thank god, looks like we're going to make it."

Roach kept his eyes on the traffic behind them. "He's still got a couple of miles to kill us."

The truck pulled off to the right as it approached the gas station then swerved back onto the highway. The gas station was disappearing behind them. Crow pounded on the window and the man made a circle with his thumb and index finger letting them know everything was okay.

"That was it!" they hollered. "Back there!"

The guy drove a half-mile before they got him to pull over.

Achy and damp they climbed out of the truck. The driver waved as he pulled away.

They walked along the highway back to the gas station, which looked to be the only structure in Gaviota. As they turned up the gravel road to the station they could hear someone pounding on metal. Crow saw the Turd on the rack in the garage and a guy under it hammering.

Crow ran up. "Hey man, what are you doing to my van?"

The guy stopped pounding and wiped his brow with his sleeve. He looked like the Skipper from *Gilligan's Island* but with longer hair. "This your van?"

"Yeah, what are you doing?"

"Well, you were parked in that tall grass, I couldn't see where I was hooking up and this bar got bent." He gestured with the mallet in his hand. "I'm trying to straighten it, shouldn't take long."

Crow stepped up to take a closer look. "What's that bar for?"

"Steering. It's pulling to the right. You can wait in there." He pointed the hammer at the office door.

Greasy hand marks covered the white paint around the doorknob and bells chimed from inside when Crow opened it. The room was half office half sitting area divided by a countertop. There was a black vinyl sofa with chrome arms and legs and a Formica coffee table. On it were a couple of *Motor Trend* magazines and an old *Sports Illustrated*. There were windows on three sides so they could see into the garage and out to the gas pumps and because of the slight elevation they could also see over the highway to the ocean. The banging started again and they sat on the vinyl sofa.

Roach picked up a magazine. "*Motor Trend*, who reads *Motor Trend?*" He flipped the pages. "I hope he knows what he's doing."

152

"All he's doing is straightening that bar. Why are you being such a drag?"

"Because I'm starved." Roach slapped the magazine down. "Look there's vending machines."

"Don't torture yourself, we don't have any money for that."

"They've got both kinds of *Fritos* too, barbecue and regular. I bet if I had a coat hanger I could reach up in there and get something."

Crow sat up and looked over the counter. "There's a closet in the corner, go look while he's banging."

Roach went behind the counter and just as he got to the closet- *-ding-ding*--a car pulled up to a pump outside.

"Duck down, Skipper's gonna see you."

The Skipper walked out to greet the customer and Roach crawled back to the sofa clutching something to his chest. "Look what I got." He held up a *Playboy* magazine.

Crow reached for it. "Lemme see."

"No way, I found it." Roach sat down and stared at the cover.

Crow scooted closer. "What are you waiting for? Open it."

"I'm looking for the bunny."

"What bunny?"

"Every cover has a bunny on it somewhere."

"Why can't you just turn to the centerfold like a normal person?"

"Hold on...there it is, on her garter. Okay, what section did you want?"

"Just open it."

Roach held the magazine up and let the centerfold fall open. "Oh man, would you look at that."

"No doubt she's a real blonde."

Suddenly the front door swung open whipping the chimes on the knob and the Skipper rushed in. He looked at them as he went to the counter. "Oh man, did I leave that out here?" He reached behind the counter. "The guy's paying with a *Master Charge*, I need carbons." He pulled up a bundled stack of carbons and rushed back out slamming the door behind him.

Crow looked at Roach and shrugged. "Turn the page."

"You want me to read the jokes?"

"No, turn to more pictures."

The car pulled away and the Skipper came back inside. "I gotta put that magazine back, it's not supposed to be out here."

"Can't we just look at it until you're done?"

"I am done." He took the magazine from Roach and put it behind the counter. "I've got it as straight as I can get it. I'll pull her down and you can take it for a test spin."

The Skipper backed the van out and Crow hopped in and drove around the station. He turned left then right and could feel it pulling, but it drove okay.

The Skipper and Roach watched as Crow came back around. "Well, how is it?" Skipper asked.

"Good enough, I guess. It's still pulling to the right."

"Yeah, you'll probably need to replace that bar."

"How much will that cost?"

"Oh, probably sixty bucks or so, but you could get one at the junkyard and do it yourself for almost nothing."

"Hey man," Roach said. "You gonna let us slide on the towing fee since our vehicle got damaged?"

"Yeah, I won't charge you. You're gonna want to keep an eye on those front tires too, in case they start wearin' funny. They're already pretty bald."

Roach nudged Crow. "Lets get some quarters for the vending machines."

Crow dug into his pocket. "Yeah, we got more than enough cash to get her fixed, and we gotta eat." He turned to the Skipper. "Do you have a roll of quarters for a ten?"

"Sure, come on inside."

"I'm gonna pull up to the pump," Crow said. "We'll fill it up too."

* * * *

They waved to the Skipper and drove down the gravel road to the highway and turned south. Roach opened a bag of *Fritos*. "Wow, a full tank of gas, a bunch of food and cash. We're ready for a surf trip."

"The van's not driving so good," Crow said. "The faster I go the more it pulls."

"Is this as fast as you can go?"

"Yeah, forty."

Roach leaned back and put one foot on the dash and the other out the window. He popped a chip in his mouth. "It's cool, I'm in no hurry. You ready for some *Fritos*?"

The closer they got to Ventura the worse the pulling got. Crow parked at the curb in front of his house and got out to inspect the tires. Sure enough the left front tire was worn down to the inner lining.

"Damn, now we need a tire too."

25
CRAB GETS BURNED

It was Tuesday morning and Crab laid in bed waiting for his dad to leave for work. He couldn't blame him for being mad, but indefinite restriction? He couldn't be kept away from the beach forever. The lecture driving home from Lance's house last night played over in his mind-- *"Now is the time you should be honing your character. You need to surround yourself with people of integrity, not hanging around with hoodlums."* But as his dad spoke, all he wanted was to be back at Lance's with his friends.

He knew going back up to El Cap was a stupid idea. How lame was it coming face to face with Gil in the ranger booth. But then Gil let them in, and driving onto that bluff was like a dream. Even surfing those little waves was fun, then being on the roof of the store and seeing Kari...he'd do it all over again.

Crab heard his mom call Timmy and Kathy. "Come give your daddy a hug good-bye." He looked at the clock, eight forty-five. What would he do for the rest of Easter vacation?

He moped around the house and it irritated his mom, so he kept doing it. What was he supposed to do, be happy? By the end of the afternoon he'd gotten to her.

"Go out and mow the lawn, now. Go!"

"But Dad just mowed it Saturday."

"I don't care, mow it again!"

He mowed the lawn then went to his room and stayed there until it was time for dinner. At the table he'd mind his manners, then go back to his room.

His dad tucked his napkin into his collar. "So, tell us about your day Mike."

156

"Mikey was a butthead today," Timmy said. "Mommy had to yell at him."

"I didn't yell at him, he just needed some fresh air. Timmy use your napkin."

Crab rolled his eyes. "It was fine, I thought about what you said, about character and stuff."

His dad straightened himself. "Well good, any conclusions?"

Crab picked up a chicken leg and sighed. "I like my friends and if--."

His dad's face-hardened. "You like them? You like characters who steal food from other people? Characters who completely disregard the orders of park authorities? Do you like that I had to drive 100 miles two days in a row to get your butt from those authorities?"

Crab stared at his plate. "No."

"Look at me when I'm talking to you."

"Settle down Frank," his mom said. She looked at Crab. "It does seem awfully silly for you to go back up there after they told you not to."

"We thought we could get in without bothering anybody."

His dad leaned forward. "So that would've made it okay? If you rob a bank but don't bother anybody, it's okay, right?"

"Oh Frank, it's not like they robbed a bank."

"I told you they're robbers," Timmy said.

"That's enough Timmy, eat your dinner."

His dad sawed the chicken thigh on his plate. "What I don't understand is why those delinquents want you kids hanging around, anyway? I'll tell you why," he pointed his fork at Crab. "They're using you. I bet they get you to do their dirty work don't they? Who actually took the ice chest?" His dad stuck the fork in his mouth and chewed, glaring.

Crab sat silent.

"That's what I thought...you're smarter than that Mikey. You don't need to hang around with riff-raff like that. Stick to kids your own age, good kids like that Eric Phelps and that other kid...Lowe, who used to come around."

"You said they were numbskulls."

"Well, they seem smarter now. I tell you what," he wiped his mouth, "tomorrow you can leave the house, go around the neighborhood and see what your old friends are up to."

"Oh gee, thanks dad." Crab picked up a forkful of mashed potatoes and plopped them back on his plate.

His dad sawed another piece of chicken from the bone. "You might as well get used to being land-locked, whether you choose to have friends or not is up to you."

"Can I be excused? I'm not that hungry."

"But you didn't eat anything," his mom said.

"Oh, let him go, he's not going to starve."

* * * *

The next morning Crab laid around, ate cereal and watched cartoons with his little brother and sister. He had no intention of seeing his old friends; he couldn't even imagine what kind of stuff they did for fun these days. At noon the cartoons ended and soap operas began. His mom made baloney sandwiches and tomato soup for lunch and turned the T.V. to *The Days of Our Lives.* "Mike, after lunch can you run to the grocery store for me? We're having Hamburger Helper tonight and I need some ground beef and we're almost out of eggs."

He stared down at his sandwich. "Sure," he droned. But getting out and riding his skateboard did sound good. His mom gave him two dollars and he grabbed his skateboard and went outside. He lifted the garage door and found a tin of graphite

158

powder. He spun each wheel and squirted the lubricant onto the ball bearings.

His thirty-inch laminated *Hobie* rode smooth and fast down the driveway into the street. *Jue's Market* was a few blocks away on Main Street and he took long strides with his left foot to get momentum. At the corner he looked down the street toward Phelps' house, nobody was around. He was glad.

He skateboarded into the grocery store careful not to turn too sharp on the slick floors. Only once he'd been told not to ride his skateboard in the store, but that's because he was chasing Lance. He rolled up to the meat counter and asked for a pound of ground beef. The butcher looked over the counter to see what he was standing on.

"You on roller skates?"

"Naw, it's a skateboard, you know, sidewalk surfing."

"Boy, that's a fancy one."

Skateboarding home with the grocery bag Crab saw the garage door was open at Phelps' house. Inside Phelps and Lowe were on the ground looking at something. They heard his skateboard and looked up.

"Hey Mike, come here," Phelps called.

On the ground was a shoebox. "What's in there?"

Phelps lifted the lid. "Gun powder."

"What are you going to do with it?"

"We're gonna light it," Lowe said. "You got any matches?"

"You gonna light it right here?" Crab asked.

"No, in the backyard. We just have to be careful moving it, it could go off just carrying it."

"No it can't," Crab said. "Guys in westerns are always riding with sacks of gunpowder."

"Hey yeah." Phelps socked Lowe on the shoulder. "I thought that sounded fishy."

159

"Well, you believed it too."

"Look," Crab said. "I'll take these groceries home and come back with some matches."

"All right, we'll be in the backyard settin' up."

Crab dropped off the groceries and told his mom he was going over to Phelps' house.

"Oh good, I'm glad you're taking your father's advice," she said.

He looked through the junk drawer in the kitchen for matches.

"What are you looking for in there?"

"I need a wrench for my skateboard."

"You know your father keeps all the tools in the garage."

He cupped a box of matches from *Cleck's Beef and Bourbon* in his hand. "All right, I'll be home before dinner." He skated back to Phelps' house and found them in the backyard behind the playhouse. They'd made a trail of gunpowder about a half inch wide and three feet long to the shoebox.

"You got the matches?" Lowe asked.

"Yep, right here."

"Let me see 'em."

"Hey, I'm lighting it," Phelps said. "Give 'em to me." Phelps slid open the box and took out a wooden match. They crouched down at the end of the trail of gunpowder. Phelps struck the match and cupped the flame then slowly brought the fire down to the powder. The match blew out.

"Aw man, lemme do it," Lowe said.

"I got it ass-wipe, back off, give me some room."

"So what's gonna happen when you light it?" Crab asked.

Lowe looked at him like he was an idiot. "It's gonna light, what else would it do?"

160

Phelps lit another match and quickly touched it to the gunpowder, but again the flame went out. "Crap, I touched it, it should've caught."

"My turn," Lowe said and tried to grab the matchbox.

Phelps pushed him away. "Get outta here, I get one more try. Each of us'll get three tries, then we'll start over."

"Pffff, like I'll need three tries," Lowe said.

Crab was excited at possibly getting a turn. He watched Phelps' last try fail and Lowe grabbed the matchbox. "Okay, now watch a pro do it." Lowe took out a match and struck it. He touched the flame to the powder; it didn't light. "What the hell, man." He took out two matches.

"You light both those it's gonna count as two turns," Phelps said.

Lowe struck the matches and touched them to the gunpowder. Nothing. "This stuff's bunk."

"Give Mike a try."

Lowe took out another match and quickly struck it straight into the box of gunpowder. They all jumped back, but the match smoldered out.

"You asshole," Phelps said. "That could've been dangerous...I guess it is bunk though, it's pretty old."

"Let me try," said Crab.

Lowe rolled his eyes and handed him the matches. "It's not gonna light dip-wad."

Crab took a match and struck it into the box and again it smoldered out.

"See it's not gonna light, you're wastin' your time."

Crab moved in over the box, he could smell the metallic aroma of the gunpowder. He put the match tip to the striker and flicked it. The match landed on the bed of gunpowder and flared up on the surface.

"See, I told you, it ain't--"

A flash of white heat suddenly blackened the world. Crab was on his back, his ears ringing. He opened his eyes and saw splotches of black and white movement. It was Phelps and Lowe hovering over him. "Are you okay? Are you all right?" Crab wasn't sure, his face, arms and hands tingled. He did a mental survey and didn't feel any pain. Phelps' face came directly over him.

"Man, your hair's all singed and your eyebrows too."

Crab leaned up on his elbows. "I guess it wasn't bunk." He got up slowly, he felt disoriented and wobbly. "I should go home."

Phelps and Lowe followed him to the garage. His skateboard was leaning on the tool bench where he'd left it. "You sure you're okay?" Phelps asked.

"Yeah, I'm fine, a little dazed I guess. I'll see you guys around." His head didn't feel fully connected to his body, there was no way he could ride his skateboard. He carried it down the driveway, his fingers around the rail felt cool. He lifted the skateboard to look at them and saw the skin on each finger pushed back from the nail to the second knuckle in neat little piles. Puss was forming over the pink flesh. He turned to Phelps and Lowe. "I think I might need to go to the hospital."

162

26

EASTER SUNDAY SWELL

"Wake up Lance," Ann said banging on his bedroom door. "Mom and dad are coming home today, we've got to clean up."

He heard the gas wall heater kick on in the hallway and threw off his blanket. "I know. I'm not retarded." He looked out the window and saw a thick fog. He opened his door and Ann was there in her nightgown standing by the heater.

"Close that door, your room's freezing," she said. "Is your window open?"

"I always sleep with it open. I'm preparing for when I live in my shack on the beach."

"What are you talking about?"

"You know, like Moon Doggy. Me and Crab have been talking about building a shack on the beach. Living for free, surfing every day."

"Oh brother, isn't that what you do now?"

"I can't wake up and look out the window at the waves."

"Maybe you should try harder in school, get a good job then buy a house on the beach."

"Yeah right, and work every day, only surfing on weekends? No way."

"Uh, maybe you haven't noticed Lance, but that's what normal people do."

"Maybe I'm not normal."

"So, you want to be a surf bum."

"What's wrong with that?"

"Nothing I guess, if you don't ever want a girlfriend."

"What chick wouldn't dig a surf shack on the beach?"

Ann rolled her eyes and shook her head. "How are you going to cook?"

"Barbecue."

"What about a refrigerator?"

"Ice chest."

"Where you gonna get ice?"

"We haven't figured out everything yet."

"Well, maybe you should watch more *Gilligan's Island* to get some tips."

"Ha, ha. We've been concentrating on how to get food and stuff first, then we'll start figuring out the other junk." He and Crab had a pretty good handle on food. There were always the food trays in the halls at the Holiday Inn. And in the dumpster behind *The Big Green House* restaurant they could usually find warm baked potatoes wrapped in foil. And they could fish. They'd become expert fisherman, but Ann wouldn't understand any of that. "Okay so, what do we need to do?"

"First, you need to go to the grocery store and get some cereal and milk so we can eat breakfast."

"With what money?"

"Mom and dad left us money for groceries."

"They did? Why didn't you tell me? Where's my half."

"Oh brother, that's exactly why I didn't tell you. And besides what do you need money for mister I'm-gonna-be-a-surf-bum-and-live-at-the-beach-for-free?"

"Okay, okay, just give me some money so I can get going."

Lance followed Ann to her room. She took two dollars from her purse. "How much did they give you?"

"Ten dollars, but I already spent seven after you and your surf bum friends went through six T.V. dinners, three boxes of cereal and a half gallon of milk."

"We did?"

164

"Yes, so hurry up. When you get back I'll need you to take out the trash, vacuum, and mow the lawn."

"And what are you going to do?"

"Clean the kitchen, straighten the house and do laundry. If you have any dirty clothes put them in the hamper. Are you ever going to wash those trunks?"

"They're fine. I'd like to get to the beach sometime today, you know."

"Maybe you don't need to go the beach every day Lance. Have you seen how foggy it is?"

He shook his head. "Like that matters?"

She handed him the two dollars. "There's more to life than surfing Lance, you know there's school tomorrow. Have you done any homework this week?"

"Geez, you're worse than mom, I think I'm gonna barf."

* * * *

It was after one o'clock when Lance finally grabbed his board and jumped on his bike. He peddled down Channel Drive to the lemon factory. The morning fog had lifted, but the sky was still grey. He was grateful for the clouds, it made the time spent doing chores less painful. But when he reached the lemon factory and saw the waves it was like a punch in the gut.

"Holy crap, a swell!" Big waves were breaking across Pierpont bay. He peddled hard and soon saw a bunch of cars at the Pier, a sure sign it was good. He rode up the hill and saw Dennis getting a clean overhead wave. He locked his bike and hurried down to the beach.

Dennis was jogging up from the water. They hadn't spoken since their talk about unstrapping Cal's surfboard.

"Hey Lance, it's unreal out there!"

"I saw that wave you just got. Are you leaving?"

"Yeah, I was supposed to pick up Noelle a half hour ago, we're going to her folks house for Easter." Dennis kept jogging.

Wow, Noelle or these waves, that's a tough one.

"Hey Lance," Dennis called. "I wanna know how your board works out there."

Lance nodded and waved then ran down the beach. He flung off his backpack and pulled out his wetsuit. Bill and one of the twins were on the beach watching the waves. "How come you guys aren't out there?"

"We've been out all day," Bill said. "Where've you been?"

"I had chores." Lance could see the current was pushing south, but all the guys in the water were huddled together next to the pilings. "Are they hanging onto a rope?"

"Yeah, Dugo and McGillis tied a rope to a piling," Bill said. "Everybody moves down the rope until it's their turn. It's genius."

Crow came up from the water as Lance zipped up his beavertail jacket. "Where the hell have you been?"

"Stuck at home. Where's the Turd?"

"Haven't got it fixed yet. We rode our bikes down. Come on, let's jump off the Pier, it's easier than paddling."

On the Pier a small group of spectators watched the surfers. They moved apart to let Crow and Lance through like they were gladiators entering the arena. Lance looked down, seven guys were hanging on the rope, their surfboards pointing into the current.

"There's only room for one," Crow said. "You go. I'll jump in when the next guy lets go."

Lance climbed over the rail and stood on the end of a crossbeam twenty feet above the water. He looked down; the current made little wakes around the pilings.

166

"Hey Lance," Roach called from the rope, "you coming out to play with the big boys?"

"Sure am," Lance said and jumped. He let go of his board mid-flight before splashing into the water. It was cold and he sank deep. When his downward momentum stopped he stroked for the surface. He flicked his hair from his eyes and found his surfboard floating a few feet away. He climbed on and paddled for the rope.

McGillis let go and drifted past looking to the outside, "Ride the Wild Surf, kid."

Lance grinned, he'd seen that movie. It was a Hollywood production about big wave surfing. Fabian and the other actors sat on surfboards in a pool on a movie set, then the film would cut to real surfers dropping in on huge waves at Waimea Bay.

Dugo and a twin let go of the rope too and Crow splashed into the water. Lance grabbed the rope behind Ringlets.

"Well, you didn't puss out," Ringlets said. "Let's see if you can make a wave."

Ringlets was being an ass, but he was right. Lance wouldn't know until he tried. He'd never surfed big lefts before.

McGillis dropped in on his wave and made it look easy, nothing fancy, just a clean bottom turn into the pocket. That's how Lance wanted to do it, clean and easy. He couldn't wait for his turn.

A three-wave set appeared outside and Q, Roach and Ringlets let go one after another. Lance moved to the end where a plastic jug buoyed the rope. He watched the three of them surf their waves and it wasn't long before Crow said, "Here comes ours."

Lance saw the waves coming. He waited a few moments for them to get closer then let go. The current carried him into the first wave's path. He paddled to adjust his position until the wave loomed overhead. He turned and stroked, the swell lifted him and

167

he felt his surfboard take hold of the wave's speed. He jumped to his feet and glided down the smooth face. He carefully leaned into his turn and trimmed down the line through the section. He heard guys hooting for him as he kicked out. He'd made the wave and his adrenaline was pumping. He kept his cool and fought the current back to the rope, but there were too many guys hanging on.

"Grab my foot," Roach said.

The guy perched on the crossbeam would have to wait.

The waves came in like gentle giants, each one rolling in just like the last. Lance's confidence grew with every ride, his board worked like a dream and he couldn't wait to tell Dennis. After every wipeout he'd go up on the beach, rest a little, then jump in off the Pier again. The amazing thing was without all the paddling his energy was saved for surfing, he and the others surfed well past sunset.

With the sky darkening the crowd was thinning. Lance took his last wave in and walked up from the water to the group of guys watching this great day end.

"What an Easter Sunday," Roach said. "A gift from the gods for sure."

"Yep, Easter Sunday, 1973," McGillis said. "We'll remember this one for a long time."

Lance looked out at the horizon, there were a few minutes of light left. He could get another wave if he went now. He grabbed his board and ran to the Pier.

"Hey Lance where you goin'? I thought we were riding home together," Crow said.

"I'm gonna get one more."

He ran out onto the Pier and looked over the rail. The rope was empty and the white jug floated on the black water. He saw Ringlets surfing a wave and Q paddling for one. He jumped in

168

and stroked to the rope. He looked out; nothing was showing. Come on waves don't abandon me now. A short lull could leave him in total darkness. This was probably a bad idea. "Come on, send me a wave!"

A dark swell rose in the purple twilight, Lance watched it grow. He let go of the rope and paddled toward it, it was hard to read in the darkness. He turned. The wave came up quick and the face was steep. He jumped to his feet and felt himself being launched with the lip. He bailed headfirst and skimmed down the face of the wave, somehow he was bodysurfing. He put his left arm out and continued down the line. He rode the wave all the way to the beach.

Crow and Roach met him at the shoreline. "That was cool," Crow said.

Lance high stepped from the water. "I don't know how I did it, I ate it on the take off and next thing I know I'm bodysurfing."

"Yeah, that was outta sight," Roach said. "Now get your board, I'm starving."

Lance looked down the beach, but his board hadn't washed in. "Ha! I beat my board." He scanned the water and down the beach he saw the white deck of his board flitter over the top of a wave far outside. "I see it, it's still out there drifting towards the jetty."

The jetty was three hundred yards down the beach. They ran to it and climbed the rocks. "Do you see it?"

"There it is." Crow pointed into the darkness. "It's still out there.

Lance saw the white deck appear over a wave. His heart pounded, he looked down at the black water and thought about diving in after it, but the current had already taken the board half way to the San Jon jetty. "Let's go to the next jetty."

"This is crazy," Roach said.

They ran to the San Jon jetty, another three hundred yards down the beach. The light was all but gone.

Lance's stomach tightened, if his board didn't wash in now he knew he might never see it again. Panting and exhausted they climbed the rocks and scanned the black ocean.

"I don't see it."

"I don't either," Roach said.

Lance stood and stared, the faint white of the breaking waves barely visible. "This can't be happening!"

"It's gone," Crow said. "Your board's gone."

Roach shook his head. "The surf gods just took it away."

PART 3

HOBO JUNGLE

27
TRAIN RIDE

After a week Lance's surfboard still hadn't turned up. He'd put the word out to everybody on Pierpont figuring that's where it'd wash up. But he'd heard nothing. Dennis told him about a guy who lost his board in Hawaii the same way. They found it a year later floating at sea with a foot of algae growing on the bottom.

Now Lance needed to make some money. Not only did he need another surfboard, he still owed Dennis a legitimate twenty dollars for the one that disappeared. On Saturday morning he lugged the push mower out of the garage and dragged it around the neighborhood offering to mow lawns at two bucks a shot. After four hours he pulled the mower back home. His dad was backing the car out of the garage and Lance waited to put the lawnmower away. His dad rolled down the window. "Hey Lance, how'd it go out there?"

"I made two lousy bucks and the lady can't pay me 'til next week. This is gonna take forever."

"You just keep it up, if people know you're coming around every weekend you'll build a clientele."

The thought made him sick.

His mom came out of the house carrying her purse. "Oh Lance, your friend Sandcrab called."

"He did, when?"

"Not too long ago. He wants you to call him. He said to tell you he can go to the beach again. Did he get in some kind of trouble?"

"He's been sick or something, he wasn't at school all week." Lance ran into the house.

"Lance!" his mom called. "We're going to *Sears*, lock the house if you leave."

"I will." He ran to the kitchen and dialed Crab's number. "Hey man, it's me. Where you been, your parents transfer you to a new school or somethin'?"

"Nah, can I come over? I gotta get out of this house."

"Sure, I'm gonna heat up some left over beef stew, you want some?"

"Is the Pope Catholic?"

Crab showed up on his skateboard with both hands wrapped in white gauze.

"What the hell happened to you?"

He told Lance about the gunpowder and the emergency room. "They almost had to take skin off my butt and put it on my fingers."

"Damn," Lance laughed, "then we could've called you ass-fingers." He told Crab about hopping the train to the shop with Crow and Roach, and about the Easter Sunday swell and his board drifting away.

"It's gotta be that tarantula curse," Crab said. "Has anything happen to Crow or Roach?"

"The Turd's messed up. Something got broken when it got towed."

"See, the curse. Is that stew ready? I wanna get to the beach and go by the shop."

Lance stirred the stew. "Uh...I should warn you, Dennis is pretty pissed at us for unstrapping that Souther's board."

"Us? You did it."

"Yeah, but you were with me. As far as he's concerned we both did it."

"Did you tell him you did it?"

"He's just mad because it happened at the shop, he's worried about his reputation. Plus, he had to fix it. He charged me the forty bucks he was gonna give me in credit."

Lance got out some bowls and changed the subject. "How come you didn't ride your bike?"

Crab held up his bandaged hands. "My bike's got hand brakes."

They ate the stew then skateboarded down Channel Drive to the railroad tracks. A freight train was coming slowly up the tracks.

"Hey, you wanna hop this train?" Crab said.

"Are you crazy, what about your hands?"

Crab looked at his bandages. "I can hang on with my elbow."

The train was short at about forty cars. It screeched and clanged past as they tossed their skateboards in the bushes.

"Okay, do what I do," Lance said. He ran alongside a freight car and caught up to a ladder. He grabbed hold and hopped on. Behind him he watched Crab grimace as he grabbed a rung and jumped up. He hooked his elbow around the ladder and waved a bandaged hand. Lance was surprised at how gung-ho Crab was. It must've been from being cooped up at home for so long.

The train was picking up speed and Lance looked back at Crab who grinned and hooted with excitement. The train's acceleration worried Lance. He began looking for a closer place to jump. The San Jon Bridge was approaching; they'd have to wait for the grass. Lance yelled back to Crab, "After the bridge get ready to jump." Crab's eyes were wide and he wasn't smiling anymore. Lance faced outward preparing to jump. He pointed to the approaching grass. "Get ready, right up here." He leapt off with one long stride and rolled as if wiping out on his skateboard. He tumbled to a stop and from the ground saw Crab

174

still clinging to the train as it snaked into the railroad trestle over the 101 freeway. Lance got up and ran, but the train was now going faster than he could run. At the trestle he watched the red light of the caboose shrink away northward. "Oh crap!"

He walked over the pedestrian bridge to the Pier. Maybe the train would slow down around Santa Barbara and Crab could jump there. The thought of Crab's dad having to drive to Santa Barbara to get him the first day he was off restriction wasn't funny. Lance walked onto the Pier. The waves were small and blown out; no one was there. He walked to the end of the Pier and looked out over the ocean. *Should I call Crab's dad? What would I tell him, that the last time I saw your son he was heading north clinging to the side of a freight train?* White caps broke over the ocean and the wind blew in his face. There was nothing he could do for now. He turned and walked back toward land.

On the way he stopped to watch a fisherman. The guy was skinny and dirty and wore grimy clothes. This guy wasn't fishing for fun; he was fishing to eat. He sat on a bench cutting a mussel for bait. Lance peeked in his bucket. It was empty. The man squinted at him with red eyes. Lance smiled. "You catching anything?"

The man just glared.

Lance could see dirt in the creases of his face. "You fish out here a lot?"

"What's it to ya?" The man snapped.

"I was just wondering...can you catch enough fish out here to live on?"

The man spit near Lance's shoe. "I'm alive ain't I? Get the hell out of here and mind your own business."

"Relax mister, I was just asking."

Lance walked back along the shoreline and as he climbed over the rocks of the San Jon jetty he couldn't help thinking that maybe he'd find his surfboard; that somehow it'd washed ashore and had been there this whole time.

At Seaward Avenue he headed up the hill to the lemon factory, crossed the railroad tracks and got his skateboard from the bushes. He grabbed Crab's skateboard too.

28
HOBO JUNGLE

Crab cursed himself. He'd missed his chance to jump and the train was only going faster.

Rumbling out of the trestle over the 101 freeway he saw a line of cars waiting for the train to pass at California Street. He wondered what would happen if this train didn't slow down until San Francisco.

The train passed Figueroa Street and was now passing the fair grounds; ahead was the trestle over the Ventura River and he saw tall bushes growing up from the river bottom being whipped around in the rush of the train. They looked thick and strong. This might be his chance. As the freight car entered the trestle Crab leapt off like Superman narrowly missing the steel structure. He hit the bushes sideways and covered his head with his bandaged hands. Branches snapped and broke as he crashed through the shrubbery and rolled down the embankment to the river bottom.

He lay still for a moment waiting for the pain; nothing felt broken.

He watched the train speeding away northward over the trestle. "That was close." Crab clambered to his feet and brushed himself off. His skin stung with scratches and scrapes. He looked up the embankment. That would be the easiest way back, along the railroad tracks. But he'd never been in the river bottom before and it wasn't far to the ocean. He started down the dry waterways that crisscrossed around large clumps of reed grass and oak shrub toward the beach. The place had a swampy odor.

A pair of boxer shorts and a ripped T-shirt lay next to a trestle piling. Across the river bottom to the northwest was the familiar outcrop of date palms and Monterey cypress trees that were visible from the Main Street Bridge. Crab always figured that's where the hobos lived.

The larger clumps of reed grass were over ten feet tall and when the paths narrowed it was like walking through a maze. He veered left then right always moving toward the ocean. Ahead on the path he saw a black kitten batting the air in play. He stopped to watch. The kitten saw him, arched its back and sidestepped into a thicket. Crab moved forward and saw an opening into the thicket big enough for him to walk through. He stepped in.

The narrow path turned slightly then opened into a large clearing. In the center was a fire pit with a makeshift cooking apparatus. Beyond that were sheltered sleeping areas with blankets and crates. His stomach tightened; luckily no one was there. He stepped in closer. Over the fire pit were iron crossbars attached to poles planted in automobile tire rims. A metal bucket hung from the lower crossbar and there was a barbecue grate over the fire pit. Two large logs lay in a wide vee shape for sitting by the fire and there was a stump to sit on while tending the cooking. A few steps away was a dining area with a giant wooden spool for a table, a couple of folding chairs and more stumps. Over it was a thatched roof. An orange cat slept under the table and a grey cat strolled across the camp. The bedding areas were divided into personal shelters built of tree limbs and driftwood with palm canopies and tarps. This was way better than the shack he and Lance had been talking about. If he wasn't so scared the place would've seemed cozy. It had to be a hobo camp.

Across the clearing was another path into the bushes; he decided to exit there since that was the direction to the ocean. Scanning the piles of junk and belongings tucked away in the shelters he noticed something behind a shopping cart that looked

178

like the smooth rail of a surfboard. He moved closer and saw a gray rail and white deck. It was Lance's surfboard.

Crab ducked under a branch into the shelter and heard a shout. "Get the hell outta there!"

His heart leapt. A man came at him from across the camp with a club-like stick.

"I'll kill you, you son-of-a-bitch!"

Crab ran for the passageway into the river bottom and didn't look back until he reached the ocean.

* * * *

Lance's parents were home when he got there. He said a quick hello and went to his room. He put a record on the turntable and laid back on his bed letting the piano notes soothe his anxiety over what to do about Crab. The vocals came in.

I sailed an ocean, unsettled ocean
Through restful waters and deep commotion
Often frightened, unenlightened
Sail on, sail on sailor...

As the record played Lance looked at the newest *Surfer* magazine and settled into thoughts of empty waves in exotic places. When the record ended he flipped it over and heard the telephone ring in the kitchen.

His mom called out, "Lance, it's for you."

"Oh no." What would he say if it was Mr. Shaw? He walked to the kitchen. He'd have to tell him the truth.

His mom held out the phone. "It sounds like Sandcrab."

"Huh?" He grabbed the phone. "Hello?"

"You won't believe what I found--"

"You're home?" Lance put his hand over the receiver. "Can we have some privacy mom?"

"Privacy? What for?"

"He's got a girl he likes...and, you know..."

"Oh goodness, not that. Well, hurry it up, the roast is almost done."

"Thanks mom." He waited for her to leave. "Okay, what happened--hurry before my mom comes back."

"I jumped into the river bottom just before the train went into the trestle."

"Damn you're lucky, who knows where you'd have ended up."

"That's why I jumped. I figured I'd rather break my leg than have to call my dad from who-knows-where. Anyway, you'll never guess what I saw in the river bottom."

"What?"

"Guess."

"I don't know, an all girl nudist colony?"

"Your surfboard."

"What are you talking about? Don't mess with me, man."

"Your board's down there in a hobo camp, I swear. Wait'll you see the place, it's deluxe, you're gonna dig it--"

"You didn't get it?"

"I couldn't, a hobo was coming at me with a billy club, I had to run."

"Did you tell him it was my board?"

"The guy wanted to kill me. I didn't hang around to chat."

"Dang, they must've found it washed up on the beach. How many hobos live there?"

"I don't know, I only saw one."

"Well, how many do you think, ten?"

"I don't know, maybe three or four."

Lance's mom came in to check the roast. "Ten what? Girls?"

"No mom, we're talking about something else now, we're almost done." Lance held the phone from his ear as he waited for her to pull the roast from the oven and place it on the stove.

"I'll give you one more minute." She walked out shaking her head.

"Okay, meet me tomorrow at Inside Point."

"All right, I'll show you where it is, but I'm not going back in there."

29

JOHN BEAR

The next morning was overcast and chilly. Lance put on brown cords over his trunks and pulled on a faded red zip-up sweatshirt over his terry-cloth shirt. He slipped on his blue canvas deck shoes and biked to Inside Point. The tide was high and the waves mushy. Sandcrab was already on the planter talking with Bill and Stoody. Lance didn't see his bike. "How you get down here so fast?"

"My mom dropped me off."

Lance locked his bike to the rail. "Did you ask these guys if they want to come with us?"

Stoody crossed his arms. "I'm not going into any flea-bitten hobo camp."

"No way," Bill added, "it's dangerous in there, a hobo'll kill you for your shoes."

Lance glanced down at his deck shoes. "Okay, you weenies stay here and pick your butts, while we go on a jungle adventure."

"Hey Lance, if you guys don't make it back can I have dibbs on your bike?" Stoody asked.

"Don't worry about us smart-ass, we'll be back in an hour with my surfboard."

Lance and Crab started up the promenade. Lance noticed welts on Crab's neck and arms. "Did you get those scratches jumping from the train?"

"Yeah."

"What'd you tell your mom?"

"I told her we were skateboarding down Catalina Street and diving into the ivy."

"Good thinking."

They walked to the end of the promenade where the concrete gave way to the dirt parking lot at the Point. The Ventura River was more than a quarter mile ahead at the tip of the Point.

"So what's your plan?" Crab asked. "You gonna just walk in there and ask 'em for your board?"

"I'll tell 'em like it is. I appreciate you guys finding it and everything, but it's mine and I need it back."

"What if they don't wanna give it back?"

"Well, hopefully they won't be there and we can just grab it and split."

"Yeah, it's Sunday, maybe they'll be in church."

The morning haze was lifting across the Santa Barbara Channel and they could see the outline of Santa Cruz Island twenty miles out. They came to the mouth of the river and looked up the dry riverbed toward Ojai.

"See the trestle?" Crab said. "The camp's just this side of it near the south bank."

"Okay, lead the way."

Flies scattered as they stepped over piles of dry seaweed stranded at the high-tide line.

Crab picked up a club-like stick. "Get one of these, just in case." He batted a rock with it. "This is a good one."

Lance picked up a thin stick with an end that looked like a bird's head. "This one's cool."

They weaved their way up the dry waterways through the overgrown reeds and shrubs. The air smelled of decaying vegetation and warmth emanated from the dense overgrowth. The sun was beginning to break through and Lance pulled off his sweatshirt and tied it around his waist.

Crab stopped. "Whoa, look...an owl." Above them perched on a branch of scrub oak was a large grey owl. It sat perfectly still,

183

if not for the glaring yellow eyes they might not have seen it at all.

"I've never seen a real owl before."

"Me neither, I didn't think they came out in daytime."

"Well, this one does."

The owl broke its stare and turned away. Crab took a step forward and the bird spread its wings and swooped down with its talons out. Crab ducked and waved his stick. The owl flapped its wings whipping the air and lifting itself away.

Crab peered over his shoulder. "What the hell was that about?"

Lance watched as the owl flew up and turned eastward. "I don't know. I always thought owls were mellow. Maybe your white bandages freaked him out."

"Maybe it's a sign, maybe we should turn around."

"I'm tellin' you it was your bandages, don't be a baby, come on."

They continued toward the trestle taking a right fork, then a left staying near the south bank. Lance jabbed his stick into the soft dirt. "I wonder how long these guys have lived down here?"

"They've definitely been here a while, their camp looks permanent, it beats the hell out of the shack we've been talking about."

"What's so cool about it?"

"It's just cool, you'll see."

"It must get washed out every now and again, remember when all the rivers flooded in sixty-nine."

"We lived in Garden Grove then."

That's right, I always forget you're a Souther."

"Better than being a hodad."

A calico cat dashed across their path carrying a black and yellow garter snake in its mouth. "There's a lotta cats down

184

here." Crab said. He looked up at the railroad trestle above them. "Hey, we passed it."

A train whistle blew and a passenger train was coming south fast. "Hurry," Lance said. "Let's get under the bridge before it goes over."

They ran up the embankment and squeezed into the nook where the trestle met the riverbank and they waited.

Crab pointed to a bra laying in the dirt and giggled. "Man, I'd liked to have seen those."

The rumble grew and everything began to vibrate. It felt like an oncoming tsunami. The thunder rose until it seemed they'd be crushed by the sound. The train rushed over and as quickly as it came it was gone. Lance's ears were ringing. "That was insane."

They staggered out from under the trestle and fell back on the riverbank. Crab shook his head. "I bet that's what it sounds like getting barreled at Pipeline."

"I bet Pipeline's even louder." Lance leaned back and looked up. "Hey look, smoke." Not far away a string of smoke rose from the river bottom.

Crab frowned. "That's gotta be the hobo camp. We better come back later."

Lance stood up. "No way, we can't leave now."

"Yeah way. I'm not going down there."

"Come on, let's just sit here a minute and think."

"I'm going back to Inside Point."

"Sshh, listen. Did you hear that?" They froze. A rustling came from the bushes and a black cat scampered down the embankment into the river bottom.

"A stupid cat, I told you there's tons of 'em down here." Crab stood up. "I'm outta here man, you coming?"

There was another rustling and Lance put his hands up signaling Crab to be quiet.

"It's just another cat, you coming or not?" Crab turned and a large man stepped from the bushes. The man grabbed him by the throat.

"What the hell are you doing here?" The man spit. He was tall with greasy black hair and a leathery face with deep lines.

Lance held up his stick. "Let him go!"

The man gritted his stained teeth. "I asked a goddam question, what are you doing down here?"

"There's no law against us being down here," Lance said. "Let him go."

The man sneered. "I make the law down here."

Crab croaked trying to breathe.

Lance stepped forward. "Look sir, we just want to get my surfboard. My friend saw it in your camp yesterday."

The man raised an eyebrow. "Your what?"

"My surfboard, it's grey and white with a blue pinstripe."

The man's face eased and he took his hand from Crab's throat. "Is that all?"

Crab fell to his knees gasping for breath.

The man shook his head and chuckled.

"Yeah," Lance nodded, "that's all."

The man pointed at Crab. "Why was he snooping in our camp?"

"It was an accident," Lance said. "He was just exploring and stumbled on it."

"I followed a cat," Crab said.

"Look, we don't want any trouble. We just want to get my board and go."

The man scratched his head. "So, you're wantin' to negotiate?"

"No, I just want to get my board," Lance said.

"Well now, you need to understand that's not your surfboard."

186

"Sure it is. He knows what my board looks like. It's mine."

The man shook his head. "It belongs to us now, we found it."

"So, you won't give it back?"

Crab sat up, his eyes watery. "Forget about it Lance, let's just go."

The man straightened. "Oh, I'm sure we can work something out. We'll have to talk to Cricket, he's the one who found it." He placed his palm on his chest and nodded. "My name's John Bear."

Lance relaxed. "I'm Lance and that's Crab."

John Bear put his hand on Crab's shoulder. "Sorry for being so rough on you, but seeing you pokin' around here again today got me a little worked up."

Crab rubbed his throat with his bandages. "It's not like I want to be here."

John Bear slid his hands under Crab's arms and lifted him to his feet. "What's wrong with your hands?"

"It's a long story."

John Bear chuckled. "Not having such good luck lately, are ya." He turned and walked down the embankment. "This way to the surfboard boys."

Lance and Crab followed him down the dry waterway to the narrow path and into the clearing. Lance couldn't believe the elaborate system of ropes, tarps and thatched palm leaves. He saw the private quarters and the common area. It was like something out of *Swiss Family Robinson*.

They walked to the fire pit in the center of the camp where a fat guy sat roasting a small animal on a spit. The animal's head was cut off and it had no tail, maybe a rabbit. Above the animal was a pot hanging from a crossbar.

A skinny guy sat at the giant wooden spool table, he had fishing tackle spread over its top. Lance looked at the man and recognized him as the fisherman he'd seen on the Pier the day before.

"I found these two gentlemen outside our camp," John Bear said. He pointed at Crab. "That's the one I chased out of here yesterday."

The skinny guy stood up holding a knife. "Did you tell 'em what we do to trespassers?"

"Turns out they're here to do business."

"Business?" the guy growled.

Lance stepped up next to John Bear. "Are you Cricket?"

The man's eyes shifted from Lance to John Bear and back to Lance.

"Look Mr. Cricket, I just want my surfboard back, I don't want any trouble."

John Bear put his arm in front of Lance. "I told 'em we might be able to work out a deal."

"What kind of deal?"

"That's what we're going to talk about." John Bear extended his arm to a log. "Have a seat boys."

They sat down and John Bear sat on the adjacent log and patted the seat next to him. "Come on over Cricket."

Cricket walked over, spit and sat down.

"Stew," John Bear said. "You keep your eye on the cookin', but feel free to pipe in."

The fat guy turned on his stump. "Oh, I'm listenin'."

Lance peered around for his surfboard. He was impressed with how organized the place was; everything seemed in order. He noticed a fishing net and glass floats in the common area that looked to have been hung there for decoration. Crab was right, it was cozy.

"Gentlemen," said John Bear, "let me introduce you to our new friends, Larry and Clam."

"It's Lance and Crab."

"And these are my colleagues, Cricket and Stewart." Cricket spit on the ground again and looked away. Stew nodded.

"What are you roasting there?" Lance asked.

Stew flashed a toothless smile. "This here's feline."

Lance winced. "Cat?"

"You bet," John Bear said. "Cat's not bad eatin', beats squirrel or rodent any day."

Stew turned the spit then stood and stirred the pot. "Yes sir, I'm makin' a feline fricassee."

"Do you eat a lot of cats?"

"Whenever there's nothing else. Cricket didn't have any luck fishing yesterday." A striped cat came up and rubbed it self on John Bear's leg, he leaned down and scratched it behind the ears. "Yep, there's plenty of these guys around."

Cricket squinted at Lance. "You were the one on the Pier yesterday, you jinxed me."

"Jinxed you? All I did was ask a question."

"We can forget about all that now," John Bear said. "It's time to get down to business. Now, what are you gentlemen willing to give us for the surfboard?"

Lance sighed. "I don't have anything to give you."

John Bear raised an eyebrow. "Well tell me, how much does a surfboard cost in today's economy?"

Lance frowned. "What's that got to do with anything?"

John Bear folded his arms. "I'm just trying to understand the value of the said item we're bargaining for, you know, to understand the playing field, so to speak."

Lance stood up. "Look, I lost my surfboard, you guys found it and now you should give it back. It's mine."

Cricket stood up and pointed his knife at Lance. "That surfboard ain't yours, understand? It belongs to us, and if you want it back you better listen."

"Okay, settle down," John Bear said. "There's no need for that. Sit back down and let's have a civilized discussion."

Lance sat down. "I don't know what you guys want from me, I don't have anything to give you."

"But you've got access to lots of things."

"What's that supposed to mean?"

"Things, like shoes and clothes. I bet your dad's got all kinds of stuff he's willing to give to the Salvation Army. We could use that stuff." John Bear lifted his foot to show them the holes in his shoes. "What else fellas, Stew what do you need?"

Stew looked up, closed one eye and scratched his chin. "Uh, lets see--salt and pepper, mustard, ketchup. Especially ketchup, I'm always cravin' ketchup."

"Oh yeah, salt and pepper and ketchup." John Bear leaned forward and put his elbows on his knees. "Cricket, what about you?"

"I want whiskey, a big bottle of whiskey, and a cigar."

"We can't get whiskey," Lance said. "I might be able to get you a cigar, though. My dad's always got cigars laying around."

John Bear nodded. "Hey now, there we go, cigars. Can you get three of 'em?"

"Sure, maybe. Can I see my surfboard?"

Cricket glared at Lance. "You'll see it when you come back with something to offer and not before."

"Okay," John Bear said. "You got a nice list of stuff there, go out and round up as much of it as you can and we'll see if you can't get your surfboard back."

Lance and Crab stood up. "All right," Lance said. "We'll be back before dark."

190

"Before dark?" John Bear smiled and rocked back on the log. "You are anxious to get that surfboard."

"I can't surf without it."

"Nope, I don't suppose you can."

"We'll see you in a while," Lance said.

John Bear stuck a finger in the air. "Maybe a hat too, a derby, or a top hat."

"A top hat?"

"Or any kind of hat..."

Crab pulled on Lance's arm. "Let's get outta here before the list gets any longer."

30

PLUNDER

"This shouldn't be too hard," Lance said as he and Crab walked down the river bottom toward the ocean. "I should be able to get most of the stuff from my house."

Crab lifted his head to expose his throat. "See any marks?"

"Nah, it's just red."

"Man, did he smell. I was gasping for air and sucking in his stink." Crab itched his nose, his bandages were brown with dirt.

"Yeah, that was pretty scary. How about that camp though? You were right, that place is deluxe. We could live there easy."

"Told you."

They walked back to Inside Point and Crab climbed onto the bike's handlebars and they rode to Lance's house. Lance's dad had the car in the driveway and was pulling down the garage door.

"Hi Mr. Stratton," Crab said jumping down from the handlebars.

"Hey, how you doing there Sandcastle? What are you two doing home this early in the afternoon?"

Lance's mom came out of the house with her purse. "Don't tell me you rode all the way from the beach like that?"

"Oh mom, we do it all the time." Lance wheeled his bike onto the porch.

She turned to Crab. "How are your hands healing?"

"Pretty good, I'm going to the doctor tomorrow."

"You're very lucky it wasn't worse," she said.

Lance rolled his eyes. "Come on let's get something to eat."

"You can heat up the leftover enchiladas," his mom said opening the car door. "Just put them in the oven at three fifty for twenty minutes."

"Okay, thanks mom."

Lance headed into the house and his dad hollered, "Leave some food for the rest of us."

While the enchiladas heated up Lance rummaged through the kitchen for things to give the hobos.

"While you raid your kitchen, I'm gonna check the T.V. Guide," Crab said.

Lance found a full bottle of ketchup in the pantry, but that was it. He couldn't take the salt and pepper shakers.

Crab yelled from the living room, "*Endless Summer's* on right now, channel nine."

Lance ran in and turned on the T.V. "Why do they always have to show it in the middle of the day?"

"We've only missed about thirty minutes." Crab plopped on the sofa. "Oh crap, I forgot your T.V. is black and white."

The movie was every surfer's dream. Two guys fly around the globe in search of the world's best wave. It played in movie houses in the mid-sixties and was now shown on T.V. a couple times a year.

They ate enchiladas and watched as Mike Hynson and Robert August surfed their way around Africa. By the time the surfers reached Australia the enchiladas were gone and during the next commercial break Lance brought in a bag of clothes from the garage that his mom was going to donate to the *Retarded Children's Thrift Store*. He dumped the clothes on the floor in front of the T.V.

"Man, wouldn't you like to live like those guys, just traveling around the world surfing?"

"They only did it for the movie, it's not like they did it all the time."

"I know numb nuts, but they still got to do it."

Lance put a sweater, a smoking jacket, a long sleeve dress shirt and a couple of old t-shirts into a sack. He added the ketchup and three *Tiperillo* cigars from a box on his dad's desk.

"You think that's enough stuff?" Crab asked.

"No, I'll need to make a couple of stops."

Lance wheeled his bike off the porch and Crab eased onto the handlebars. Lance handed him the bag and pedaled down Thompson Boulevard to the restaurant at the Vagabond Motel. Lance parked the bike. "I'll be right back."

He went inside and as usual, being a kid, was ignored by the waitresses. He went to the closest empty table, grabbed the salt and peppershakers and walked out.

"They'll never miss 'em," he said adding the shakers to the paper sack. "Now we'll go to Retarded Children's for some shoes."

"Are you going to steal those too?"

"You saw that big ol' bag of clothes my mom's gonna give 'em. I don't think it qualifies as stealing when they get all the stuff for free in the first place."

"That doesn't mean you can just go in there and take it."

"Sure it does, last week me and Stoody went in there just wearing our trunks and came out fully clothed. Where do you think I got this cool terry cloth shirt?"

"Oh brother."

"My mom gives 'em stuff all the time."

"Doesn't make it right."

"Look, that stupid pair of shoes is gonna help me get my surfboard back and right now that's all I care about."

"You're stealing from retarded people."

194

"Just get on."

Crab adjusted himself on the handlebars and they continued across Plaza Park, up Chestnut Street past the Ventura Theater. Lance turned down Main Street and stopped at the Top Hat hamburger stand a half block from the thrift store. Crab hopped off and Lance parked the bike.

"Man, those burgers smell insane," Crab said.

"Well, you stay here and try not to go crazy, I'll be back in a minute." Lance kicked off his canvas deck shoes and put them in the paper sack.

"So who are you getting the shoes for?"

"I don't know, John Bear needs 'em, but I guess it's all up to Cricket to decide. I'll be right back."

Lance walked into the store barefoot, at the front was a gray-haired security guard dozing off. Lance went to the shoe section and tried to decide what kind of shoes would be best. Something durable, comfortable and good-looking. For size he'd just get something too big for himself. He saw a pair of brown wingtips. His dad wore wingtips every day and he always said if you took care of them they could last you twenty years. Lance slipped his bare feet in. With his brown cords they looked pretty good, if you liked that sort of thing.

Lance walked casually down the center aisle trying not to clomp as the loose shoes slid around on his feet. Near the front he snatched a light blue golf hat off a rack and continued out the door. Crab was standing to the side of the burger stand watching people get their food. Lance grabbed the bike, picked up the sack and wheeled the front tire between Crab's legs. "Hey, let's go before you go looney."

Crab turned. "That was quick."

"Piece of cake." Lance held up a foot. "How do they look?"

"Like clown shoes." Crab looked over Lance's shoulder. "Did anybody see you?"

"No way, I was out of there before they even knew I went in."

"Well, there's a security guard standing out front looking this way...now coming this way!"

Lance turned around and saw the security guard walking toward them. "Oh crap, get on."

Crab hopped on the handlebars as Lance pushed the bike for momentum, his feet slipped around inside the shoes. He got on the pedals and stood up for power, the blue golf hat flew off.

"You boys come back here," the man yelled gaining on them.

Lance turned left at the corner and immediately saw his mistake. It was Palm Street, the steepest street in Ventura. He couldn't turn around; they had to go up. Lance pedaled up the incline as far as he could. Crab jumped off and Lance, in the wingtips, scrambled to push the bike up the hill.

Out of breath he reached the top where Crab stood looking down. "He gave up."

Lance looked back, the security guard stood panting with his hands on his hips a third of the way up the hill. Lance kicked off the wingtips and slipped into his canvas deck shoes. "Phew, put these in the bag, let's get outta here."

They pedaled down Poli Street behind the San Buenaventura Mission and past Holy Cross School. There they cut down the dirt hill back to Main Street and rode to the bridge over the Ventura River. Lance locked his bike to a chain link fence and they headed down to the river bottom.

31
RED

At the railroad trestle Lance and Crab looked over the river bottom toward the ocean. There was no smoke.

"We'll find it," Lance said. He put the sack down and reorganized the things inside.

"What are you doing?"

"I'm making sure the salt and pepper are standing in the corners. I want the cigars on the bottom so they'll be a surprise, and I want the ketchup on top so it's the first thing they see."

"You think it matters?"

"Yeah, I want 'em to start with something good and end with a nice surprise." Lance rolled up the top of the sack and they started down the embankment. Crab led the way through the tall clumps of reed grass. They knew they were close when a cat darted across their path and around the next bend they saw the opening.

"You're getting to know your way around here pretty good," Lance said.

Crab stopped and put his hand out. "After you."

Lance stepped into the thicket and called out. "John Bear-- Cricket--Stew, it's us. Anybody home?" They entered the camp and no one was there.

"Quick, let's get your board and split!" Crab said.

"But we gotta give 'em the stuff."

"Just leave it, come on, let's get your board."

Lance followed Crab to a bedding area where a dirty sleeping bag and blankets lay on the ground surrounded by crates.

"It's gone," Crab said. "It was right there next to the shopping cart."

"Where would they hide it?" Lance scanned the camp and saw a strange man emerge from the bushes across the way.

"Oh Jesus, who's that?" Crab gasped.

The guy's hair was red and matted on one side. He wore overalls and a grimy long-sleeved shirt.

"Hey," Lance called. "You know where John Bear and those guys are? We got some stuff for 'em."

The man cautiously started toward them.

"They're expecting us," Lance said.

The man's eyes were fixed on the bag. He stopped in front of Lance and reached for it.

"This is stuff for Cricket and John Bear," Lance said. "Do you live here too?" Lance held the bag up. "This is stuff we brought to trade for my surfboard back, do you know where it is?"

The man grabbed the bag.

"Hey, what are you doing?"

He took out the ketchup bottle, dropped the sack and unscrewed the cap. He tilted his head back and shook globs of ketchup into his mouth.

Lance picked up the bag and backed up to where Crab stood. "That's weird."

"And I thought Roach ate sick stuff."

The man stopped for a moment and licked his face.

"What's going on?" John Bear said standing at the entrance to the camp. Stew came up behind him.

The red haired guy pulled the ketchup close to his chest.

John Bear's eyes widened. In a calm voice he said, "That's our ketchup you got there Red." John Bear held his hand out and stepped toward him. "Come on Red, give me the bottle."

Red watched him for a moment then put the bottle to his mouth and ran.

"Stop him," John Bear yelled.

198

Red tried to make for the exit, but Stew blocked his way. Red cut back and came around toward Lance and Crab who stood in front of the other exit.

"Stop him boys."

Lance put his arms out and Red made a move and ran straight into Crab. They toppled into the reeds. John Bear hurried over and pried the bottle from Red's hands. Red jumped up like a scared dog and ran from the camp.

Lance leaned over Crab. "You okay? Your head's bleeding."

Crab sat up and touched his forehead. "It's just ketchup, he did clobber me though."

John Bear held up the half empty bottle of ketchup and examined it. "Del Monte, that's a good brand." He took a moment to sniff it then took a drink.

"Save me some of that," Stew said.

John Bear handed the bottle to Stew and wiped his mouth on his sleeve. He looked at Lance. "So what else you bring?"

Lance held up the paper sack. "Who was that guy?"

"We call him Red, he lives out here." John Bear took the bag. "He never says anything. I'm not sure he can talk." He carried the sack to the spool table. "He can be a nuisance. We have to run him outta here every now and again."

Lance looked over at Stew letting the last drops of ketchup fall into his mouth. "Why do you guys like ketchup so much?"

John Bear emptied the bag on the table. "It's full of flavor, we don't get a lot of spices down here." He spread out the clothes, shoes, salt and pepper and cigars. "Stewy's a good cook but there's only so much he can do. Look Stew, salt and pepper."

John Bear sprinkled a dash of each into his mouth. "Umm, um, there's nothing like real salt meltin' on your tongue." He put the shakers on the table and Stew came over and took a dash of each as well.

"Stew look, little cigars with plastic tips, one for each of us."
John Bear put one in his mouth. "And wingtips." He sat on a
stump and tried on the shoes. "They fit too. Try on that sweater
Stew."

Lance watched John Bear and Stew. "Shouldn't Cricket be
here before you guys start divvy-in' up all this stuff?"

"Oh, he's gonna be real happy with this, yes indeed. Real
happy."

"Well then...you think I could get my board?"

"Sure, sure. Go ahead and get it."

Crab was holding his forehead. "He moved it, the surfboard's
gone."

"He did?" John Bear looked puzzled. "You know where he
put it, Stew?"

Stew shrugged. "He musta hid it. Probably protecting his
interest."

John Bear stood up and slipped on the smoking jacket over his
dirty sweatshirt. "Stew, why don't you start the fire. We can heat
up the fricassee, smoke our cigars and visit with the boys here
while we wait for Cricket." John Bear winked at Lance. "We
don't get many visitors."

Crab turned to Lance and took his hand from his forehead.
"How's my head look."

"Boy, you gotta knot," John Bear said.

"I think he hit me with the ketchup bottle."

"Dang that Red. He's a hard one to figure out, kinda like a
ghost, he just drifts around. I can't help but feel sorry for him. I
leave food out sometimes. Cricket hates it when I do that. He
thinks we ought to put him out of his misery."

"For real?"

"Sometimes I wonder, Cricket's got tendencies." John Bear
lowered his voice to a whisper. "He told me once he got sent to

200

Camarillo and they gave him shock treatment. He doesn't like talking about it."

"Camarillo, the mental hospital?"

John Bear nodded and stood up. "Excuse me while I light my cigar."

Stew had the fire going and John Bear walked over and took out a burning stick. He pressed the cigar into the ember end, then held the stick out for Stew and they stood by the soup pot smoking. John Bear bent over and smelled the fricassee while Stew stirred it. They took another puff on their cigars then John Bear sat down on a log. "Come on over boys, have a seat."

Lance peered into the pot before sitting down. "Is that the feline fricassee?"

"Sure is," Stew said.

"Stew's an expert at chowders and such," John Bear bragged. "He's worked in almost every restaurant in town."

"You're a chef?"

Stew shook his head. "Naw, I'm a dishwasher. I'd keep a bucket under the sink and early in the evening when the plates started coming in I'd pick a theme, then scrape off the stuff I wanted into the bucket--rib bones, potatoes, corn, beets--you'd be surprised how many people don't eat beets. At one place they put a slice of beet on every salad, and I tell you almost all those plates came back empty, except for that beet. Anyway, I'd bring the bucket back and turn it into somethin'."

Crab scowled. "That doesn't sound like cooking."

"Oh, don't kid yourself," John Bear said. "It takes real skill to come up with some of the concoctions he does. You know what his specialty is?"

Lance shrugged.

"Bullfrog chowder, woo boy is it good." John Bear rubbed his belly and blew out smoke.

"Is frog better than cat?"

"Oh yeah," John Bear said. "They serve frog in fancy restaurants, cat meat's kinda stringy. Wasn't until I had Stew's feline fricassee that I started liking it. It comes out tasting like somethin' between chicken and squirrel." John Bear leaned over to Lance. "He's got real talent."

Lance could smell John Bear's earthy odor. He leaned back and looked to Stew. "So what do you put in that fricassee?"

Stew took a long puff on his cigar and adjusted himself on the log. "It varies. This one's got two kinds of seaweed--red and green, potatoes, a couple of oranges, some lemon…"

"Where do you get oranges and lemons?" Crab asked.

"You kiddin' me?" John Bear said. "Just a mile up river from here is a hundred acres of orchards." He lowered his voice. "I know where there's a house with five avocado trees. I go there in the morning sometimes and pick ripe avocados right off the ground."

"And the potatoes," Stew said, "we get them from the dumpster behind The Big Green House, that's one of the restaurants I used to work at."

"Hey, we've gotten baked potatoes from that dumpster before too," Crab said.

Lance nodded. "Yeah, we're kind of practicing how to live like you guys. You know, for free, finding food wherever we can, so we can surf whenever we want."

John Bear rocked back with his hands on his knees. "How about that Stew, these boys have aspirations to live like us."

Stew blew out a puff of smoke. "Can't blame 'em."

There was a rustling in the bushes and Cricket entered the camp with a gunnysack over his shoulder. He knelt down on his bedding and began emptying the sack.

202

John Bear called out. "Cricket look who's here, and they brought stuff."

"They bring whiskey?"

"Well no, but there's a cigar here for ya."

Cricket tucked the gunnysack away and came over to the fire. John Bear reached into the breast pocket of his smoking jacket and handed Cricket a cigar. Cricket winced. "Looks like a woman's cigar." He bit off the plastic mouthpiece and spit it out. He took a stick from the fire and lit the cigar then turned to Lance. "So what else you bring?"

"Uh, there's salt and pepper on the table. There was ketchup, but--"

"Red got to it before we got here," John Bear interrupted. "Drank almost the whole bottle."

Cricket looked at the wingtips on John Bear's feet and the smoking jacket, then at Lance again. "You think I'm gonna give you that surfboard for a woman's cigar and some salt and pepper?" Cricket shook his head and flashed his ragged teeth. "I want whiskey, you bring me a bottle of whiskey then we'll talk." He spit and moved away back to his personal area.

"Well, there you have it," John Bear said.

Lance frowned. "I can't get a bottle of whiskey. I don't have any money and even if I did I can't buy it."

John Bear leaned back and blew out a cloud of smoke. "I know a way you fellas can earn some money, and surely you can find somebody to buy you a bottle of whiskey."

"What, mowing lawns?" Lance asked.

"Hell no. What I'm talking about is easier, and pays better too."

"Does it involve a gun?" Crab sneered.

"Oh no, it's not illegal, per se...you could liken it to digging for buried treasure."

Crab laughed. "Ha! You gonna give us a treasure map?"

John Bear smiled. "No need for a map." He leaned forward and whispered, "The treasure's in all the washing machines in all the laundromats."

"Huh?"

"Every washing machine has a trap under the agitator that catches all the loose change from people's pockets. All you need is a three-eighths inch hex wrench. You take the cap off the agitator, lift up the agitator and there's the treasure."

"Oh brother," Crab said. "What do you get, like twelve cents?"

"Sometimes, and sometimes a dollar twelve; even two twelve, depends on when they were cleaned out last. Say there's ten machines per facility; and who knows how many facilities?" John Bear took the last puff of his cigar and flicked the butt into the fire. "You do the math."

Lance looked at Crab. "That's a possible twenty bucks per laundromat. I can think of three, no four, right off the top of my head."

Crab rubbed his forehead and looked at John Bear. "If it's so great why don't you guys do it?"

John Bear smiled. "When you live without soap and water and pressed clothes for a time, folks start taking offense, you're not welcome anywhere for too long, you gotta keep movin' or the cops show up. You kids won't have any problems lingering in a laundromat."

"It's perfect," Lance said. "Thanks John Bear, we gotta go. Tell Cricket we'll be back with the whiskey."

"I'll tell him. And thanks for the smoking jacket, the shoes and the cigar."

"You sure you don't want to try some of this fricassee?" Stew offered.

204

"No thanks," Lance said. "My mom doesn't like it when I spoil my appetite."

Stew shrugged.

Lance stood up. "If this laundromat scheme works, we'll get you more ketchup too."

32
HOME FOR DINNER

Lance walked into the house and smelled dinner cooking. He headed for the kitchen. A large pot was boiling on the stove and his mom pulled a loaf pan from the oven.

"Hi Mom, meatloaf?"

"Yep, your dad's favorite." She closed the oven door. "Did you and Sandcrab go back to the beach?"

"Yeah."

"What do you do down there all day long without a surfboard?"

"I borrow other guy's boards, but the waves weren't that good today, so I just hung out."

She took the steaming pot from the stove and poured the hot potatoes into a colander in the sink. "Don't you ever just want to hang out at home? You could've helped your father and me plant flowers in the backyard."

Lance opened the refrigerator door. "Boy, that sounds way funner than being at the beach."

"What are you looking for? We're going to eat soon."

"I'm hungry now."

"You'll live until dinner." She dumped the potatoes back in the warm pot and started mashing them. "Why don't you go in the backyard and tell your dad to get cleaned up for dinner."

Lance opened the back door. "Hey Dad, dinner's almost ready."

"Lance, I didn't say yell for him. Go wash your hands."

When Lance came back to the kitchen he sat at the table and watched as his mom searched the cupboards. "I know we had a new bottle of ketchup in here somewhere."

The back door opened and Lance's dad came in. "Boy, that smells good."

"Jim, didn't we just buy a new bottle of ketchup?"

"I thought we did, but who knows the way food disappears around here."

"One of Lance's friends probably ate it," Ann said entering the kitchen. "They eat everything in sight."

"They do not," Lance snapped, "why do you say stuff like that?"

"That's enough," his mom said, "everyone sit down, dinner's ready."

Lance plopped a dollop of mashed potatoes on his plate. "We don't even need ketchup, we've got gravy."

"Your sister doesn't like gravy."

"What kind of freak doesn't like gravy?"

Ann glared at him. "It's okay Mom, I can eat my meatloaf plain."

His mom dug a nearly empty bottle of ketchup from the refrigerator. "There's a little left in here." With her knife she scraped the inside of the bottle. "I grew up during the Great Depression, we never wasted anything." She dribbled a few drops of ketchup onto Ann's meatloaf. "My mom would've swirled a little warm water in this bottle and let me drink it. We used everything."

"You drank ketchup?" Ann asked.

Lance smiled and stabbed a bite of meatloaf.

"When you're hungry you'll eat anything. You remember, don't you Jim?"

"Well..." He smiled. "We were never that hungry, but we didn't waste anything either."

"Your father was fortunate, your grandfather had a job throughout the depression."

"I bet there were a lot of hobos back then," Lance said.

His dad took a forkful of meatloaf and dipped it into his mashed potatoes. "They were all over the place, every day somebody was knocking on the door asking for work or a handout."

"Did you ever want to be a hobo dad?"

His dad choked.

"What kind of question is that?" his mother asked. "Why would anyone want to be a hobo?"

Ann laughed. "Lance has some romantic notion that hobos have it made--no responsibility and all the freedom in the world."

Lance glared at his sister. "You don't know what you're talking about, and what's romance got to do with anything?"

His dad gathered himself. "No Lance, becoming a hobo is not something I've ever considered." He chuckled and shook his head. "Does it appeal to you?"

"I was just asking. I see a lot of hobos at the beach, they seem pretty happy."

His mom wagged her spoon. "You stay away from any hobos you see down there. Tell him Jim."

"Your mother's right. Those men are desperate. They'll lie, cheat and steal to get whatever they can. Hell, they'd kill somebody for a pair shoes."

"Why do you say that, it's not true."

His dad's face hardened. "You bet your life it's true. They'll take anything, anyway they can get it."

Lance moved the peas around on his plate.

"You remember that story in the paper last year about the man who washed up on the beach?" his mom asked. "They said he was murdered in Hobo Jungle."

Lance stabbed at a pea. It was dumb to bring up hobos with his parents. They could never appreciate the freedom of living in the river bottom. He smiled at his plate wondering what John Bear and those guys would think about a meatloaf dinner like this. It was time to change the subject.

"Guess what me and Crab watched today, *Endless Summer*."

"That's such a good movie. You remember that one Jim. The two surfers traveling around the world looking for the perfect wave."

"Crab says it's in color."

"I bet it's beautiful in color."

Ann looked at her dad. "You realize we're the only people in Ventura without a color T.V.?"

His dad sat back in his chair and grinned. "Color T.V., who cares about T.V.? I'm thinkin' about quittin' my job and ridin' the rails. Who's with me?"

Lance rolled his eyes. "Oh brother dad."

33
JUNKYARD

The next day after school Lance rode his bike to Crow's house to tell him about the laundromat scheme. If it worked, not only could he get his surfboard back, but they could both pay back Dennis the money they owed him. Crow lived on the east side of town. Lance cut through the mall parking lot, crossed Mill Road to Dean Drive and turned onto Westmont Street where Crow lived. The houses were nice here, ranch style with large manicured lawns. He saw the Turd ahead, parked on the street, the front end up on blocks.

Lance rang the doorbell and Roach answered eating a sandwich.

"Hey Lance, what's up?" He yawned. "Come on in."

"You just wake up?"

"Yeah, guess where we spent the night last night."

"In jail?"

"The junkyard. But wait for Crow to get out of bathroom, he'll tell it better. Hey, Stoody said you found your board in Hobo Jungle."

"Yeah, some hobos have it and won't give it back until I bring 'em some whiskey."

"Ha! They're holding your board hostage, you gonna get it for 'em?"

"Well, yeah, I want my board. What kind of sandwich is that?"

"Peanut butter, mustard and peach, you want one? I just opened a can."

"Sure, but I'll make it."

210

Lance followed Roach into the kitchen. "Geez, doesn't anybody do dishes around here? Crow's mom still in Palm Springs?"

"Yeah, she came home for a few days, but then she left again."

Lance looked over the mess on the counter and found the can of peaches. "You got a rag to wipe the counter?"

"Probably in the sink."

"I'm not touching anything in there."

Roach took out two slices of bread and held one in each palm. "Here, I'll hold 'em, you spread."

Lance spread on the peanut butter then neatly placed four peach slices on the bread.

Crow came in and leaned against the doorjamb, he stretched and yawned. "Roach tell you what happened to us last night?"

"Not yet," Roach said, "I was waitin' for you."

Crow folded his arms. "We got stuck in the junkyard and had to spend the night in the back of a van."

"What the hell were you doing?"

"Getting parts for the Turd."

"You were stealing 'em?"

"Those guys are the thieves. Most of those cars they just clean up off the highway. It's not like they pay for 'em."

"It's freaky in there man," Roach said. "All these wrecks with broken windshields and bloody hair stuck in the glass. It's creepy. Hey Crow, you want a sandwich?"

"Sure. So this is what happens--we go out there yesterday to buy the stuff, but the guy's a real ass--"

"What stuff?"

"A steering bar and a tire. Anyway, I tell the guy what I need and he says to go look around there's plenty of vans out there."

"The place is bigger than a football field," Roach said.

"So, we find a van with a good spare on the front and I get underneath and check the steering bar and it's good. So we go tell the guy and he says six bucks for the tire and twenty for the steering bar. I told him I only had twelve bucks, but he wouldn't budge."

"It's cause he saw us drive up in your mom's Mercedes," Roach added.

"You snuck your mom's car out?" Lance asked chewing his sandwich.

Crow nodded. "I had to. So, I tell him I can only get the tire and asked to borrow a cross wrench. 'You gotta bring you own tools kid,' he says. So, we went and got the cross wrench from my mom's car and I grabbed some pliers and we went back in. While Roach took the off the spare, I got underneath and took out the cotter pins from the steering bar. That's all that holds it in, a couple of cotter pins and it just slides off these rivets."

"So, if you stole it why'd you have to go back last night?"

"We didn't steal it, we bought the tire and went back last night for the steering bar."

"I tell you man, it's scary in there at night," Roach said. "You know there's gotta be ghosts in there."

Crow took a bite of his sandwich and looked at Roach. "You put mustard on this?"

"Yeah, I gave you the works."

"Not bad."

"Where's this junkyard?" Lance asked.

"It's on the way to Santa Paula, on Briggs Road near the Santa Clara River," Crow said. "It was pitch black out there. We had to walk along a chain link fence about ten feet high until we found a place where the barbed wire was flattened down and we could climb over."

"Did you guys have flashlights?"

212

"Yeah, but we didn't use 'em until we got to the van," Crow said. "There was a flood light at the front of the junkyard, it was far away but it made shadows so we could see a little."

Roach shook his head. "I swear you could go nuts in there, your mind starts playing tricks on you."

Lance ate his last bite of sandwich. "So, why were you there all night?"

"I'm gettin' to that," Crow said. "We find the van and I get under it and get the steering bar, then we climb inside to get some vent knobs and other stuff I need. All of a sudden Roach flicks off his flashlight and says, 'Shhh listen.' We're sittin' there and can't see anything, but we hear a growl."

"It was the scaredest I've ever been," Roach said. "I just knew it was a werewolf or a zombie or something."

"What was it?"

"The junkyard dog," Crow said. "A Doberman. He's just sitting in front of the van watching us and growling."

"What'd you guys do?"

"We got down on the floor in back and waited for him to leave, but he wouldn't."

"We ended up falling asleep," Roach said. "When we woke up we could see the outline of the hills, we looked out and the dog was gone. We got our stuff and ran as fast as we could to the fence."

"That was the scariest part," Crow said. "I knew that damn Doberman was gonna come out of nowhere and tear us apart."

"But he didn't." Lance grinned.

"Yeah he did. As soon as we got to the fence that dog came snarling out of nowhere. I'm clinging to the fence holding the steering bar and he's nipping at my feet. Then a light comes on in the corner of the junkyard and there's voices. We jump over the fence and run, and that damn dog's chasing us on the other

213

side, then all of a sudden there's three guys running with him. They're yelling in Spanish and waving crowbars. We got in the car and I floored it. In the rear view mirror I saw 'em come running out after us."

"That was our night," Roach said.

"You got the steering bar?"

"Yep, and a window handle and some vent knobs. The Turd's gonna be in good shape," Crow said.

"And you've still got six bucks."

"No," said Roach. "We stopped at *Carrows* on the way home and got steak and eggs."

34

THE SCHEME

Lance followed Crow and Roach onto the front lawn. A newspaper plopped on the grass at Crow's feet as a kid rode by on a stingray bike with canvas bags stuffed with newspapers hanging on his handlebars.

Crow tossed the newspaper on the porch and looked at Lance. "I heard you found your board in Hobo Jungle."

Roach laughed. "The hobos are holding it ransom, tell him Lance."

"What do they want for it, beer?" Crow joked.

"Close, whiskey. Crab and me already took 'em some cigars, clothes and ketchup.

"Ketchup?"

"Yeah, they like ketchup, and salt and pepper too, but now they want whiskey."

"How many of 'em are there?" Crow asked.

"Three, and another crazy one, but he doesn't live with 'em."

"They're probably gonna try to work you for all they can get."

"Yeah, I thought about that. But one of 'em, John Bear, told me about a way we can make some quick money."

"Financial advice from a hobo?" Roach chuckled. "This ought to be good."

Lance lay down on the grass. "Come on, I'll tell ya."

Crow plopped down. He plucked some grass and tossed it at Lance. "They don't have you selling river bottom real estate do they?"

Lance craned his neck. "Who's that guy across the street looking over here."

Crow waved. "Hi Mr. Weinberger, anything I can help you with?"

Mr. Weinberger stood with his legs apart and his hands on his hips. "I'm wondering how much longer we have to look at that eyesore parked there."

"I'm hoping to have it running today, sir."

"Well you better, because if you don't I'm going to have it towed as a derelict vehicle."

Roach hollered, "What do you care mister, the van's not bothering anybody."

Mr. Weinberger's face reddened and he shook his newspaper. "It's bothering me young man and I'm sure your mother won't be pleased to hear you had her car out all night, Steven. I saw you drive in this morning at seven thirty."

"Oh crap." Crow stood up. "Like I said sir, I'm hoping to have it off the street today."

"Good, and tell your friend to learn some manners."

"Why don't you tow your ass back in the house and mind your own business," Roach hollered.

The man batted the air with his newspaper and marched into the house.

Crow collapsed onto the grass. "Great, he's gonna tell my mom," he socked Roach on the shoulder, "and you weren't helping any."

"Who does that guy think he is?"

Crow shook his head. "Forget about it...what's this money scheme Lance, I gotta get busy on the Turd."

"According to John Bear all laundromat washing machines have a change trap under the agitator--the big thing that turns in the middle--you can take that off with a three-eighths inch hex wrench and get the coins from the trap."

216

Crow and Roach looked at each other. "And how many pennies we gonna find in there?"

"He says it depends when they were last cleaned out. You might find two cents; you might find two dollars. Think about it, if there's ten machines per laundromat..."

"Hmm, it's worth a shot," Roach said.

Crow jumped to his feet as if he'd just caught a wave. "How many laundromats in this town? Let's get the Turd fixed and go do some laundry."

* * * *

Crow took his hands off the steering wheel as they drove down Telegraph Road to Crab's house. "Look at that, she's driving straight as an arrow." He veered right through the Five Points intersection where Telegraph Road turned into Thompson Boulevard and got into the left hand turn pocket. "Do you see what I see?"

To the left in the supermarket shopping center next to the fish'n chips place was a laundromat. Crow pulled in and parked in the middle of the lot where they could see in.

Lance leaned between the front seats to look out. The sun was low and the sky was turning orange. Inside the laundromat two women sat reading magazines. A bored kid stared out the window. "Should we wait for them to leave?"

"I say we just go in and do it," Roach said.

"Yeah, what do they care?" Crow opened his door, Lance slid the side door open and they walked between the parked cars.

"You got the wrench?" Lance asked.

Crow patted his breast pocket. "Yep."

The door was propped open and they entered silently, but both women looked up from their magazines. The little boy watched them. The lids were open on all the machines not in use and sure enough there was a metal cap on the top of each agitator and in the center was a place for a hex wrench.

Crow put the short end of the wrench into the cap. "It fits." He tried to turn it. "It's really on there." He leaned into it putting his weight on the wrench.

"Maybe it turns the other way," Roach said.

"Hold the agitator, I don't want to break it."

Roach held the agitator. Crow leaned on the wrench and fell forward. He held up the wrench. "Damn piece of crap, it stripped."

Roach tried to turn the cap. "It's still on there. I hope they're not all this hard."

"Come on, we can borrow another wrench from Crab's dad, his won't be aluminum."

"I knew this sounded too easy," Lance said.

35

LAUNDRY MONEY

Crow parked the Turd around the corner from Crab's house. Lance grabbed Roach's skateboard and climbed out the side door.

"Don't forget to get the hex wrench," Crow said.

Lance waved and skateboarded around the corner to Crab's house, the third one down.

He rang the doorbell and Mr. Shaw answered with a napkin tucked into his collar.

"Well, hello there Lance, we're having dinner right now, so--"

"Oh, I'm sorry Mr. Shaw. I was just in the neighborhood and thought I'd stop by to see how Crab's doctor visit went."

Mr. Shaw leaned out the door and looked up and down the street. "Where's the rest of the musketeers."

"You mean Crow and Roach? I don't know. I don't think Crow's got the van running yet. It got messed up when it got towed."

"Hey Lance, what's up?" Crab stepped in front of his dad. "Check it out." He held up his hands and the big bandages were gone, just his fingers were wrapped.

"Wow, you're almost healed."

Mrs. Shaw joined them in the doorway. "Why hello Lance. We're having dinner, have you eaten?"

"Uh...no ma'am."

"Well, why don't you join us."

Lance dropped the skateboard on the front porch and followed them in. Crab's little brother Timmy sat at the table in a booster seat and his sister Kathy was in a highchair. Timmy stuck his tongue out at Lance as he sat down. Mrs. Shaw got him a plate.

"Help yourself Lance there's plenty, here's some rolls." She handed him a basket.

"This looks great, I've never had white spaghetti sauce before."

"It's clam linguini," Crab said. "You'll like it, it's like clam chowder on noodles."

"I don't like it," said Timmy.

Lance looked at Timmy's plate, there were two noodles and three peas.

"Timmy, eat your noodles." Mr. Shaw looked at his wife. "Can't he eat two damn noodles? How many rolls has he eaten? He's going to turn into the Pillsbury Dough Boy."

Lance shoveled his food knowing Crow and Roach were waiting; he sopped up the clam sauce with his bread.

"My goodness Lance you must've been starving, would you like more?"

"Oh, no thank you Mrs. Shaw, I'm stuffed. That was great." He drank the last of his milk. "Hey Crab, you want to go skateboard the wave behind the market?"

"You care if I go Mom?"

"Oh, I don't mind. Just be careful, it seems like everyday you come home with more bumps and scratches."

"Thanks Mom." Crab slid his chair out. "I gotta take a whiz and get my skateboard."

"Mikey, I don't want to hear that kind of language." His mom said picking up the empty plates.

"Thanks again Mrs. Shaw…that clam stuff was good." Lance waited for Mr. Shaw to finish taking a sip of his beer.

"Mr. Shaw, do you think I could borrow a three-eighths inch hex wrench while we're skateboarding?"

Mr. Shaw's face lit up. Lance knew he was proud of his tool collection.

220

"A hex wrench, you mean an Allen wrench? Sure, what do you need it for?"

"My skateboard keeps loosening up and I forgot to bring one."

"I'll get it for you. Three-eighths inch...you need me to take a look at your skateboard?"

"Oh no, I know what the problem is, thanks though."

"Just be sure and have Mike bring it home, it belongs to a set."

"I will, thank you sir."

Lance and Crab skated down the driveway and at the bottom Lance turned right.

"Where you going? It's this way," Crab said. "Hey, is that the Turd?"

Crow started the engine before they opened the door.

"Where the hell have you guys been?"

"My mom invited Lance in for dinner."

"Damn, I wish I'd have gone to get you," Roach said. "What'd you have?"

"Clam linguini," Lance said rubbing his stomach.

"Did you get the wrench?" Crow asked.

Lance held it up.

"Oh no," Crab said, "don't tell me we're going to do the laundromat thing?"

"Yeah, what's wrong with that?"

"It just seems like no matter what we do something goes wrong."

"Don't worry," Lance said, "things are getting better. The Turd's running, your bandages are almost off, I'm gettin' my board back, and we're about to score some serious cash."

Roach rubbed his hands together. "Let's hope so."

The van rolled side to side as Crow turned into the shopping center parking lot. "Nobody's there, let's hurry."

Crab frowned. "Can we get in trouble for this?"

"For what?" Roach said. "Picking up lost change?"

Crow turned around in his seat. "If anybody gets suspicious I'll just say my mom lost her wedding ring and we're looking for it."

Roach slapped him on the shoulder. "That's good."

They walked across the parking lot and Lance pushed open the laundromat door. It smelled of soap and lint.

Crow went straight for the second machine.

"Go easy this time," Roach said.

Crow inserted the wrench into the cap and gave it a tug, the cap turned. "It's coming."

They all leaned in. "Back off, give me some room to work here." Crow unscrewed the cap and handed it to Roach. He pulled on the agitator. It didn't move. He pulled on it again, nothing. "Damn."

"Do it again," Roach said. Crow pulled and Roach hit the base of the agitator with his fist, it popped up.

Crow lifted the agitator off and underneath was a circular crevice lined with coins. Lance and Roach scrambled to dig out the change.

"Hey," Crow said. "We need to be organized. Let Roach get this one. Lance, you get the next one. You guys can alternate. Crab keep an eye out for cops or anybody coming. If somebody does come, remember we're looking for my mom's ring. When we're done we'll divide the money four ways."

"Not yet," Lance protested. "First, we get the whiskey, then you and me pay Dennis back, then we start splitting it four ways."

"No way, I'm not paying your debts." Roach echoed from inside the washer drum.

"This was my plan."

222

"Lance is right," said Crow. "It's his plan, and you guys should help pay for the Turd fiasco." He went to work on the next machine; unscrewed the cap and pounded out the agitator.

Lance bent into the machine. The coins were wedged into the trap, and he had to pick them out one and two at a time. "Seventy-two cents," he called out as he stuffed the coins into his pocket. He replaced the agitator and screwed the cap back on. He walked past Roach bent in the next machine as Crow pounded out another agitator.

"Woo-hoo," Roach called out. "Dollar forty-three."

"Keep it down," Crab said. "A guy from the fish 'n chip's place just came over and looked in."

The heavier Lance's pants got with wet coins the lighter he felt.

They got eleven of the twelve machines open and while Lance filled his pockets with the coins from the last washing machine, Crow gave that first stubborn machine another shot.

His adrenaline flowing, Lance jumped onto the washing machines with his pockets bulging. He pounded his chest like Tarzan and walked across the tops of the machines. At the back of the laundromat was a soda pop machine. "Hey Crab, you want a soda?"

"Sure, get me root beer."

Lance jumped down holding his pockets to keep his pants up. He pulled out a handful of coins and plucked out five nickels. He slipped them into the slot, yanked out a bottle of root beer and plugged the machine with five more nickels.

"I got it," Crow called out unscrewing the cap of the first machine. He pulled off the agitator and Roach bent in.

"There's at least two bucks in here!"

"All right, let's get out of here," Crab said.

"Wait," said Crow. "I say we count it here. It'll be a lot easier than in the dark van." He pointed to the folding tables.

"Good idea," Roach said. "Let's get a soda and start counting."

"What if somebody comes?" Crab complained.

"So what?" said Roach. "What's some lady gonna care if we're standing here counting change?"

Lance and Roach emptied their pockets onto the folding table and made four piles of coins.

"Do quarters and dimes in dollar stacks, nickels in twenty-five cent stacks and pennies in ten cent stacks," Crow said.

Lance picked out the quarters first and stacked those. He counted a dollar seventy-five. He moved to dimes--a dollar ninety. He started stacking nickels, "Who wants another soda, I'm buying." They all raised their hands and continued counting. Lance grabbed four stacks of nickels and went to the vending machine. He got four sodas and with two bottles in each hand he turned and saw a man enter the laundromat. The man was bald with keys hanging from his belt. He glared at the boys counting change. Lance put the bottles on the table and began stuffing stacks of change into his pockets and whispered, "Somebody's here, I think we gotta go."

"Where'd you boys get that money?" The man said narrowing his eyes.

Crow grinned. "We were looking for my mom's ring and we found some change."

"Any change you found here belongs to this establishment."

They hurried to stuff coins in their pockets. Crab struggled with his bandaged fingers and coins dropped on the floor.

"Stop right there," the man demanded.

"It's not your money," Roach said. "It's money people lost."

"It's my property. Now stop or I'll have to call the police."

224

An aisle of back-to-back washing machines separated them. Lance figured the guy wanted to stay closer to the door in case they tried to run. He stuck his finger into his root beer bottle in case they did.

Crow scraped the last couple stacks of pennies on the table into his hand and said, "Okay mister, we don't want any trouble. I'm keeping my mom's ring though."

"Sorry sonny, I can't let you do that." Seeing Crow's cooperation the man eased toward them from around the machines. "If your mom lost a ring here she'll have to come down and claim it."

Crow sifted through the pennies in his hand as if looking for the ring. "Okay, but don't lose it." Crow stepped forward holding his hand out then tossed the coins in the man's face.

"Run!" Crow yelled. The man shielded his eyes as pennies rained down on the machines and floor.

Lance ran behind Roach as Crow hit the door. They were suddenly out of the florescent light and in the dark parking lot. "Split up," Crow yelled.

Lance ran between the parked cars and looked back, he saw Crab still inside jockeying around the washing machines with the man. Across the lot Crow was standing by the Turd with the door open.

"I'm going back for Crab," Lance called.

When he pushed the door open the bottle still attached to his finger tapped loudly on the glass. The man looked surprised and stepped back. Lance swung the hand with the bottle and hollered, "Go Crab!" The man moved toward him and Lance popped his finger from the bottle shooting a gush of root beer into the man's face. He flung the bottle over his shoulder and rushed out behind Crab. Over the man's cursing he heard glass shatter.

They ran into the parking lot and the Turd drove past with the side door open. They jumped in, Crow hit the gas and Roach slammed the door closed. Crow sped onto Thompson Boulevard and veered into the left lane through the five points intersection onto Telegraph Road.

Roach climbed into the passenger seat. "Damn, that was close."

"The fish 'n chips guy must've called him," Crab said.

Crow looked back in the rearview mirror. "How the hell'd you guys get outta there."

"Easy," Crab said, "Lance came in, blasted the guy with root beer and we ran."

They giggled like a bunch of girls.

36
BOB'S BIG BOY HAMBURGERS

"Hey, Bob's Big Boy's up here, I say we get burgers and reorganize." Roach said.

"Yeah, we gotta rethink this and I'm starved," said Crow. He looked back. "You guys can just get something to drink if you're not hungry."

Crab and Lance looked at each other. "No way, we're eatin'."

In the restaurant they cupped their hands over the coins in their pockets to keep them from jingling as they followed the waitress to a round booth in the back. She laid out their menus.

"Can I get you gentlemen anything to drink?"

"Coffee, please," Crow said.

"Make that two," said Roach.

She looked at Lance and Crab. "Anything for you boys?"

"Uh, sure, I'll have coffee," Lance said.

Crab scowled. "Coffee? I want a vanilla milkshake."

"Me too," Lance said. "Coffee and a chocolate shake."

"I'll have strawberry," said Roach.

Crow nodded. "Chocolate for me."

She smiled. "Okay, I'll get the shakes started and be back with the coffee."

Crow watched her walk away then leaned forward. "We need to count the money again and see exactly how much we have."

They dug the coins from their pockets and spilled them onto the table. They began stacking.

The waitress came back with the coffee and raised an eyebrow. "You boys break into your piggy banks for a big night out?"

They looked at each other.

She flashed a grin. "Just promise you won't tip me in pennies. I'll come back with your milkshakes and get your order."

Lance grabbed the sugar dispenser. "I forgot about the tip, how much do we have to leave?"

"Don't get out much, do ya?" Roach said watching Lance pour the sugar. "Hey, you having coffee with that sugar? Save some for us."

"Ten percent is normal," Crow said stacking dimes, "less if they're crappy."

"Ten percent of what?" Crab asked.

"Of the bill, Fig Newton," Roach replied,.

The waitress came back with their milkshakes, each one piled high with whipped cream and a cherry. Lance plucked the cherry off his and popped it into his mouth.

"So, what can I get for you boys?"

"Big Boy Combo's all around," Crow said.

"And what dressing for your salads?"

"You guys should try ranch if you haven't had it," Roach recommended.

"No way, I like bleu cheese," Crab said.

"I can get you a side of both if you'd like to try it," she offered.

"Really? Thanks." Crab handed her his menu.

"I'll be back to refill your coffees."

Roach leaned in. "That's the great thing about coffee, they keep refilling it."

Crab sat back. "She's definitely ten percent."

Crow spooned whipped cream into his mouth. "We need to get a few things straight. The next laundromat, we get in, we get out. No sodas, no counting coins, no horsing around." He looked at Lance. "Okay Tarzan?"

Lance slurped his milkshake and nodded.

228

"After this we'll go to *Sears* and get three hex wrenches. Crab, you cool with being lookout?"

"I guess."

"We need to be professional," Crow said.

Roach saluted. "Aye, aye Cap'n Crunch."

Lance took a dime from his pile. "Let me out, I gotta call my mom and let her know I won't be home for dinner."

Roach slid out of the booth and Lance walked to the pay phone.

"Hey Mom, it's me. We're at Bob's Big Boy, I'm gonna eat here."

"Who's paying for it?"

"Oh, Crow's taking us out to celebrate getting his van running."

"Well, that's nice of him. What time will you be home?"

"I don't know, we're going skateboarding at the Holiday Inn parking lot after this."

"Don't you have homework?"

"No--I gotta go Mom, I think our food's coming."

Back at the table he found the guys quietly sipping their drinks. Roach got up to let him in and Lance slid into the booth. "What's going on? Why are you guys so quiet?"

"Nothing's going on," Roach said. "Why are you so paranoid?"

Lance saw that his coffee had been refilled. "You guys are acting funny."

"The only thing funny around here is your face," Crow said. "Hey, here comes our burgers."

Lance pushed his pile of coins aside.

The waitress set a coffee pot on the table and dealt the plates. "Four combinations, one with dressings on the side. Anybody need more coffee?"

"I could use a little more," Roach said.

She topped off his cup and left them to their double cheeseburgers.

"Dip your fries in the ranch," Roach said. "It's better than ketchup, I bet those hobos have never had ranch."

"Man, they'd freak out over a meal like this," Lance said.

Crab picked up his burger. "They wouldn't even need menus, they could just drink the ketchups and eat the gum off the bottom of the tables."

"Hey, we wouldn't even be here right now if wasn't for them." Lance raised his milkshake. "I say we drink a toast to John Bear."

Crow raised his shake. "To John Bear, laundromats, and more buried treasure."

They clinked their milkshakes.

Lance dipped a fry into his ranch and followed it with a mouthful of double cheeseburger.

"So, what do those hobos eat?" Roach asked.

Crab put down his burger and wiped his mouth. "They were cooking feline fricassee yesterday."

Lance tossed another fry in his mouth. "It's like cat stew."

"Whoa, they eat cats?" Roach laughed.

Crow held up his hand to speak as he swallowed. "There's lots of places in the world where people eat cats."

"Sure, people who're starving," Crab said.

Crow continued. "My dad got served cat in the Philippines when he was in the Navy. A guy invited him over for dinner and they cooked the family cat in his honor."

Roach sat back. "I wonder what it tastes like."

"John Bear says it tastes like something between chicken and squirrel."

230

Roach reached for the sugar jar. "I'd try it." He tipped the jar over his coffee and the lid splashed into his cup spilling coffee and sugar over the table. "Crap!"

Crow and Crab burst out laughing. Crab looked at Lance. "That was meant for you."

Roach stood up and grabbed napkins from the dispenser. "Damn, it backfired."

Lance held his napkin to the edge of the table to stop the dribbling. "That's what you get for trying to booby-trap me."

The commotion attracted the waitress' attention and she came over with a wet towel. "Do we have a spill?"

She looked at the mess, picked up the cup and put down the towel. Lance and Roach's coins were bathing in coffee and sugar. Her smile turned to disgust. "I have a three year old at home that doesn't make such a mess." She called to a busboy, "I'll need more towels over here."

She wiped the table and put the bill between the salt and peppershakers. "I'd appreciate it if you boys could finish your meal like adults."

They finished eating in silence and Crow stuffed his last fry into his mouth then picked up the bill. "Twelve eighty-five. How much do we have?"

"Thirteen-thirty," Crab said. "How much does that leave for a tip?"

"Not much," said Roach.

They walked to the register and Crow put the bill on the counter. The waitress punched the amounts into the machine. "Twelve eighty-five."

Roach stepped up with the coins in the belly of his shirt. He spilled them onto the counter. "It's all there and the tip too. We wanted it to be more."

She waved them away. "That's fine, just go."

As they walked out Lance turned to her. "You might want to rinse those, some of 'em are kind of sticky."

37
SURF LIQUOR

The next day after school Crow, Roach, Lance and Crab piled into the Turd and headed to the Bank of America on Main Street. Crow had five dollars in a savings account there. Last night after Bob's Big Boy they'd hit a laundromat on Telegragh Road, then bought three hex wrenches at Sears and hit another laundromat on Main Street. Crow parked behind the bank and took a sack full of coins inside to exchange for paper money. He returned with the coins and a handful of paper coin rolls.

"She said we've got to separate the coins into these rolls before I can cash 'em in." Crow dumped the change onto the floor in the back of the van and they began separating them and filling the rolls. Crow took the rolled coins back into the bank and exchanged them for two tens and four ones.

They drove down Seaward Avenue to Surf Liquor where Crow pulled into the Mohawk gas station on the corner of Seaward and Pierpont. "I'll get gas then park in the alley behind the liquor store."

Lance opened the side door and he and Crab jumped out with their skateboards.

"Remember," Roach said, "don't ask anybody who might be a narc."

"Yeah, yeah, don't worry, we'll find a cool old lady to do it." Lance dropped his skateboard and he and Crab pushed across the gas station to the small cement wave on the side of the liquor store. Lance hit the little embankment hard, came off the top backside and laid into a cutback. His composite wheels screeched as the board slid out and he hit the cement.

Crab came around in a sweeping turn and stopped next to a palm tree growing from a square bed cut in the sidewalk. "How much total do you think we made last night?"

Lance checked his pants for holes as he got up. "Uh...let's see, we just cashed in twenty-four bucks at the bank, we spent thirteen somethin' last night at Bob's, the hex wrenches cost thirty-seven cents each. Then whatever Crow threw at that guy in the first laundromat, and whatever you dropped--"

"I didn't drop that much."

"I'd say forty bucks, easy."

"Wow, three laundromats and forty smackers. We may never have to get real jobs. I can't wait 'til we start splittin' the money."

"Me too. Maybe tonight. Hey look, this dude looks cool." A guy with curly hair and round shades was coming up the sidewalk.

Lance picked up his skateboard and stepped into the guy's path. "Hey man, you think you could buy us a bottle of whiskey?"

"Whoa man, aren't you guys a little young to be hittin' the booze?"

"It's not for us, we owe it to somebody. We need a six pack of beer too."

"What's in it for me?"

"I don't know what do you want?"

"How much money you got?"

"Ten bucks."

The guy looked up and down the street. "A six pack for me and I'll do it."

"Is there enough for that?"

"Yeah, I can make it work."

Lance looked at Crab. Crab nodded.

234

"Okay," Lance said.

"All right, give me the money." The guy looked around. "Hurry up and don't be obvious."

Lance dug the ten out of his pocket. "We'll be in the alley in a brown van with surf racks, you can't miss it."

"Yeah, yeah, I'll come find ya."

The guy disappeared around the corner.

Crab put his skateboard down. "How come you're gettin' beer too?"

"Insurance, I wanna make sure I get my board back."

Lance and Crab skated around the back of the liquor store to the van.

"What happened, where's the stuff?" Crow asked.

"The guy's in there gettin' it right now."

"And you left?"

"Yeah, what was I supposed to do, stand there pickin' my nose?" Lance sat on the edge of the open van and leaned on the door.

"You saw him go in, right?"

"No, I figured he could find the door."

Crow pounded the steering wheel. "The guy might've split."

"Go look inside just in case," Roach said.

Lance skateboarded to the front of the store and peeked in the window. There was no one at the beer cooler or at the front counter. The man working the register was reading a magazine.

He skated back to the van. "He's gone! Quick, drive down Pierpont, maybe we can catch him."

"Son-of-a-bitch," Roach said.

Crow drove down Pierpont and they looked down every lane until the street dead-ended at the north jetty of the marina. "Well, that sucks."

"Ten bucks down the tubes," Roach said.

235

Crow cranked a u-turn. "Now we gotta spend the other ten."

"Hey," Lance said. "There's another laundromat next to the Big T supermarket."

Roach looked at Crow. "Let's do it."

A few minutes later Crow parked the Turd in front of the Sandy Laundromat next to Big T. "All right, let's make this quick."

"Hey, that's my sister's old boyfriend in there reading the paper. He could buy for us."

"He's old enough?"

"Yeah, I saw him buy beer before. I'll ask him."

Lance walked into the laundromat. "Hey Alan, what's going on?"

Alan put down his magazine and smiled. "Lancelot, what's shakin'?"

"We just pulled up and I saw you in here, I miss you coming over to see Jean."

"Yeah, me too. I was bummed when she moved to San Diego."

"Hey man, can you do me a favor?"

"Uh...sure...what?"

* * * *

A few minutes later Lance opened the laundromat door and waved the guys in from the van.

Alan shook hands with Crow. "So, this story about Lance needing whiskey to get his surfboard back is true?"

"Yep, we're headin' down to Hobo Jungle as soon as we get the booze."

"All right, it just sounded a little weird. I don't wanna be contributing to Lance's delinquency." Alan winked at Lance.

236

Roach handed Alan a ten dollar-bill. "Just get a fifth of something cheap."

"And two bottles of ketchup too," Lance said.

Alan left the laundromat and headed to Big T. Before the boys could get out their hex wrenches a man came in through the back door with a tool box and placed it on a machine that had an Out of Order sign on it. They groaned and went back to the van to wait.

"What the hell could be taking him so long?" Roach said. "You sure you didn't give our money to another thief?"

"No way, Alan's cool."

"Here he comes." Crow leaned out his window. "Hey, over here!"

Alan came up to the window. "Sorry man, they took my fake I.D., I only got the ketchup." He handed the sack to Crow.

"You're not twenty-one?"

"Not for a few months. I used to have all the information memorized, but nobody ever asked. The lady called the manager and they threatened to call the cops. It was probably because I was buying whiskey in the middle of the day."

"Man, that sucks," Lance said.

"Here's the change."

Crow and Roach looked at each other then back at Alan. "Keep two bucks, man," Crow said. "Sorry for the hassle."

"Thanks." He started back to the laundromat then turned. "Hey Lance, tell Jean I said hi."

"I will."

"What a drag," Roach said.

Suddenly there was a tap on the side window and someone was peeking through the curtains.

Lance slid the side door open. "Hey, you're the dude that took off from the liquor store with our money."

"What are you talkin' about man? I came out and you guys were gone. I sat there and drank a beer in case you came back."

"You did?"

"Yeah. Then I happened to be walking home this way and saw the brown van with racks."

"I looked in the store and you weren't there," Lance said. "I thought you took off."

"I had to take a leak, I was using the toilet. Anyway, here's your stuff." He held up a grocery bag.

Crow shook his head. "Hey man, get in, we'll give you a ride."

38
BACK TO HOBO JUNGLE

The sun was getting low over the ocean as they drove down Harbor Boulevard toward the Ventura River. Crow parked the Turd on Main Street at the south end of the bridge over the river. "How far is it from here?"

"It's on the other side of the railroad trestle." Lance rolled up the top of the grocery bag and they all climbed out of the van.

The ocean breeze blew in their faces and the sun glared in their eyes as they walked along the levee toward the trestle. Ahead, a black cat licked its paw; it stopped, watched them coming then dashed into the river bottom.

When they crossed the railroad tracks Lance saw smoke rising from the overgrowth. "There's the camp."

Starting down the embankment Lance stopped at the crook where the trestle met the bank. "I say we stash the whiskey here, then when we've got my board we bring 'em back here, out of their territory to make the final transaction." He put the whiskey wrapped in its own brown paper bag amongst the other garbage and covered it.

* * * *

Meanwhile, inside the camp Cricket leaned back on a log puffing a cigar butt while John Bear scrubbed an iron skillet with salt water and sand. Stewart cleaned a bonita Cricket had found washed up on the shoreline. He dangled fish guts over the three cats clawing at his pant legs and chucked the guts into the bushes. The cats hissed and scratched after them.

John Bear brought the pan over to the fire. "It's going to be a feast tonight fellas. How's that cigar, Cricket?"

Cricket blew out a puff of blue smoke. "Damn good one."

"Damn right it is. I found it in the ashcan outside the Sportsman Bar last night. The chewed end was still wet, that's how fresh it was." John Bear set the pan on the grate over the fire.

Stew tossed the fishtail and head in the direction of the cats then stuck two fingers into a can of animal fat and wiped it around the pan. He flopped in the bonita and wiped his hands on his pants.

"Sssshhh, you hear that?" John Bear whispered. "Somebody's coming."

A voice called out, "Hey John Bear... Cricket... it's me Lance, we've got the stuff."

John Bear's eyes widened. "Come on in boys, we been waitin' for ya."

"I hope they brought more ketchup," Stew said.

"They'd better of brought the whiskey." Cricket spit and puffed on his cigar.

* * * *

Lance led his friends into the clearing and saw John Bear standing by the fire pit wearing his smoking jacket. Stew stood next to him and Cricket was on the ground leaning against a log smoking a cigar.

"Well, hello there," John Bear said. "We're just cookin' up some dinner. Whaddaya got for us?"

Cricket stood up and dropped the cigar butt on the ground. He twisted it out with his foot. "You bring whiskey?"

"We brought it," Lance said. "And a six pack of beer." He held up a bag. "Not to mention a couple a bottles of ketchup."

"All in that bag?" John Bear asked.

"No, this is just the ketchup."

"Well, where's the rest of it?" Cricket snarled.

"Not so fast pal," Roach said. "You're not gettin' anything until we have his surfboard."

John Bear held up his hands. "Easy gentlemen. There's no reason for hostility. This is a friendly negotiation." He looked at Roach. "I don't believe we've had the pleasure."

"That's Roach," Lance said. "And this is Crow. You remember Crab."

"Nice to meet you boys. And these are my associates, Stewart and Cricket." John Bear rubbed his hands together. "So, where's the whiskey and beer?"

"Not until we get the surfboard," Crow repeated.

"No offense John Bear," said Lance, "but shouldn't we be dealing with Cricket?"

"Oh, it's fine son. We split everything three ways. Cricket does the findin', I do the negotiatin' and Stewart does the cookin'. Right fellas?"

Cricket spit and Stew nodded.

"All right then." Lance held out the bag. "Here's the ketchup, get my surfboard and we'll get the beer."

"What about the whiskey?" said Cricket.

"We stashed it on the way here. You give me my board and we'll give you the beer, then we'll take you to the whiskey."

John Bear handed the ketchup to Stew. "Fix up the fish with this." Then he nodded to Cricket. "Get him his surfboard."

Cricket pointed to an opening across the camp. "In there. Go get it."

Lance walked across the camp and looked inside the dark hollow. He could see his board lying on the ground to one side. He stepped in and was almost knocked over by the smell. "It's their crapper!" he called out. He held his breath and continued in, grabbed his board and hurried out to fresh air.

The board was dirty and there were a few new shatters, but over-all it looked in good shape. "Get 'em the beer Crab."

Crab ran out of the camp and returned with the bag. He handed it to John Bear.

John Bear sat down on a log and pulled out the six-pack. "These are still cold." He gave one to Cricket and one to Stew. "Take it slow and easy boys." John Bear yanked off the pull-tab and took three big gulps. He followed it with a rumbling three-gulp burp.

"Now that's a fine malt beverage."

"We should get going now," Crow said.

"Yeah, I gotta get home," Crab added.

"Now, hold on there. It's you boys who busted in here at our dinner hour and that fish is about done."

"It is done," Stew said as he pulled the pan from the fire while taking a swig of beer.

John Bear took three more gulps and tossed his can into the bag. "You boys sit down and converse with us while we enjoy our repast."

Lance looked at his friends. "Come on, we can stay for a minute." Lance set his surfboard against the end of the log and sat down facing the bums.

Stew came over with the skillet and sat between John Bear and Cricket. He put the pan on the ground. The fish was covered in ketchup and they each tore off meat and stuffed it into their mouths. John Bear handed out the last three cans of beer. "Well, how about some conversation." He took a big gulp of beer and washed down the fish. "You boys like beer?"

"Not that kind," Roach said.

John Bear looked at the can. "What's wrong with this kind?"

"It's malt liquor."

John Bear looked at Stew then Cricket. "How 'bout that boys, a connoisseur."

Roach slouched. "No, I just don't like malt liquor."

"Well," John Bear smiled, "that's unfortunate for you. Every beer I drink is the best I've ever had." He held up the can and admired it, then took another swig. "One of the many beauties of livin' down here is takin' nothin' for granted."

"You act like you like living down here?" Crow said looking around the camp.

"Hell yes I do, beats the hell outta livin' in the rat race." John Bear reached for more fish.

"Ah, come on," Roach said, "you wouldn't trade this for a comfortable bed and a refrigerator full of food?"

"They've got plenty of food," Lance argued. "Look at this place, it's deluxe.

"Yeah, they've got it made," Crab added, "and it's all free."

Roach grinned. "Those are some deluxe bathroom facilities."

A railroad horn echoed across the river bottom and the rumble grew quickly before a passenger train sped across the railroad trestle.

John Bear smiled. "This is the way man's meant to live, the way he's always lived, in the open, commingling with nature. I think there's something noble in it--"

"There's nothing noble about scrounging for whatever you can get," Roach interrupted.

John Bear glared at him. "You've got a lot to learn sonny if you think nobody up there's scrounging for what they can get.

243

And believe me, the more they get the more they want, and the less they care who gets stepped on...at least *we're* honest about it." He stopped himself and took his last drink of beer. He crushed the can in his fist and mumbled, "No good crooks is what they are."

"That's enough chatter," Cricket said tossing his empty can. "Let's get the whiskey."

"Yes sir." John Bear stood up. "Good fish, Stewart. Thank you for the beer and ketchup boys. Now, if you could, lead us to the almighty whiskey."

Lance picked up his surfboard and led the group out of the camp. Cricket followed close behind and would have the honor of breaking the seal on the whiskey bottle. It was almost over. Lance turned to Cricket.

"So where'd you find it?"

"Find what?"

"My surfboard, where'd it wash up?"

"On the beach, I don't remember--why you always askin' questions?"

The trestle loomed overhead, they turned the corner and there at the base of the embankment was Red tipping back the whiskey bottle. "No!" Lance shouted.

"Who the hell's that?" Roach cried.

"Get him!" Cricket yelled.

Red jumped up and staggered into the overgrowth.

The three hobos chased after him yelling curses.

Lance clutched his surfboard. "Let's get outta here!"

39
CRICKET

Later that week, after school, Lance paddled into the lineup at the Pier. The waves were good and everybody was out, even Crab, who wore orange Playtex gloves over his bandaged fingers. Crow and Roach rode their bikes down because Crow's mom had taken the keys to the Turd away when she found out he had driven her Mercedes.

It'd been three days since they'd delivered the whiskey to the hobos and already it seemed a distant memory. Thoughts of curses and hobos were over. Crab was healing, the Turd was fixed and Lance had his board. As soon as Crow got the keys back they'd hit some more laundromats and pay off Dennis.

Lance thought he saw a set forming outside and paddled through the pack past everyone. Sure enough, waves were building. He was farthest out and would have his pick of the waves. As the first wave approached he heard McGillis behind him. "This one looks good, you goin'?"

"Nope, it's all yours," Lance called back. He paddled up the face and at the wave's crest surveyed the next three. As he suspected, the third and fourth waves looked best. He stroked hard, but he could hear McGillis close behind. Paddling over the lip of the second wave he saw the third wave already feathering, catching it was out of the question--he just needed to get over it.

"Should've gone," McGillis shouted.

Lance stroked hard up the face of the third wave as it began to throw. He punched through the lip and came out the other side. No way McGillis made it over. He could relax, the last wave was all his.

He turned at the base of the swell and took two hard strokes. He felt the mass lift him and the board accelerate, he jumped to his feet. Sliding down the face he delayed his turn to avoid hitting McGillis stroking up the wave. McGillis lifted his feet as Lance streaked by. He came off the top then crouched forward speeding through the section. On the inside the wave walled up and as a finale he tried to bash the lip and got launched in the shallows. He tucked his head and rolled, bounced off the bottom and popped up laughing. He looked on the beach to see who'd witnessed his wipeout. Bill and Stoody raised their fists in approval.

Lance's board lay fin-side-up near the Pier. He high-stepped from the water excited to get back out. A figure stepped from behind a piling and stood over the board. It was Cricket.

"Hey Cricket, what's going on?"

"You still owe me whiskey," he snarled.

"You didn't get it from Red?"

"No! You didn't deliver and this surfboard's mine 'til you do."

"Oh no, no way. I'll get you another bottle, but you're not taking my board." Lance bent to pick up it up and Cricket slammed his knife into it.

"What the hell are you doing? I said I'd pay!"

"You're damn right you will," Cricket snapped.

"What's going on?" Bill called. He and Stoody were running over.

Cricket pulled the knife from the surfboard and pointed it at Lance. "You get me my whiskey, or else." He backed away, moving up the beach through the pilings.

"Who the hell is that?" Stoody asked.

"Is that one of your hobo friends? He looks crazy." Bill said.

246

"He is crazy." Lance stared at the gash in his surfboard. "Damn him."

Stoody pointed to the water. "Hey, look at the wave Crab's got. It just keeps getting better out there."

Lance picked up his surfboard. "I gotta get some ding tape to put over this. I'll see you guys out there."

By the road Lance saw Cricket looming under the Pier watching him. "I want my goddam whiskey!" Cricket spit. He raised his knife, then turned north toward the promenade and Hobo Jungle.

Lance ran up the dirt hill to the pedestrian bridge, trembling.

* * * *

Dennis was behind the counter in the shop. "Hey Lance, waves are good, huh?"

"Yeah, it's good. Hey, you think I could get some ding tape? I got a gash in my board."

"Ouch, looks like somebody stuck a knife in it. What happened?"

"Oh, it was Crow's fin, he dropped in on me and--"

Dennis raised an eyebrow. "If he dropped in on you why is this gash on the bottom of your board?"

"Well, maybe he wasn't dropping in--"

"Lance, stop jerking me around. I know what a fin gash looks like; this is from a knife. What happened?"

Lance looked down at his sandy bare feet. "A crazy hobo did it. Remember when I told you somebody on Pierpont found my board...I lied." His voice trembled. "Some bums found it and they had it in Hobo Jungle. They wouldn't give it back unless I got 'em some stuff. I did, but now they want more stuff and one of 'em just stabbed my board."

247

"What the hell?" Dennis leaned back on the counter and crossed his arms. "Explain to me exactly what you're talking about."

Lance took a deep breath. "I thought we could just sneak into their camp and get it. I didn't want to say anything because I knew you'd make a big deal about it."

Dennis ran his fingers down his mustache. "Well, I'm glad it hasn't turned into a big deal."

Tears welled up in Lance's eyes. "I don't know why I do the stuff I do...I lied about Crab unstrapping that board, I did it. I just keep screwing up."

Dennis put his hand on Lance's shoulder, "Look Lance, everybody makes mistakes, the key is to learn from them. That's what growing up is."

Lance nodded fighting back tears.

"Look, what's done is done. Why don't you tell me the whole story from the beginning."

Lance took another deep breath and told Dennis how Crab saw his board in the hobo camp, about John Bear and Stew and the ketchup, the thrift store, the laundromats, Surf Liquor, right up to Red drinking the whiskey and Cricket stabbing his board.

"So you've been down to this hobo camp three times?"

"Yeah."

Dennis shook his head. "This is going to end now." He frowned and pointed to the door. "Run over and see if that Cricket guy is still around the Pier. If he is, tell him to wait there, you've got some whiskey for him. I've got a bottle of Jack Daniels my uncle gave me for my birthday. While you're doing that I'll close up. I was going to close early to get some waves anyway."

248

Lance ran over the pedestrian bridge, but Cricket was gone. He ran back to the shop. Dennis was coming down the ladder of the boat with the bottle of Jack Daniels. "You find him?"

"Nope, he's gone."

"How long would it take us to get to the camp?"

"I don't know, fifteen minutes maybe."

"Get in the car."

Lance climbed into the Karmann Ghia, his wetsuit was almost dry. Dennis put the Jack Daniels on Lance's lap and started the engine. He put it in gear and the car bumped onto the pavement.

"Thanks for doing this," Lance said. "The other hobos aren't that bad, you'll like 'em."

Dennis glared at him. "We're not going down there to make friends Lance, we're going down to end to this." He accelerated into a left turn onto Thompson Boulevard.

Lance looked down at the Jack Daniels bottle and nodded. "This would all be over if it wasn't for that stupid Red. He's the one that keeps screwing everything up, the other guys aren't that bad...wait'll you see their camp, it's cool, they've got a deluxe fire pit and all these cats they can eat anytime--"

"Look Lance, this isn't some Huckleberry Finn adventure. These guys are dangerous. You need to get serious. Now let's talk about what we're gonna do."

"Okay, but I'm just saying they're not all that bad."

"Wake up, Lance! One of them just stuck a knife in your surfboard. They're dangerous, you understand?"

Lance nodded and looked down. Through a hole in the floorboard he saw the pavement speeding by. "Yeah, you're right."

40

WHISKEY AND BLOOD

As they walked along the levee Lance could hear the waves breaking in the distance.

"Hear that?" Lance asked.

Dennis smoothed his mustache. "Yeah, let's make this quick so we can get out there."

They crossed the railroad tracks where a black cat lay cut in two. The front paws and head had made it across, but the back half lay between the rails. Lance bent down to take a closer look, he could smell the decay.

Dennis put his hand over his mouth. "Come on, we're missing waves."

Before heading down the embankment Lance checked for smoke from the camp; there was none. He started down and Dennis followed. Lance stopped at the bottom.

"What's the matter?" Dennis asked.

"I was just thinking. You know how in those Dudley Doright cartoons Snidley Whiplash is always tying Dudley Doright's girlfriend to the railroad tracks, did people really do that?"

Dennis frowned. "Are you kidding me?"

"Just think about it, head over here, feet over there."

Dennis gripped Lance's arm. "Dammit Lance, this is serious! Stop messin' around!"

"Okay...sorry. That cat just got me thinkin'." Lance kept quiet until they reached the entrance to the hobo camp. "It's in there, I'll let 'em know we're here." He called out, "Hey John Bear--Cricket--Stew--it's me, Lance."

A voice responded from beyond the reeds. "Come on in Lance, welcome my friend."

Lance led the way into the camp where John Bear stood in his smoking jacket by the spool table.

"Well, I didn't expect to see you back so soon. Who's your friend?"

"This is Dennis."

John Bear squinted at Dennis and rubbed his chin. "Dennis?...you the one who owns the surf shop?"

"Yeah, how'd you know?"

"It's a small town." John Bear looked at the bottle of Jack Daniels in Dennis's hand. "That for us?"

"No," Lance said. "It's for Cricket. He just stuck a knife in my surfboard. He says I still owe him cause the last bottle got broken."

John Bear frowned and nodded. "It got broken all right, Cricket smashed it on Red's skull, it's a wonder he's still alive." John Bear turned and called out, "Hey Stew, we got visitors."

Stew emerged from the toilet area buttoning his pants.

"They brought us Jack Daniels."

Stew's eyes widened and he hurried over. "You open it yet?"

"It's for Cricket," Lance said. "I can't give it to you guys."

"Don't you worry, Lance my boy," John Bear said, "you can be sure he'll get his full share of that."

"No way man, he threatened me."

The waves cracked in the distance and Dennis looked at Lance. "We can't wait around."

Lance turned to John Bear. "Look, he stuck his knife in my board, then pointed it at me. This whiskey needs to get to him."

John Bear scowled and shook his head. "He's taken this way too far. Stewart and I will take full responsibility from here. That bottle is your payment in full. Once we take possession of it, Cricket won't bother you any more. You have my personal guarantee."

Dennis looked at Lance and shrugged. "We don't have much choice." He held the bottle out to John Bear. "You gave us your word."

John Bear grinned and took the bottle with two hands. He squinted at the label. "See here Stew, charcoal filtered." He twisted off the cap and took a swig then handed the bottle to Stew.

"Hey, careful there," Lance said.

Stew handed the bottle back and John Bear took two more big gulps. "Woo wee, that's tasty." He wiped his mouth with his sleeve. "Cricket gets too wound up over things." He took another gulp and handed the bottle back to Stew.

"Okay," Dennis said. "This is in your hands now, we're outta here."

"You guys better slow down with that," Lance said. "Make sure you save some for Cricket."

John Bear grabbed Lance by the arm and pulled him close. "You know, he almost killed him."

Lance twisted from the stench of rotting gums and whiskey. "Huh?"

"Red, Cricket cracked his damn skull."

"I know, you already said that."

Stew took the bottle from his mouth. "It was just like he'd done to Smitty, but Smitty wasn't so lucky."

John Bear turned still holding Lance and took the bottle from Stew. "Enough about Smitty, we don't talk about Smitty."

Dennis knocked John Bear's hand off Lance. "Sorry fellas, we're done here, we gotta go." Dennis turned. "Who's this?"

Cricket stood across the camp surveying the scene, his skin looked gray and his eyes black. He glared at John Bear. "You talkin' about Smitty, drinkin' my whiskey and talkin' about Smitty?"

252

"Hell no, we weren't talkin' about nuthin'. Come get some whiskey."

Cricket pulled the knife from his belt and walked toward John Bear.

Lance and Dennis stepped back.

John Bear held out the bottle. "Look here, it's Jack Daniels, the rest is for you."

Cricket took the whiskey and guzzled what was left. He smashed the bottle on the rocks around the fire pit.

John Bear stepped back. "What'd you do that for? You got glass all over the place."

"What'd you tell 'em?" Cricket said pointing the knife at John Bear.

"We didn't tell 'em anything." John Bear moved away. "Put that thing down."

Stew crept behind the giant spool.

"They didn't tell us anything," Lance said.

"Shut up! I'm not talkin' to you." Cricket swiped the knife at John Bear.

John Bear staggered and fell. Cricket went at him, John Bear kicked to keep him away.

"We didn't say anything, I swear to ya," John Bear gasped.

Lance looked to Dennis.

Cricket stuck the knife into the hard sole of John Bear's wingtip shoe.

John Bear cried out, "We didn't say anything, tell him Stew."

Lance picked up a burnt log from the fire pit.

Cricket yanked the knife from John Bear's shoe. John Bear rolled and Lance threw the log. It spun end over end and struck Cricket in the back. Cricket turned, his eyes were glazed and his mouth agape like a rabid dog.

Dennis picked up the broken Jack Daniels crown. "Relax mister, nobody wants to get hurt!"

Cricket came at Dennis, they circled around with their weapons out. Behind them John Bear crawled to the bushes.

Cricket swiped at Dennis.

"Leave him alone!" Lance yelled and picked up the iron skillet from the grill.

"Stay back Lance," Dennis ordered.

Cricket lunged at Dennis. Dennis jumped back and stumbled to the ground. Blood streamed from his arm.

"No!" Lance screamed. He raised the frying pan and ran at Cricket.

Cricket turned panting. He pointed the knife and hissed, "I'll send you all to hell." Suddenly a rock careened off Cricket's head. His eyes rolled back and he dropped to his knees. The knife fell from his hand and he toppled face first at Lance's feet. Lance watched blood pool and spill over from a dent in Cricket's skull. He looked up and saw Red standing motionless, a second rock dropped from his hand.

"Jesus Christ," Dennis said tossing the Jack Daniels crown into the fire pit.

Tears filled Lance's eyes. He looked at the blood on Dennis's arm. "Are you okay?"

"Yeah, it's not deep."

John Bear stumbled toward them from the bushes. "You fellas should get outta here."

Dennis grabbed Lance's arm and they stepped around Cricket and past Red. Lance saw blood caked in Red's matted hairline.

They hurried from the river bottom to Dennis' car and drove in silence back to the shop. Dennis unlocked the door and went to the back room. He came out with a first aid kit and tossed

Lance a roll of ding tape. "Let's get bandaged up and get in the water."

Tears welled up in Lance's eyes again. "I'm sorry...I didn't expect any of this...I'm sorry."

"I know you didn't. It's over Lance, let's just go surfing and clear our heads."

"I can't surf right now, I don't feel good."

Dennis took him by the shoulders and looked him in the eyes. "Look, what happened down there was heavy, but we're here now and we're safe. We can sit around and dwell on all the what-ifs, or we can get in the water. There's waves and I'm telling you, it's the best therapy."

Lance put a strip of ding tape over the gash in his board. "What are we going to tell everybody?"

"Nothing, for now. You go get in the water. I'll be down after I get bandaged up."

Lance picked up his board and walked out the door, he felt nauseated.

41
CAL

Lance left the Surf Shop and walked over the pedestrian bridge. He couldn't shake the image of Cricket's broken skull. If Red hadn't shown up it probably would've been him lying there. He felt sick.

He looked down from the bridge at his friends in the water, small black dots huddled together. A wave was rising on the outside and they moved as a pack toward it. He came down the dirt hill and saw Crab running toward him.

"Lance, what took you so long, the waves are insane. I heard Cricket stabbed your board. Where you been?"

"I had to get some ding tape," he said flatly.

"You don't look so good."

Lance's stomach churned and his head was spinning. He dropped to his knees in the sand and laid his board down. "I think I'm gonna get sick."

"Whoa man, what's wrong?"

Lance vomited.

"Oh no, Lance, get up, get up man, we gotta go!"

"It's cool, I'll be down in a minute, you go ahead."

"No Lance, behind you, we gotta go, it's that Souther. Get up."

Lance spit, a string of mucous hung from his mouth. He turned and saw Cal coming around from the passenger side of the white El Camino. Lance wiped his mouth. "Crab, take my board and run."

Crab picked up the surfboard and back peddled away.

"Well, if it isn't Heckle and Jeckle."

256

"Leave him alone, he's sick," Crab called out.

"Ahh, the punk doesn't feel good?"

Lance, still down on all fours, started to get up and felt a violent blow to his ribs. He fell onto his back in the sand.

"You think that was funny unstrapping my board? You're not laughing now, are you asshole?"

Lance felt another kick to the ribs. He groaned and rolled onto his stomach. Clutching the sand he raised himself to his knees.

"You're making this too easy, punk."

Cal cocked his leg back and Lance hurled sand into his face.

"You son-of-a-bitch!" Cal covered his eyes and bent over spitting sand. "Josh, get him!"

Josh leaned against the idling El Camino with his arms crossed.

"Stay right there, Josh," Dennis said standing at the top of the dirt hill in his wetsuit and holding his surfboard.

Cal straightened trying to open his eyes. "That you Dennis?"

"Leave the kid alone Cal."

"This is none of your business, we're not in your neutral territory now," Cal said.

Dennis came down the hill and stood between Lance and Cal. "You're done here Cal, time for you to split."

"What's your problem man, the kid's gotta pay."

"I've already charged him forty bucks for the repairs."

"Well, that's great for you, but it doesn't do shit for me."

"Life isn't always fair Cal."

"Look man, you may think you're hot crap in this podunk town, but you don't tell me what to do."

Dennis put his board down. "You don't want to mess with me right now Cal."

"Or me," Crab said stepping up next to Dennis."

"Oh Jesus. Josh, get over here and hold Dennis while I finish up these punks."

Josh shook his head. "Sorry Cal, this is your deal."

"Dammit Josh, get over here, you saw what they did to my board!"

Josh leaned back on the El Camino and crossed his legs. "Yeah, and they didn't touch mine. You gotta big mouth Cal."

Cal looked at Dennis, his eyes watery and red from the sand. "Don't expect me to drop another dime in your rat hole shop."

McGillis walked up dripping holding his surfboard. "What's going on here?"

"Nothing," Dennis said. "These guys are just leaving."

Josh opened the car door and got in. "Come on Cal, I think you're done here."

Lance got up and brushed the sand from his wetsuit. "Hey McGillis, he's the guy with the blue board that cut you off that day during the Santa Ana's. Remember?"

McGillis stabbed his board in the sand and approached Cal. "I've been lookin' for you asshole."

Josh put the car in gear and leaned out the window. "Better jump in back Cal."

Cal ran after the car and McGillis ran after Cal. Cal dove into the bed of the El Camino and it sped away.

McGillis punched his hand over his head and walked back triumphant.

Dennis said, "I was trying to set an example here."

McGillis picked up his board. "So was I."

Lance picked up his surfboard, he felt a dull ache in his ribs. Emotionally he was drained, his anxiety gone. He followed Crab and Dennis to the water.

Paddling into the lineup felt like the most natural thing in the world. He paddled past everyone and sat farthest outside, alone.

258

"Hey Lance, whaddaya waiting for, a tidal wave?" Ringlets teased.

He turned and watched as his friends scanned the horizon for the next wave. He looked beyond them to the sandpipers on the shoreline scurrying toward the water, burying their bills in the sand before being chased up the beach by the next wave. He thought about John Bear and Stew and Red. He wondered how many times a similar scene had gone down in Hobo Jungle. He wondered about Cricket lying in the dirt.

He looked at the people on the Pier strolling and fishing. Seagulls soared overhead, squawking, searching for scraps. A swell rose up beneath him, it was a wave he should've caught. He laughed out loud and watched as his friends scrambled for it. Tears welled up in his eyes again and he turned to the orange sun setting on the horizon. He was so damn lucky.

42

SAFE AT HOME

Lance couldn't shake the thought of himself, or Dennis, lying dead in Hobo Jungle.

"Lance, what's the matter?" his mom asked, "you haven't touched your dinner."

He looked up from his plate. "Oh nothing...I guess I'm not that hungry."

"Not hungry, you?" his dad chuckled, "we better check your temperature."

"It's no big deal, I'm just not that hungry."

"I bet it's a girl," Ann teased.

His mom frowned. "A girl? He's not interested in girls yet, are you Lance?"

He rolled his eyes.

His mom's face hardened. "Lance, did you get into a fight today?"

He fidgeted in his chair. "Uh, kind of." *How does she know this stuff?*

She clutched her napkin. "Are you all right?"

"Yeah, I'm fine."

"How do you *kind of* get into a fight?" his dad asked. "Does that mean you took the other guy out so fast there was no fight?"

"No Dad." Lance stared at his plate. "Remember when I told you about Crow getting into a hassle with a Souther a few months ago? Well, that guy came back."

His mom held her napkin to her chest. "What did he want?"

"Revenge, I guess. He saw me and Crab and started hassling us. He knocked me down and kicked me."

"He kicked you, where? Jim did you hear that?"

His dad leaned back. "Honey, boys get into fights, if Lance was hurt he'd tell us."

"He kicked me in the side, it's no big deal. Dennis and McGillis were there, they stopped it."

Lance picked up his fork and took a bite of casserole. His mom watched him.

"There's something you're not telling us, Lance."

He put his fork down and took a deep breath. "I have to go to Youth Authority tomorrow, one of you has to come with me."

"Youth Authority? What for?" she asked.

Ann said, "A guy at school got caught with marijuana and he had to go to Youth Authority, it's like juvenile court."

"Lance," his mom gasped.

His dad cleared his throat. "Let's not get excited. Lance, tell us what happened."

Lance slouched in his chair.

"Sit up straight and tell us what happened," his dad snapped.

"I got a ticket for stealing an ice chest."

His parents looked at each other. His dad turned to him. "Why the hell would you steal an ice chest?"

"Because we needed food, we took it from a campsite."

His mom crossed her arms. "When was this? And who's we?"

"Me, Crab, Roach and Crow."

"Sandcrab was in on this?"

"Yeah, we all got tickets. It happened at El Cap."

"El Cap?"

"It's a state beach up north."

His mom put her elbows on the table and clasped her hands over her mouth. "When did you go there?"

"Over Easter break."

She turned to Ann. "You let him go up there? Did you know about this?"

"I didn't know what he was doing."

"You were supposed to be watching him."

"It's not her fault, she didn't know anything."

"Lance, you know better than this." His dad's tone was stern. "We'll go down there tomorrow and talk with the Youth Authority people and you can spend the next week thinking about it. You are not to leave this house for a week. Do you understand me?"

"Yes sir."

His mom adjusted her napkin. "Have you done this kind of thing before?"

"No mom, that was the first and last time." He scooted his chair out. "If you don't mind, I think I'll just go to my room."

He took his plate to the sink and left the kitchen. He stopped outside the doorway and listened to his dad. "It's normal for boys to want to test their boundaries. I remember when I was a kid we stole two of the neighbor's chickens. We hid 'em in my friend's shed until we could build a coop. Boy, was my dad mad."

"That wasn't very smart," Ann laughed.

"This kind of thing is normal at his age."

Lance walked back into the kitchen and faced his family. "Mom--Dad--Ann, I just want you guys to know...I love you, and I'm sorry."

They stared in silence. He turned to go to his room and heard Ann say, "That was *not* normal."

43
CLEAN SLATE

After a week of restriction Lance rode his bike to the beach. It was Saturday and he saw the Turd parked at the Pier and Crab's bike locked to the railing. He was excited to get back in the water and see his friends.

Crow, Roach and Crab hooted at him as he paddled out.

Crab grinned. "How was restriction?"

"It sucked. Didn't you get in trouble?"

"Nah, I already did my time. My dad even took me out for a burger afterward."

"I did," Crow said. "My mom kept the keys to the Turd for an extra week because of it. I just got 'em back today."

Lance sat up on his board. "So you guys didn't clean out all the laundromats without me?"

"Nope." Roach craned his neck looking outside. "You lucked out."

They all started to paddle.

"We'll go tonight," Crow said. "I've got it all planned out."

* * * *

After dinner Lance skateboarded to the asphalt wave in the alley behind the supermarket. Crab was already there and soon the Turd pulled up. Crow and Roach jumped out with their skateboards and took a few runs before they all piled back into the Turd ready for business. Crow held up a piece of paper. "I went through the phone book and made a list of all the laundromats we haven't hit yet. Here they are lined up in order. There's four between here and Ojai. We should be able to get enough to pay back Dennis and score some cash for ourselves."

"How much do you guys owe him?" Crab asked.

"I owe him twenty-five for getting the Turd from Gaviota."

"And I still owe him twenty for my board," Lance said.

"Finally," said Roach. "I'm sick of working for free."

Crow steered the van west down Thompson toward the Ventura Avenue.

* * * *

The next morning Lance rode his bike to the Surf Shop, his backpack was heavy with coins. It was Sunday and the shop didn't open until eleven. He found Dennis standing on the deck of his boat checking the surf.

"Hey Lance, what's cookin'?"

"I got your money."

"Come on up."

Lance parked his bike, laid his board down and climbed the ladder. He stepped over the rail and looked down the gangway. There was a little stovetop, a dining table and sofa, but no Noelle. He sat down on a bench seat. "This is cool, you must like living here."

"It was fun at first."

"What do you mean, this is the coolest pad ever." He ran his hand over the unvarnished wood rail.

Dennis smiled. "It doesn't work very well with a girlfriend."

"Noelle doesn't like it?"

"The novelty wore off for her as soon as she found out she had to use the bathroom in the shop."

Lance leaned back on his palms. "Why, is the toilet busted?"

264

"No, but you can't really use it on dry dock, all the waste goes into a tank and stinks up the place. Then there's issues with mold in the ice box, anyway..."

Lance opened his backpack and handed Dennis two rolls of quarters.

Dennis' eyes narrowed. "Is this from the laundromats?"

"Yeah, we went out last night, Crow'll be paying you back today too."

Dennis shook his head. "How much did guys get?"

"Sixty-nine bucks. Enough to pay you off and still pocket six dollars each."

"Damn, what size hex wrench did you say it takes?"

"It's too late for you man, we've already cleaned out every laundromat between here and Ojai. Tonight we're going to Camarillo and Oxnard."

Dennis shook his head and ran his fingers down his mustache. "There's something not right about it, but it's too comical to be criminal." He stood up. "Well Lance, I gotta shower before I open up."

"Do you shower aboard?"

"That's another thing, no hot water. The shower's in the shop too."

Lance nodded. "Hey, do you mind if I leave my board inside? I've got some stuff I need to do downtown."

"Sure."

* * * *

Lance rode his bike across Plaza Park to Main Street and stopped at the Top Hat hamburger stand. He bought three cheeseburgers and three fries and paid with two rolls of nickels.

He put the warm bag on top of his wetsuit in his backpack and rode down Main Street to the river.

He locked his bike and walked along the levee to the trestle. The severed cat was still on the tracks, the fur was coming off and the flesh was sunken in around the bones. Lance looked out over the river bottom and saw a string of smoke rising from the camp. He paused. *This'll be the last time ever.* He sucked in a deep breath and started down the embankment.

"Hey, Lance my boy, is that you?"

He stopped and turned. John Bear and Stew were standing by the cinderblock wall across the railroad tracks. Lance ran over and John Bear and Stew sat down against the wall each chewing a stalk of grass.

"I didn't think we'd see you again," John Bear said.

"I didn't think I'd come back. What are you guys doing over here?"

"We're waitin' for the 11:10."

"A train?"

"Yeah, it's time for a change of scenery."

Lance looked down the tracks. "Did Red...is Cricket..."

John Bear poked a stick in the dirt. "It's better if we don't talk about it. I appreciate what you and your friend did, I don't think I'd have come out of it too good."

Stew nodded and looked down.

John Bear squinted into the overcast sun. "I've got something for ya." He opened his bundle and handed Lance a sort of tiki head on a string. "I carved it from an avocado seed, you can say it's a surf god or something."

Lance held it up and admired it. "It's cool, thanks." He slipped it over his head and pulled off his backpack. "I brought you guys something too."

"Oh, don't tell me," Stew said licking his lips. "I smell hamburgers."

"I been smellin' it too," John Bear said rubbing his hands together.

Lance reached in the bag and handed them each a cheeseburger wrapped in white paper.

John Bear and Stew peeled back the paper as if they were uncovering treasure. "Look at that," Stew said, "pickles, cheese and onions too."

Lance handed them each a bag of fries and pulled out two brand new bottles of ketchup. "I got you each a bottle."

"Hee hee, you thought of everything," John Bear said. "What a feast."

Lance unwrapped his burger. "I would've given this one to Red if he was here."

"He hasn't come around since that day, I'm not sure where he is," John Bear said. "He's a mysterious one."

Lance looked back at the smoke rising from the camp. "How come there's smoke if you guys are leaving?"

"Jolly and Roger are down there, they just came up from San Diego, they'll be staying for a while. We like to move around, that way you don't wear out your welcome in any one place. Usually move north in the summer and south in the winter."

A train horn sounded in the distance.

"Well, here she comes, we sure appreciate the hamburgers."

"And the ketchup," Stew added screwing the cap back on.

Lance looked down the tracks at the approaching train. "Will you guys ever come back to Ventura?"

John Bear smiled. "This is our home town, the wind always blows us back here."

* * * *

The next morning Crow turned the Turd down Seaward Avenue on the way to Santa Barbara.

"Can we get in trouble for this?" Lance asked.

"Only for ditchin' school," Roach replied. "I don't think we can get in trouble for walking around Santa Barbara High looking for somebody."

Crow looked at Lance in the rear view mirror. "Yeah, all they can do is kick us off campus."

"It doesn't matter," Crab said. "This is something we've got to do, who knows when we'll have this much money again, this is our one and only chance to impress the girls."

"Nobody'll even notice us," Roach added. "There's gotta be a lot of guys with bleached hair like ours at their school."

"Hey, we could even stop in Carpinteria and hit another laundromat on the way up," Crab suggested.

"Now your talkin'," Roach grinned.

Lance crept forward in the van and took the carved avocado seed from his backpack. He reached up and hung it over the rearview mirror where it swung with the motion of the van.

"What's that?" Crow asked.

Lance sat back, "Just a little something for good luck."

ACKNOWLEDGMENTS

Thanks to Myrna Oakley, my mentor and guidance counselor. Jane Manchee, artful critic and compadre in writing (look for her book, *HARNEY COUNTY*, coming soon).

Early readers--Adam Stratton, Jillian Weiseneck, Gina Bevilacqua, Scott Trimble, Steve Tollefson, Chuck and Sandra Corbridge, John Astor, Brent Clark, Drew Lage, and Garrett Wyatt.

For moral support and advise--Rudolf Bekker, Kendall Conrad, John Golson, Mike Lang, Linda L. Peterson and Jeff Schroeder.

Carla Bartow for the cover art. Check her out at carlabartow.com.

Scott Trimble and Gabe Timm for web advice, support and general guidance.

Of course, none of this could have been possible without the never-ending support and patience of my lovely wife Renee, and daughters Colette and Audrey. I will always cherish those drives to the beach with Renee reading aloud and the girls in the back seat giggling and asking, "Dad, did you guys really do that?"

"Of course not," I'd say, "I told you, it's fiction."

And a special thanks to Paul Alary, George Billinger, Brent Clark, Dan Daly, Cameron Fox, Steve Monahan, Chris Quam, Steve Skates, Matt Tipton, Richard Vanderwyk, and all you guys I hung out with at Schoolhouse, the Pier, and Inside Point. I love you guys.

Bruce Greif grew up an avid surfer and skateboarder in Ventura, California. He currently lives in Portland, Oregon, with his wife and two daughters.

Made in the USA
Monee, IL
21 May 2022

96713108R10166